UNLIKELY

THE UNLUCKY ONES

MARLEY VALENTINE

Marley
Valentine

unlikely

usa today bestselling author
MARLEY VALENTINE

Cover design by PopKitty Design
Photographer: WANDER AGUIAR :: PHOTOGRAPHY
Model: Dina & Evan
Edited by Shauna Stevenson at Ink Machine Editing
Proofreading by Hawkeyes Proofing

This book contains mature content.

DEDICATION

To all of you taking a chance on a new genre just because I wrote it.

It's the right time.
It's the right person.

— MARLEY VALENTINE

AUTHOR'S NOTE

Like many of the books in this series Unlikely is a story about love and healing but also deals with some heavy topics. Please note that the following occurs off page:

- Stillbirth

Please note the following occurs on page:

- Grief and Loss
- Reference to Stillbirth
- Reference to Rape of a Main Character's Parent.

Even though the author has written these stories with as much accuracy as possible, please remember this is still a fictional piece of writing.

If you need any extra information on the subject matter in this book, please email the author at marleyvalentine@marleyvbooks.com

PROLOGUE
ZARA

I can't stop the tears.

No matter how hard I try, they won't stop falling, and I *need* them to stop falling.

"Mom." The voice of Raine, my sixteen-year-old daughter, is full of worry and trepidation, and I hate to be the one to make her sound that way.

"I'm fine, babe." I try to keep my voice steady, to reassure her. "I'll be out after my shower."

Slowly, I rise up off the toilet and step out of my underwear, ignoring the drops of blood that drip down my leg, my mind too fixated on the heaviness of my leaking breasts.

They're too sore to touch, and alleviating the fullness feels more like a punishment than the guaranteed relief I know it would bring.

It's been three days since I gave birth to a sleeping Lola, and every part of me feels like I died with her. The grief is nuanced and complex, and as a surrogate for my daughter's father and his husband, I'm struggling to sort through what are my feelings and what are everybody else's.

They lost a daughter.

Our daughter lost her sister.

But what about me? I lost someone too, hadn't I? I was more than just a vessel for this baby, and I don't know how to untangle that thought from the rest of it. Our lives are so intertwined, our love for one another unconventional, and I have never hated it more than I do right now. I have never doubted my role in this life I chose, but I don't know what feelings I have a right to feel and what ones I don't.

I don't know when I can cry and when I can't.

I don't know if I can complain about the changes and the pain in my body.

I don't know if I can share a single thought without guilt and regret consuming me.

I hate it here. I hate how we got here. And I hate what we all lost.

Turning the shower on, I wait for the stream of water to reach the right temperature. Stretching my leg, I climb over the lip of the tub and just stand there under the spray, knowing the responsibility to wash and take care of myself lies solely on my shoulders, and yet I can't get a single muscle of mine to move.

The heat of the water scalds my skin, and it's still not enough to rid my chest of the cold, empty, hollow feeling. I'm a living and breathing contradiction, simultaneously wanting the aches and pains to stay and desperately wanting them to go. I want every reminder to somehow immortalize Lola's existence, but I also selfishly want to wind the clock back to a time where everything didn't hurt this badly.

My eyes spill with tears as my body purges the remainder of the pregnancy. I massage my tender breasts, watching the milk spill through my fingers, tortured by the instant relief.

"Zara." The familiar voice calls my name, followed by the rattling of the door. "Zara, I'm coming in."

No. No. No.

"Zara." The voice is closer, and I turn to find Jesse, my best friend, my daughter's father—Lola's grieving father—standing there staring at me.

Not at my body.

Not at my heavy chest.

Not at my marked-up stomach.

Just *me*.

"What are you doing here?" I ask flatly. "You should be at home."

There's nothing but anguish on his face, the tired eyes of a man whose world has forever been altered. He drags a towel off the rack—always the gentleman—and leans into the shower to switch off the water and wrap it around me.

"Raine's worried about you," he says, the four words his only explanation. "She says you've been in the bathroom for an hour."

Had I been?

"I'm fine," I lie. "I'm just moving a little slower."

"Let me help you," he says. "Sit down. We can start with washing your hair."

I glance down at the towel covering my body, disoriented and confused. "This towel's going to get wet," I say.

"Nothing a wash can't fix," he says, turning on the tap and adjusting the temperature. "I'm going to go get a cup from the kitchen. Will you be okay until I get back?"

I manage to nod.

Raising my hand, I reach for my hair and, for the first time, I realize the wet, matted bird's nest that it's become.

I hear Jesse come back in, closing the door behind him. He sits on the edge of the bathtub and begins to wash my hair—wetting the knotted mass, lathering up the shampoo, and rinsing. Once. Twice.

He adds the conditioner, and before I know it, he's running a comb through the locks, detangling them.

Grateful he can't see my face, the tears return and I swallow down a sob, not wanting to break down in front of Jesse.

New cracks form in my heart, and older ones deepen, as I think of the man who's expertly brushing my hair, a skill he was so determined to learn as a girl dad.

A skill he absolutely would've used with Lola.

"There," he says as he rinses the last bit of conditioner out. "I can braid it when you finish your shower. Keep it out of your face and stop it from knotting up." When I don't respond, he adds, "Do you want me to help you shower?"

Do I need his help? Probably. Am I going to ask for it? Absolutely not.

I shake my head. "I'll manage. Just tell Raine not to worry. I won't be long."

He doesn't get up immediately, and I don't know if he's lingering because he's concerned or because he has something to say.

I try to wait him out, but the silence stretches, neither one of us having the energy to muster an actual conversation.

Eventually, he speaks. "I'll be outside if you need anything."

He doesn't wait for an answer, and I don't give him one, but when I hear the snick of the door being closed, my body loses some of its tension.

I can't be this broken mess. I can't afford to be. Not if it's scaring Raine enough to call her father. Because he's an amazing man and an even better father, and he will come running for her, every time.

Sighing, I stand up and let the towel drop to my feet. I turn the water back on and dig deep within myself to find any morsel of strength to wash my body and leave this bathroom. I do my best not to focus on the pain, literal and metaphorical, and robotically go through the motions.

Finally dressed in sweats and an oversized tee, I make my way to the living room and see Jesse standing in my kitchen, cooking with Raine.

They're both silent, moving around each other like a well-oiled machine.

Raine notices me first, and I can't help but wince at the way she anxiously chews at her bottom lip. I know without even asking, she's waiting for me to be angry at her for calling Jesse.

I want to be angry at her, but that doesn't help either of us, and quite frankly, it isn't fair. I'm raising a beautiful, smart woman, who is worried about her mother, despite losing her sister three days ago.

My shame and embarrassment and inability to deal with my feelings is not her responsibility.

Needing to reassure her, I make my way to both of them. Standing behind her, I wrap my arms around her, squeeze her to me, and kiss the back of her head.

"I love you."

She places her hand over mine. "I love you too."

I turn to face Jesse, who's frying some ground beef. "I can finish this," I tell him. "You go home to Leo."

He shakes his head. "Go sit on the couch. I'll finish this up and then I'll leave."

Not wanting to argue, I nudge Raine. "Do you think you can braid my hair?" I ask her, offering an olive branch.

She offers me a soft, sad smile and leads me to the couch. She runs to the bathroom and grabs a comb and some elastic bands before sitting down and gesturing for me to sit on the floor between her legs.

"I think I've mastered a fish braid," she says. "Can I try it on you?"

"Sure."

We sit together in the quiet, all three of us, sharing the same air, sharing the same heartache, the same grief. Raine combs my wet hair and starts sectioning it into pieces, tugging and weaving strands to create the perfect style, and my eyes never leave Jesse.

There's no way he's not broken inside. I know him as well as I know myself, but I sure am jealous of the way he always manages to put himself together for everybody else.

I want his strength more than I want my next breath.

He glances up and catches me looking at him. His smile is so sad, it actually hurts to look at. "Please go home to Leo," I say again. "We can finish the rest."

Raine pipes in. "I can finish the rest, Dad. Thank you for coming."

His lips tip up ever so slightly, and I have no doubt he's looking at Raine right now and thinking of Lola. Everything he has with one daughter and everything he won't have with the other.

"Okay," he says, nodding. "Just call if you need me."

I know he's really talking to Raine, knowing the last thing I'll do is call him. And I know my daughter well enough to know she's giving him a subtle nod, a secret between the two of them.

I let them have it, determined that this will be the one and only time either of them will see me so vulnerable.

Jesse washes his hands and walks over to us. He kisses us both on the forehead, and we both watch him head to the front door and wave goodbye before he opens it and steps over the threshold.

The sound of the door closing echoes through the house, heightening the silence between Raine and me. She finishes off the braid and we both sit here, her hands resting on my shoulders, a sliver of awkwardness between us that's never been there before, an awkwardness that I need to erase. But before I can find the words, Raine says, "Mom, I'm sorry."

"Hey," I say a little too firmly, standing as quickly as I can and turning to face her. Extending my arm, she takes my hand and I pull her up off the couch, guilt consuming me that I didn't do a better job of hiding my heartache. "You do *not* need to apologize for a single thing."

"I just..." Her breath hitches, and I see the unshed tears pooling in her eyes. Her pain and devastation, splitting me right in two. She tries to turn away, but I place my hands on either side of her face, forcing her to look at me.

"You don't need to hide your feelings from me," I tell her. "Especially not now. I'm sorry I put you in an uncomfortable situation. I'm sorry that for a single second I made you worry about me."

The stoic facade she inherited from her father cracks, the carefully placed mask slipping, her grief as obvious and prominent as mine. Tears spill, streaming down her face, her shoulders shaking.

My thumbs skim across her cheeks, trying to soothe her. I want to tell her it'll all be okay and this too shall pass. I want to reassure her with asinine clichés that for some reason make us feel better, even though, right now, not a single one of them holds true.

Because it won't be okay.

And it won't pass.

Time won't heal.

"I've got you," I whisper, wrapping my arms around her and pulling her close to me. "You cry for as long as you need, you hear me."

I don't know if she was waiting for permission or just needed to know I would be here to catch her when she falls. Her body rattles against mine as she struggles to find her breath through the onslaught of tears; her sadness and grief, palpable and painful.

This is why I need to do better. She is the reason I need to get out of bed every morning.

My body will heal, the hormones will level out, and the additional stretch marks—old ones lined up right next to the new—will remind me that a woman is capable of many things, but putting my needs above my daughter's isn't one of them.

Not even for a single second. A mother knows better... *I* know better.

It doesn't matter how hard it is or how much it hurts or that I, too, loved and lost.

It doesn't matter that grief will forever be a permanent fixture in our lives or how all of our hearts will have the same Lola-shaped hole for as long as we live.

My loss is not hers, and hers will always be greater.

1

CLEM
TWO YEARS LATER

My body thrums, alcohol swimming in my veins, the bass of the music making my chest thump and my pulse flutter. Without a care in the world, my body sways to the music, eyes closed, arms raised in the air.

It isn't often that I exchange an early night in my bed for a night out—drinking and dancing in a club isn't typically my scene—but it's my twenty-fourth birthday, and every now and then I need an excuse to step away from the monotony that is my life and the constant hurdles of reality.

Sensing someone near me, I open my eyes to see my friend Nina and her boyfriend of the month, Nick, making out on the dance floor. Some of our other friends are scattered throughout the mass of undulating bodies, but truth be told, they're more her friends than mine, and I'm enjoying the noisy solitude.

My mind empty, my body in sync with the beat.

Surprising me, a hand presses against the small of my

back, and I open my eyes to find Nina and Nick right beside me.

Leaning into me, she moves her mouth closer to my ear and tries to shout above the music. "We're going to get some drinks. Same as before?"

I'm extremely particular about what I drink and how much. I'm also a twenty-four-year-old who earns twenty-two dollars an hour as the manager of a café, and I don't have the option to be frivolous with my money or buy multiple drinks for anyone other than myself tonight.

I shake my head at her and mouth, *"I'm good."*

Nina rolls her eyes and slides her hand into mine, now dragging both me and Nick across the dance floor and to the bar. "Don't be so stubborn," she chides as we stand in line. "We're here on my father's dime tonight, remember?"

My cheeks flush in embarrassment, and I turn to look away from her, hating that she could see right through me. I'm not poor or struggling, it's just that my money was often accounted for before I got a chance to spend it on myself.

Nina is a close friend of mine... well, as close as I let people get. I met her about three years ago when she started working at the same coffee shop as me, only to find out she was a trust fund baby who didn't need to slum it with the rest of us but for some reason was very willing to do so.

This meant that every so often she liked to splurge on her friends... namely me.

It's a point of contention between us, because I don't know how to differentiate between pity and her love language. In my world, there are no such things as good deeds, and everything has a price, one that is too often too high. But after three years of knowing each other, I'm slowly learning to trust that outside my immediate family, there are such things as friendship and unconditional love.

"Fine," I concede. "A vodka orange, please."

Nina attempts to wave down the bartender and then turns to hand me her credit card. "Can you order for us? Just get me my usual and Nick another whiskey on the rocks," she instructs. "I broke the seal about an hour ago and now I can't stop peeing."

Laughing, I pluck the black card out of her fingers. "Rookie mistake."

She shrugs. "We'll be back."

I glance between them. "Do you need Nick's help to pull your panties down? Is that why he's going with you?"

They both smirk, and Nina pretends to scratch the slope of her nose with her middle finger. Shaking my head, I watch them retreat back into the crowd and am left wondering how long I'll have to wait with the drinks before they get back.

As I wait patiently for the bartender to serve me, there's a man quick to fill up the empty spot beside me. Expecting him to try and push me aside to get his drinks before I do, I'm unpleasantly surprised when he turns his body toward me, leaning his chest against my shoulder.

"Can I buy you a drink?" he shouts into my ear.

Turning my head, I take in his clammy skin, heavy eyelids, and blown pupils. He's a mess. A mess that reminds me why I end up always hating coming out to places like this.

I try to move away from him amid the sea of bodies surrounding me while also trying not to lose my spot at the bar. Instead of leaving, which is what I want to do, I offer a quick, short response and hope he moves along.

"I'm good. Thank you."

"You are good, aren't you," he slurs. "I bet you'd be a good fucking girl too."

My spine stiffens at his unwelcome candidness and my lungs expand, air filled with disgust and anger.

"Let me get you a drink," he insists.

I shake my head. "I've already ordered."

The alcohol mixed with the arrogance that men in bars seem to possess is of no surprise, as he completely dismisses my discomfort.

"But why won't you let me buy you a drink?" he asks, agitation in his tone. "We can get to know each other."

This time I remain silent, and fight the strong, inherent urge to people-please and coddle him.

I know I can step out of the line. Nina isn't going to be mad that I removed myself from an unpredictable and potentially unsafe situation; drinks aren't worth that much. But the fact that the onus is on me—the person who is standing here, minding her own business—and not him, to read the room and fuck off, is infuriating.

"You're being a bitch," he spits out, the insult not even a little bit surprising. "I'm just trying to be nice to you."

Just as I turn and face this fucker, ready to tell him where to go, I feel a hand curl around my waist, warm skin skimming against my bare midriff, and a body slide in the space behind me. It's a soft, gentle touch, featherlight almost, and their presence is more soothing than over-whelming.

The man's eyes dart to the person behind me, and I can't help but turn and follow his gaze. Expecting to find Nina or any of the other people I arrived with behind me, my heart stutters and I almost swallow my tongue when I come face-to-face with a woman I've never seen before.

Her eyes are a deep, rich brown, her hair wavy,

cascading down and around her face and shoulders. She's only a few inches taller than me, and the soft, shallow laugh lines around her eyes and pillowy-looking mouth hint that she might be a little older than me too.

Noticing my perusal, she licks her lips, the corner of them tipping up into a barely-there smirk, before glancing between me and the man behind me.

"Sorry," she says, keeping her eyes focused on mine. "The bathroom line was ridiculous."

I stare at her, completely dumbfounded, my tongue tied.

Unfazed, she steps closer to me, and my hands gravitate to her waist, keeping her still, as she leans her head over my shoulder.

"Can I help you?" she says to the man behind us, the challenge in her voice unmissable, even in the noisy club.

"Are you her girlfriend?" he asks.

At his question, she peers back at me, almost like she's either asking me or giving me permission to answer him. Dropping my hands, I turn to face him, my back now in line with the front of her, the limited space between us providing an unexpected and yet welcome sense of security.

His salacious stare makes me feel uneasy, and I don't realize I've inched my body backward until I feel arms protectively wrap around my waist. The intrusion on my personal space should bother me—it normally would—and yet no part of me has any desire to move. Instead, I find myself leaning into her, placing my arms over hers and playing the part.

"Yes," I say, eventually answering the man's question. The words roll off my tongue effortlessly, almost eagerly. "This is my girlfriend."

Not wanting to give him a single second more of my time, I shift in the woman's arms, almost expecting her to let me go, but when she doesn't, we just stand there, staring at one another.

We're a breath apart, arms still loosely wrapped around each other, my gaze getting lost in hers. It's as if the noise and the crowd cease to exist, until a voice behind me interrupts the trance.

"Kiss her," he says. "If you're together, I want to see you two kiss."

Between his insistence to be so abrasive and his complete disrespect for anyone other than himself, rage coils around my spine. My jaw tightens, but before I have the chance to turn around and tell him exactly how I feel, hands rest on either side of my face, stopping me, calming me.

Worried that she's going to pander to this man's request, I open my mouth to object, but she shakes her head imperceptibly, almost like she's telling me not to.

I'm not known for my ability to take orders, but curiosity silences me, and I wait to see her next move. My eyes dart down to her mouth for a sliver of a second, the thought of kissing her in any other circumstances strangely appealing.

Moving her hands down to my waist again, she shifts me to the side and steps forward, maneuvering herself in between me and the man.

I watch as she leans into him, her mouth near his ear, and his face lights up, like she might possibly be entertaining his disgusting thoughts. When his face falls, a wide, unmissable smile stretches my lips.

I have no idea what she said to him, but his expression

is priceless, anger and shock written on every inch of his face.

Without a second glance, she grabs my hand, curling her fingers around mine, and walks us away from him. I dutifully follow, completely swept up in this moment and this woman. Hand in hand, we walk through the crowd and up a flight of stairs that leads to the rooftop.

The air is balmy but still cooler than inside the crowded club, the music now nothing more than a muted beat below us.

She leads us to the bar that's in the middle of the open-air space. "What do you want to drink?"

I glance between her, the bar, and the direction we came from, a little frazzled by the quick succession of events. "I have to buy drinks for myself and my friends," I manage to say.

"Okay." Completely unbothered, she sidles up beside me, shoulder to shoulder, closing any distance between us. "Tell me what you're all having."

I drag Nina's credit card out of my pocket and bring it between us. "It's okay, I got it."

She plucks it from my fingers and slides it back into place. It's a light graze against my backside, nothing indecent, but it's enough to change the air around us.

"Sweetheart." Her tongue peeks out to wet her bottom lip, and my eyes don't miss the movement. "I can't buy you a drink if you pay."

The endearment makes my cheeks fill with heat, and I almost turn my face to hide it. I'm not necessarily shy by nature, but I'm also not someone who ever finds herself disorientated in the presence of other people. Truth be told, people outside my friends and family barely ever hold my attention; my mind is too full, my days too busy.

But this nameless woman has more than just my attention. She has me captivated; the damsel in distress completely in awe of her knight in shining armor.

"I think I should be buying you a drink," I tell her. "To say thank you for whatever it is you said to the sleazeball back there."

She waves me off. "You have nothing to thank me for. If anything, I should be thanking him for giving me an excuse to talk to you."

I purse my lips together and try to hide my smile, the heat from earlier now permanently staining my cheeks. It's obvious she's flirting, and it's not that nobody ever flirts with me, I just don't usually like it.

Feeling courageous, I nudge her. "Are you hitting on me?"

Her smile is confident, completely unfazed by my question or even the possibility of rejection.

Holding my gaze, she shrugs nonchalantly. "I'm seeing where the night takes me."

My skin pebbles with goosebumps as I lock my eyes on hers. I like that answer. I like that there's no pressure or awkwardness, and no expectations.

It is the very antithesis of what the man from earlier expected of me, and is in complete synchronicity with this woman seated beside me.

Her presence feels safe and calming, despite the loud music, sweaty bodies, and the free-flowing alcohol.

My phone buzzes in my pocket, and I'm quick to retrieve it, remembering I'm no longer where Nina left me, and she's probably looking for me.

Declining her call, I offer my new friend an apologetic smile and quickly type out a text.

I'm upstairs at the rooftop bar.

"Sorry about that," I say, letting my cell rest on the bar. "My friend was looking for me."

The words are barely out of my mouth when I feel arms over my shoulders. I turn to find Nina's face inches away from mine.

"I'm back," she sing-songs. "Thank goodness you haven't bought the drinks yet."

"Long line in the bathroom?" I joke.

"You have no idea."

"Let me guess," I say. "You don't feel well and you're going to head home early."

The smile on her face doesn't even falter as she carries on with the lie. "Seriously. It must've been all the food we ate for dinner."

"And Nick is going to take you to his place and make you feel better?"

She winks at me. "You know it."

We both laugh, and it's only then she must notice the woman beside me. Her eyes curiously dart between us. "Do you want to ride share?"

I glance back at my savior, taking in her patient expression. She's so at ease, waiting and watching, and I don't want to leave that just yet. I just don't really know why I want to stay either. She's interested in me, that much is clear, and I don't know if my interest in her is quite the same, but it's enough for me to let myself enjoy the moment.

She expects nothing of me, and that means everything.

"I'm going to stay," I tell Nina while openly admiring the woman in front of me. "I think I'm going to see where the night takes me."

2

CLEM

Our lips curl into matching smiles as I repeat her earlier sentiment back to her. Nina isn't one for questions, and I'm grateful she's a little too mesmerized with Nick to pay me any mind, but that doesn't mean she isn't still protective of me.

"You make sure you call me if you need anything," she says. "I'll come right back."

Nodding, I reach for her credit card and hand it to her. Shaking her head, she returns it to my back pocket, and the woman raises an eyebrow at me with a knowing smirk, reading my mind and taking us both back to that earlier moment.

"Keep it for emergencies," she says into my ear. "And call me tomorrow."

Nina then plasters an exaggerated kiss on my cheek before leaning over and whispering something into the woman's ear.

Her head tilts to the side as my best friend looks at me mischievously. "Have a good night."

I watch Nina retreat down the stairs as the bartender

reaches us and tips his chin in our direction. "What can I get you both to drink?"

"We'll take two shots of tequila for the birthday girl, please."

"She told you it was my birthday," I shout.

She nods as the bartender slams the two shot glasses on the bar and pours the alcohol till it's spilling over the sides, adding a slice of lemon on each rim.

One hand holding the lemon, the other holding the drinks, we raise them in the air.

"The only thing I don't know yet is your name," she says.

"It's Clementine," I reply, probably a little too softly, feeling vulnerable at telling her my full name. I hate the name as much as I love it, usually preferring for people to call me Clem, but tonight I don't really feel like Clem. I feel like a version of myself that I didn't even know I could be.

Spontaneous.

Light.

Free.

She clinks her glass against mine. "Happy Birthday, Clementine."

My eyes remain locked on hers as we both down the liquid. It scorches my throat as it slides along, that little reminder of just how little alcohol I usually drink. I quickly slip the slice of lemon between my teeth and let the sour taste soothe the burn.

"Not a fan?" she asks.

I try to school my features, but I fail, and this has us both laughing. "I don't drink much," I confide. "I kind of only save it for special occasions."

"I would say a birthday is a special occasion."

Feeling bold, I lean toward her. "You know what I'd like for my birthday?"

"Hopefully, something I can give you," she says, the slightest hint of seduction in her tone.

"Your name."

Her smile widens, small dimples forming on either side. "Easiest gift I've ever given," she says. "I'm Zara."

"It's nice to meet you, Zara."

She tucks a wayward strand of hair behind my ear. "It's really nice to meet you too."

The air thickens around us, and I feel my pulse stuttering over itself in excitement. I'm completely out of my element, and feeling a little drunk off it. My thoughts are a jumbled mess, my body nothing more than skin, bones, and mixed signals.

"Are you okay?" Zara asks me. "Let me get you some water."

I open my mouth to tell her I'm fine, but instead I hear myself say, "Do you want to dance?"

If this surprises her, she doesn't say anything. Instead, she takes a step back, putting distance between us, and for the first time, I manage to get a good look at her. From head to toe there isn't an inch of her that isn't put together.

Tall in heels, she's wearing black high-waisted pants, paired with a black bodysuit. She has a silver necklace, with a lock and key pendant, perched perfectly between her cleavage. Every item of clothing is seamlessly styled together, accentuating every curve of her hourglass figure. With her long tresses falling to the small of her back, she holds herself with a confidence I could only dream of.

She's all sex and class; her beauty a little intimidating. But even in my white crop top, shorts, and fishnet stockings, her eyes sweep over me as if I'm the beautiful one, as if I'm someone worth staring at.

She extends her hand out to me. "Are we going to dance or what?"

Slipping my fingers through hers, we walk back down to the main area of the club. The dance floor is full and the noise is loud enough that maybe I won't overthink my every move.

I keep my hand in Zara's as I lead us farther onto the dance floor; the music is familiar and the beat perfect to dance to. When I release my hold on her, her hands find my waist as she moves in behind me.

"Is this okay?" she says into my ear.

Her insistence of making sure I'm okay, makes her all the more attractive. They're simple questions. Questions that are second nature to most of us, and yet, many people ask and don't ever really mean it.

Raising my arms above my head, I nod, welcoming her touch. We start moving together in sync, my back against her front, our hips swaying from side to side.

One song rolls into another and then another, and by the third one, my body is aching to have more of her hands on me. I don't know if it's the alcohol or the close proximity, but her touch is both subtle and intimate, and it's maddening.

My stomach fills with butterflies every time she skims her fingertips across the piercing in my belly button, and when she rests her palm against my midriff, bringing me closer to her, I want to melt into her.

When the music changes to a more seductive beat, I give in to temptation and turn to face her. I wrap my arms around her neck while she casually slips her hands into my back pockets. Unlike before, she cups my backside and slips one of her legs between mine, her thigh pressing deliciously against the apex of my thighs.

I stare into her smokey eyes, taking in her flushed cheeks, as the air around us continues to crackle. I search for an explanation as to why I'm in this woman's arms and why I hate the idea of her letting me go.

Is this what life is like when I remove one mask and wear another?

Desire simmers in my veins, an unfamiliar feeling, one that I haven't been acquainted with in such a long time— one that almost feels like it doesn't belong.

It's clear I'm attracted to Zara, that I *want* Zara, I just don't know how to make that leap from point A to point B. I live in a world where sexuality is fluid and who you're attracted to doesn't define you, but that doesn't mean I saw this moment coming.

Objectively speaking, I have been able to appreciate the beauty of a woman my entire life, but until now, the needle has never moved beyond that, and I'm nowhere near confident enough to know what comes next.

My heart beats hard against my rib cage as we dance, her chest pressed against mine, our bodies practically melding into one another. Sweat trickles down my back as every one of my nerve endings goes on high alert. I need to get out of my own head before I ruin the night by trying to perfect the moment.

"I'm going to grab us a drink," I shout over the music. "I'll be right back."

Zara's eyes dart between mine, a small little crease forming between her brows, almost like she can see right through me and the frenzy within.

Surprising me, she kisses me on the cheek, soft and yet full of purpose. "I'll go," she says into my ear. "You dance."

My body continues to move as my eyes stay glued to her retreating form, she's so careful and caring, and even though I don't know her, I've seen enough from her to know she'll wait for me to find my feet and make the first move.

Before I can even think twice about it, I chase after her, grabbing her arm and pulling her to me.

Zara's expression shifts from startled to pleasantly surprised as I place one hand on the small of her back and slide the other into her hair. With a desperation I try to keep hidden, and feigned confidence, my mouth finds hers.

Her lips are soft and welcoming, and my anxiety settles at the ease and comfort I find in her kiss. Our mouths straddle the line between the perfect balance of right now and what's next.

And I want, so desperately, to know what comes next.

Unfastening my mouth from hers, I bring my lips to her ear, wishing we weren't surrounded by all this loud music.

"I don't know what I'm doing," I confess. "But I really want to do that again."

Zara takes the lead now, her lips on mine, hands gliding down my back and resting on my backside. She squeezes and caresses my ass, pressing me into her as my tongue slides past the seam of her mouth, eager to taste her.

With the faint taste of tequila still clinging to our lips, our tongues move in tandem, the kiss deep, the need evident. When Zara's thigh slips between my legs again, purposefully grazing against me, the pulse in my aching clit becomes my new heartbeat. Rapture replaces rationale.

I *need* more.

More of her. More of this. More of whatever it is that's making me feel *so* good.

Zara pulls back from the kiss, her chocolate-colored eyes searching mine. "Want to get out of here?" she shouts.

Wordlessly, I slip my hand into hers and lead the way, pushing through the crowd, not caring about anything but reaching that exit. As soon as we step out into the cool air, she tugs on my arm until I'm pressed against her, her mouth on mine.

"I've got a hotel room," she murmurs against my lips. "Spend the night with me?"

There is no way for her to know just how much weight her question holds or that I don't ever sleep anywhere but my bed—and thankfully, she will never know, because tonight isn't about Clem and all her hang ups.

Tonight I'm Clementine, and Clementine is hers.

3
ZARA
SIX MONTHS LATER

"Are you coming home for dinner?" I ask before taking a quick sip of my do-it-yourself iced coffee.

"No," Raine says while stuffing the last bit of her grilled cheese sandwich into her mouth. "I'm closing tonight, so I won't be home till around ten."

"I love it when you work late," I lie. "I'm always up for a night of no cooking."

Not for the first time, nostalgia wraps itself around my heart and squeezes. We've been in Los Angeles for almost six months and I've yet to find my groove. I thought the most obvious changes—new job, new friends, new house— would be the hardest things to adapt to. But it turns out watching your daughter learn how to fly in order to leave you, is not at all how I thought it would be.

I thought I'd prepared myself. I thought the excitement of watching the girl I raised blossom into a beautiful young woman would override the anticipated sting of becoming an empty nester.

But every day is more bittersweet than the one before.

I had Raine when I was sixteen, and I've now lived with her for more years than I've lived without her. I'm at that age where I can see how my world will always orbit around her but hers would no longer consist of just me.

And it shouldn't. Logically I know that, but my head and my heart are still trying to find a place where both grief and pride can coexist. Where I can still mourn the loss and change of my old life, yet eagerly want to watch Raine immerse herself in her new one.

"Dad said to call him if you're free this morning," she informs me.

I glance at my cell on the counter. "Does he have an issue calling me himself?"

"He said something about not wanting to annoy you, but I don't know what that even means, and I've got to go, or I'm going to be late to class." She kisses me on the cheek. "Love you, Mom."

"Love you, babe."

My eyes follow her as she putters around the house, picking up her bag and water bottle, slipping her arms into her jacket, and tying her long brown hair into a top knot on her head. It's always surreal watching her—a literal carbon copy of myself—perfectly executing the independence I've spent my whole life instilling in her.

"Have a good day," I call out.

She raises her hand up in a wave before walking out the door, and I take it as my cue to start getting ready for the day. I don't start work till midday, but as always, there are one hundred errands to run and a never-ending list of things I refer to as "life and house admin."

The things that are a complete bore but are an absolute necessity.

Finishing off my breakfast, I clean the kitchen and go through the house, writing down a shopping list and flipping laundry. Before I jump in the shower, I grab my cell and lie down on my bed before tapping on the name of the person I call the most.

"Hey," Jesse answers.

My mouth immediately curves up at the edges at hearing the smile in his voice. "Hey yourself. Are you busy?"

"For you, never."

"Such a charmer," I tease.

"Hey, Leo always thinks so."

Something akin to a chuckle and snort leaves my mouth. "It's a good thing you married him, then, huh? But I didn't call you to discuss your husband's undying love for you. I called because you know how much I hate when you leave messages for me with Raine."

His voice loses its jovial tone. "If you answered when I called, I wouldn't have to tell her to tell you to call me."

"I answer," I argue.

"You answer every third or fourth day and text me in between like it's enough."

He isn't intentionally trying to guilt me, but the truth makes me feel guilty. It's been six months since Raine and I left Seattle to come to L.A., and my struggle to adapt has become my biggest secret, one that I don't want my best friend and father of my child to catch wind of.

"I'm just busy," I lie.

"Well, I miss you," he says, his revelation gnawing at my resolve. "I'm still struggling with not seeing you or talking to you almost every day."

Jesse and I were sixteen when I fell pregnant with Raine. A night we would both rather forget ended up in a teen pregnancy that has bound us together for life. I knew he was my best friend then, but there isn't a person on this planet who encapsulates the true essence of what being a true best friend is like Jesse does.

It also means he knows when I'm lying, and he isn't above calling me out on my shit.

"I'm worried about you," he says. "I know why you moved, Zara, but I don't like that you're struggling."

I swallow past the lie. "I'm fine."

"I'm going to fly down next week."

This has me shooting upright. "Absolutely fucking not."

"I can come and see Raine if I want."

"That's not what you're doing," I counter. "And you know it."

He sighs in resignation, and we both sit in silence.

"I'm fine," I say again, trying to appease him. "It's a little harder than I thought it would be, but I'm going to get through it."

"It's just that you were there for Leo and me, and I want to do the same for you."

I think back on the last two years, how much Leo and Jesse and their marriage suffered. I know he wants to return the favor and be the rock he thinks I need, but as much as I miss my best friends, and my daughter misses her fathers... I *need* this time apart.

I need this moment to reconnect with the woman I used to be. To resuscitate her. To love and nurture my broken heart until my mornings start with hope and anticipation, and the nights end with an exhaustion that can only be found when you're fulfilled and sated.

I'm not there yet, far from it, actually, but I have hope it's possible. I just need time. Time Jesse doesn't know how to give me. I know there is a big part of him that feels responsible for my unhappiness, and without bringing up the most painful parts of our shared history, there is no way to appease him of that guilt.

Not till I've well and truly come out the other side.

"Jesse," I say, my voice holding firm. "This is normal. It's a big change, for all of us. I have lived in Seattle my whole life, and we have lived in each other's pockets for more than twenty years. It's going to take a minute.

"The main thing is that Raine loves it here. She's enjoying college, making new friends, and making her own money. She's doing the damn thing, and I'm so privileged to be able to be here watching her take on the world. And you are always welcome to come here for her. You know you don't need my permission for that."

I chew on the inside of my cheek, mulling over my next words, knowing I don't want to say them any more than Jesse is going to want to hear them.

"Please don't come out here for me."

There is an impossibility to my request, because whenever he visits Raine, he will still be indirectly checking on me. But the words make the boundaries real, and I know Jesse, at the bare minimum, will try to respect them.

"Okay." I can hear the reluctance in his surrender, but I'm still appreciative. "We'll stick to the schedule we've already set, and I'll see you in six weeks, but if you need me—"

"I'll call you, I promise," I assure him. "But I've gotta start getting ready for work now anyway."

"Thank you for calling me back."

"Of course," I tell him. "Tell Leo I said hello. Love you."

"Love you too."

Hanging up, I throw the cell on my bed and fall back

onto the mattress. I hadn't intended on starting my morning in such a funk. Every night, I vow to myself that the next day will be better. Extending my arm, I reach for my nightstand drawer, opening it and feeling around for my necklace, only to remember it's still missing. Trying–for the hundredth time–to remember where I left it, my hand comes across my vibrator instead, and an exasperated chuckle leaves my mouth.

It's true, this thing could get me off just as good as any woman could, but it's a reminder of the aching loneliness that I had no time to feel when I was raising Raine. Jesse and I were single for the first ten years of Raine's life, living as a platonic couple, not giving any mind to romance and relationships.

It worked until it didn't.

The same way sporadic dates and one-night stands worked for me, and now they don't.

Six months ago, I flew up to L.A. on my own. We had settled on our new place here, and I wanted to deep clean it before Jesse, Leo, and Raine drove up here with all our furniture. I had also secured a job here at an upscale hair salon in Beverly Hills and they wanted to welcome me to the team.

We had dinner and drinks, ending the night at a club called Zero in Hollywood. It was everything I expected the night to be—food, alcohol, and dancing—but I didn't expect the blond-haired woman with the lithe body and the tipsy smile. She had caught my attention from across the room, and one look around the club told me I wasn't the only one.

My gaze flickered to her every chance I got—in between drinks, in between dancing, in between conversation. And each time made me feel a little more off my game. We weren't in a queer bar, and, of course, that made it difficult to navigate interactions with people of the same sex, but I wasn't in the closet and hadn't been for a very long time.

For the most part, women were receptive to being hit on by other women, even flattered by it, as it didn't come attached with the toxic masculinity that often tainted the interactions between straight and gay men. And a lifetime of affectionate platonic friendships between girlfriends often softened any rejection.

Of course, like everything, there were outliers. Moments when exposing your sexuality didn't always work in your favor, but I was beyond privileged to have been brought into the world by supportive parents—setting the standard for the type of people I have always wanted to surround myself with in everyday life.

In that circumstance, I didn't really know how it would go, but when the perfect scenario presented itself to me, it felt like the universe was telling me to shoot my shot.

And I did.

More than once.

Quickly glancing at the time, I pluck out my vibrator instead. I slip my hand into my pajama bottoms and turn the lipstick-shaped device on and press it against my clit. A low hum reverberates throughout the room as I close my eyes, the face of the blond beauty burned onto the back of my eyelids.

The whole night was like an unexpected gift, and not for the first time in the last six months my mind and my body reminisce.

Her cherry lips.

Her soft, pale skin.

The way she felt around my fingers.

The way she sounded when she came.

My clit throbs and my pulse thrums as I slide my hand up my shirt and tweak my nipple. I increase the speed on my vibrator, imagining, wishing—even just for a moment —for someone else's hands on me.

Her hands on me.

My muscles coil at the thought, at the images, at the memories. And the nerve endings in my body flutter rapidly as I rub the sculpted tip against myself, harder and faster, eager for my release. My thighs stiffen as heat courses through me, all the blood in my body rushing to my center.

"Fuck," I pant into an empty room as my back arches off the bed.

The orgasm hits me harder than I anticipate, and my body quivers through it, every part of me pulsating. Pleasure is a high that I love indulging in, and I momentarily revel in that relaxed feeling, my chest rising and falling as I catch my breath. But just as quickly as the pleasure raced through me, the familiar feeling of emptiness is quick to replace it.

The endorphins are useless against the onslaught of my reality.

Sliding my hand up and out of my pants, I place my vibrator on my nightstand and drag myself off the bed and into the shower. I don't feel shame about self love, but I'm starting to regret allowing myself that small moment of reprieve, because the fall off the edge was bliss, but the landing was brutal.

I push all thoughts of the stunning woman to the recesses of my mind, where she belongs, where the simple idea of her doesn't have me spiraling into an existential crisis about being alone versus being lonely.

Truth be told, I know there is supposed to be a difference between the two, but between the empty side of my bed, and the ever-present silence in my house, I couldn't find it.

4
CLEM

"Holy fucking shit, that never gets easier." I slide the key into the front door and unlock it. "I literally can't feel my legs."

"It wasn't that bad," Arlo, one of my foster brothers, says as he follows me into the house. "You only asked for me to kill you once this time. It's progress."

Entering the house, I force my tired legs to carry me down the hallway and into the living room, where I throw my exhausted self onto the couch. "I fucking hate you."

"You know you love me," Arlo retorts.

I keep my gaze on him as he drags his sweat-stained tank top over his head and throws it haphazardly into his bedroom before making his way to the kitchen. On the days our schedules align enough to work out together, Arlo and I have a pretty good morning routine. We wake up early, exercise, then come back to the house, where he makes breakfast for whoever is home.

Emptying the fridge of almost all its contents, Arlo starts cracking eggs and chopping up vegetables to make omelets. "Can you tell the other two that if they're not up in ten minutes, I'm eating their omelets and mine?"

I have four foster brothers in total, but only three of them live with me. Truth be told, even if we aren't blood siblings, referring to them as foster brothers always feels like an underwhelming description of what these men mean to me.

After growing up together in a group home, the bond we share borders on co-dependant, but when you grow up trusting next to no one, you tend to latch on to the most important people in your life and refuse to let go.

Arlo and Frankie are older than me at twenty-seven and twenty-six, while Remy and Lennox are younger, at twenty and twenty-two respectively. And for all intents and purposes, I'm the middle child, and yet I never feel more like the only adult than I do with them.

Dragging my body off the couch, I trudge across our living room to Lennox's bedroom and rap my knuckles against the wooden door. It's too early for me to be catching him in any compromising positions, but from experience, I know you can never be too sure.

"Lennox," I shout while knocking again. "Rise and shine, sunshine. I'm coming in."

I push the door open just as he pops his head up from underneath his pillow. His face creased from sleep, his eyes barely open.

"What do you want?" he groans.

"Arlo's cooking omelets, are you in?"

"What's the time?" he asks.

"I don't have my phone on me, but it's probably around eight thirty."

He groans again and then drops his head back onto the

pillow. "I'll be out in a second," he says. "I'm just going to shit and shower first."

"Awesome," I say sarcastically. "I definitely needed those details."

Closing the door, I move on to Remy, loudly knocking on his bedroom door.

"Come in," Remy calls out.

I swing the door open to find him awake, freshly showered, and sitting at his desk, tinkering with an old camera. The complete opposite of Lennox.

"Morning," I greet. "Arlo's got breakfast if you're interested."

Wordlessly, Remy gently places the camera down on the desk and pushes his chair out to stand.

He's the quietest out of all of us. We all have a different story, a background, and a past that has irrevocably changed the people we've become, and it's never more evident in how quiet and reserved Remy is.

He puts everything around him back into place before walking past me and heading straight to the kitchen. Lennox is only seconds behind him, and I decide I need a shower before he and Arlo finish all the hot water.

"I'll be out in ten," I call out to them before closing the bedroom door behind me.

Our place sometimes feels no bigger than a shoe box, but after years spent in the foster system and growing up in group homes, it's always felt luxurious to me. Occasionally, it pays off being the only girl growing up among a bunch of boys, because they always prioritize my privacy and well-being over theirs.

My en suite bathroom is a perfect example.

It's a rarity to be able to afford anything with two bathrooms in Los Angeles. In fact, it was a stroke of luck that allowed us to afford a place in the heart of L.A. at all, but thanks to Arlo and Frankie, who aged out of the system first, they bit off more than they could chew for the first few years so Lennox, Remy, and I didn't have to struggle with the transition from foster children to adults.

The place is now our sanctuary.

It has four bedrooms, a cozy living area, and a functioning kitchen. We all pay rent, we have a color-coded chore wheel—thanks to Remy—and we all make the effort to try and eat a meal together as often as we can.

It's home, and they are my family. We aren't perfect, but our circumstances are perfect for us.

Stripping out of my sweaty workout gear, I throw it into my hamper before turning on the shower and waiting for it to warm up. I mentally run through the list of things I need to get done today before I go to work and everything I'll have waiting for me when I get back.

Stepping into the spray, I quickly wash my hair and my body, conscious of the others needing the hot water and the omelet Arlo is making for me. I dry myself off and then search through the piles of folded laundry for the clothes I want today. I drag my underwear up my legs and opt for a racerback tank with built-in support instead of an actual bra.

My work shirt is a plain, black short-sleeve button-down. It could do with an iron, but I just don't have time for that. Paired with some black skinny jeans and some high tops, this is the best I'm going to look today.

Sticking my hand into my bedside table, I feel through the different fabrics until I find what I'm looking for. Checking myself out in the mirror, I place the necklace over my head and tuck the pendants into my undershirt, as if to keep them safe. I gather my hair into a ponytail, then grab my bag and head out to the kitchen.

The dining table is all set, the three of them already seated and eating. I slip into my usual place and pour myself a glass of orange juice before cutting into my omelet.

"I'm working the graveyard shift at the gym," Arlo says. "So I won't be home tonight. But if you're lucky, I'll be home in time tomorrow to make you breakfast."

Arlo is a recovering addict who has spent the last four years turning his life around. He now runs a gym that is designed specifically for others embarking on their journey to recovery.

"I won't be here either," Lennox says. "I've got training tomorrow morning and then we have our big game against USC in the afternoon."

"Shit," I say, my forkful of egg in front of my mouth. "I totally spaced out. We're understaffed and I'm doing another double."

"It's fine," Lennox appeases, his mouth still full of food. "How many times do I have to tell you, you don't have to watch any of my games. You hate football anyway, so at this point it's just torture."

"I don't hate football," I argue. "I just haven't found the time to learn the game."

"That's a lie," Remy interjects. "Because the last time we were at Lennox's game and I tried to tell you what was happening, you said to only bother you if Lennox had the ball."

I grab a nearby napkin and throw it in Remy's direction. "Way to sell me out, Remy. I really appreciate it."

Throwing the napkin back, he chuckles. "I'm just

saying, you'll regret not knowing the rules when Lennox goes pro."

"Don't worry. You're safe," Lennox says, glancing my way. "Because I'm not going pro."

"You never know," Arlo says. "Scouts have been showing interest."

"Yeah, but *I'm* not interested."

It's the same discussion, week in and week out. Arlo and Remy trying to convince Lennox he wants to play professional football, and Lennox reminding them the only reason he went for a football scholarship at UCLA is because he couldn't afford college without it.

I often find myself in the background of these arguments, because I really don't know enough about it all to form an opinion. But what I do know is Lennox, and if Lennox says he doesn't want something, Lennox means it.

"Well, Remy, since you're Lennox's biggest fan, does that mean you'll be at the game tomorrow?"

Surprising me, Remy shakes his head, his cheeks turning crimson. "I've actually decided to take a photography class at the community college," he reveals. "There's an orientation class thing tomorrow that I want to attend."

Lennox nudges him. "That's awesome, man. I can't wait to see all the photos you take."

Remy is the baby of the group, and it's obvious he's still finding his feet, but the one thing we're all good at is helping one another learn how to stand.

The conversation moves effortlessly from person to person, each of us giving the others little reminders of where we'll be and when to check in.

"Okay, I'm done," I announce, picking up my empty plate and half-drunk juice and taking them to the sink to quickly wash them. "I also won't be home till late because

I'm closing the coffee shop, but I'll see you all sometime tomorrow."

Arlo comes up behind me and adds his dishes to the sink before pushing me out of the way.

"Get out of here," he says with a kiss to my cheek. "We can finish these. We'll see you tomorrow."

———

"Oh, look what the cat dragged in," I call out as Raine, my friend who also works with me, walks into the shop, school bag hiked over her shoulder, her top knot bouncing on her head with every step.

"Sorry I'm late," she says. "I'm seriously considering investing in a scooter, because this shuttle bus is more of an urban legend than a functioning service."

"You will do no such thing," I say as I continue wiping down empty tables.

"I've already got a mom," she replies. "You're supposed to be my best friend and down for whatever I want."

"I'm not down for dying," I quip. "I'm sorry, your mom sounds like a very smart lady, and I'm going to have to side with her."

Raine is one of my more recent hires. She's a new UCLA student, who moved here from Seattle for her first year of college. Despite the small age gap, it was love at first sight, for both of us. Almost five months of friendship, and I'm certain she's my platonic soulmate. She is a kindred spirit who seems to understand the side of me everyone else doesn't.

It isn't often that I connect with strangers, let alone share my life with them, but with Raine it was give and take, a piece of her history for a piece of mine.

Slipping her apron over her head, she ties the strings behind her back and makes her way toward me. She grabs the wet cloth and spray bottle out of my hands.

"Go have lunch," she orders. "This is your fourth double this week."

"Excuse me," I pout. "But I'm your boss."

She continues wiping the tables while talking to me. "Any interviews lined up?"

"I haven't heard anything from management," I tell her. "But Billy is supposed to email me a whole bunch of applications tonight."

I've worked at Wonderwood Café since Lennox started college. Near the campus, it started out as a place where he and his friends would hang out when they weren't in class, and it was an easy meeting point for whenever we wanted to meet up and catch the bus home together.

Three years later, I now work here full-time, was promoted to café manager, and any thoughts I've ever had of pursuing something different have been put on pause. It doesn't help that I'm twenty-four and haven't quite yet worked out what that something different is.

It's funny, because in every aspect of my life I feel older than my age—more mature, more experienced. And yet when it comes to making decisions for myself, I feel inadequate and undeserving in almost every way. I tell myself living for everyone else's happiness is enough, when the truth is, prioritizing everyone else has started taking its toll on me.

"I'm not going to bitch about how you shouldn't be working on the applications after hours," Raine says, interrupting my thoughts. "But I'm going to take your lunch break if you don't."

I put my hands up in surrender. "Fine. I'm going."

Fidgeting with the necklace hiding beneath my shirt, I head toward the staffroom. Gripping tightly to my reminder of what it could be like if I put myself first.

I love Clem. She's familiar. Solid and reliable.

But I want to go back to that night and forever be Clementine, because she was fearless.

5
ZARA

Closing the front door behind me, I'm surprised to see the television on and Raine lazily sprawled out on the couch.

"Hey," I greet excitedly. "I didn't know you were going to be home tonight."

I drop my bag to the floor and toe off my shoes. Raine turns her head just as I start unbuttoning my shirt.

Years as a hairdresser means I always take my clothes off before I step any farther into the house. Countless haircuts have my clothes and shoes full of hair. It's a bitch to clean up, so keeping them away from everything else in the house is always my safest bet.

I'm standing in my underwear as we finish the conversation.

"I switched shifts with one of the other girls," she informs me. "So tomorrow is an early morning wake up for me."

Feeling a little disheartened, I put my shoes away underneath the stairs and grab my dirty clothes.

"If I had known you'd be home, I wouldn't have agreed to go out."

Raine sits up in a rush, her head peeking up from over the back of the couch. "You're going out?"

I narrow my eyes at her. "Why do you look so shocked? I can cancel the date and spend the night in with you."

She doesn't miss my slip-up, and her eyes widen incredulously. "Did you say date?"

If I wasn't feeling so anxious about it, I could probably share in her excitement.

"I didn't know we were dating," she continues.

This makes me laugh. "We aren't anything, babe. And it's nothing."

"Why didn't you tell me?" she inquires. "You've never dated before."

"That's not true," I say, a little too defensively. "I've dated."

"When?" she challenges.

"Plenty of times," I lie. "I just never told you because you were young and usually spending time with your dads. They never went anywhere, so there wasn't any real point in talking about them."

While she mulls over my words, I head to the laundry room and start my usual after-work routine of putting my clothes in the wash before heading upstairs for a shower.

If I needed proof that Raine is wholeheartedly invested in this conversation, her sudden appearance in the doorway confirms it.

"Is this serious? Was I the reason you never dated? I don't want to be the reason you don't date."

"Babe," I say soothingly as I place my hands on her shoulders, willing her thoughts to slow down. "When you were younger, I chose not to date because I was busy enjoying being your mom, and nobody really caught my attention."

"And now?"

"And now you and I are at different stages in our lives, and the possibility of me growing into a single, crotchety old woman is very real."

This makes her laugh, and the sound makes me smile.

"You don't need to worry about me. Okay?" I reassure her. "Besides needing a shower, I'm fine."

"Can I pick out your outfit for your date?" she asks.

"Sure, but nothing too over the top, because it's just casual. Dinner and drinks."

I guide her out of the laundry room, and she's hot on my heels as I make my way up to my bedroom.

"How many dates have you been on already?"

"None. This is our first."

"Mom," she scolds as we reach the landing. "You're not even trying, are you?"

"What?" I ask, walking away from her and feigning ignorance. "It shouldn't matter what I wear anyway. We're either going to hit it off or we're not."

"Where did you meet her?" she asks before I step into my en suite bathroom.

"She's a client."

"So what you're saying is she wants discounts on haircuts."

Chuckling, I close the door on her, a loud sigh of resignation filling the space on her side. Raine was right. I'm not as thrilled as I should be about the date. But I'm starting to acknowledge that the right woman isn't going to just fall into my lap while I sit at home watching television, waiting for my daughter to fit me in between college, her new friends, and her new job.

I need to put myself out there. Discomfort be damned.

It doesn't matter if it doesn't eventuate into anything, I'm just getting my feet wet. Wading into the water until someone catches my attention enough to make me want to dive right in.

———

Raine picks out a black maxi dress with a sporadic floral print that has extended sleeves and wraps around my waist to accentuate my figure. The neckline is low and I can't help but think of how good my necklace would look with this outfit. It also has a long split that has one of my legs playing peek-a-boo whenever I take a step.

I feel good, sexy even. It's the confidence booster I need to make me want this date to work out.

Entering the restaurant, I take in the expensive decor and the almost luxurious ambience. It's a lot more than I'm used to, but working in a high-end salon means my clientele very much indulges in expensive things. Aubrey, my date, included.

"Good evening, miss. Do you have a reservation?"

I glance around, and when I spot Aubrey, I point in her direction. "I'm with her."

Nodding, the maître d' leads me to our table. She elegantly pulls my chair out for me and then lays the cloth napkin over my lap before allowing me to tuck myself in. It's all a little too much, and not at all my scene, but there's nothing to complain about when someone is going out of their way to wine and dine you.

"You made it," Aubrey says, her smile wide.

Her lips are painted a beautiful ruby red, complementing a gorgeous full face of makeup. She's pulled out all the stops, and I'd be lying if I said I don't find her effort and persistence extremely endearing.

"This place looks amazing," I tell her. "Thank you for suggesting it."

She waves me off. "It's completely self-serving. You finally agreed to go out on a date with me, and there's no way I'm not going to do everything I can to make sure we have a good time."

My cheeks heat at her words as I bite the corner of my lip to try and hide my smile, her forwardness not at all unwelcome. I wanted to apologize that she had to ask me out twice before I agreed, but I don't want to intentionally steer the conversation toward my laundry list of reasons of why I hesitated.

This is nice. *She* is nice. And good food, good wine, and good conversation do not need to go to waste.

"Well, I'm impressed," I say truthfully. "I couldn't tell you the last time I ate in a place like this."

The conversation between us is a steady flow of questions and answers. *How old are you? What age did you know you were into women? What's your relationship history like?*

Everything is informative but not too intrusive, the back and forth surprisingly effortless.

An hour into our date, my cell vibrates on the table. I don't even hesitate to pick it up when I see Raine's name on the screen.

How's your date going? Does she like your dress? Do you need me to bail you out?

Glancing up at Aubrey, I offer an apologetic smile. "I'm sorry, it's Raine."

"Is everything okay?" Aubrey asks.

"Yes," I say with a laugh. "She's actually asking how the date is and if I need her to call me and bail me out."

Aubrey nervously skates her teeth across her bottom lip. "And do you?"

I quickly type out a response and rest the phone back on the table. "I told her I don't really want to miss dessert."

Aubrey's infectious smile returns. "So what you're saying is I need to delay dessert to spend more time with you."

I shrug. "That sounds about right."

"I like how close you are with her," she says. "Did you ever contemplate siblings? Finding another donor or asking her father?"

The question is unexpected, life punching me in the stomach when I least expect it. I attempt to swallow past the unwanted boulder of emotion that sits in my throat, but the residual pain makes it too hard to ignore.

"Did I say something wrong?" Aubrey says quickly, clearly picking up on my discomfort.

"No." I shake my head, schooling my features. "You're fine. What about you? Were you and your ex talking about kids before the divorce?"

If Aubrey notices that I never truly answer her question, she doesn't say anything, instead launching into an explanation of why kids aren't for her and how she's glad the timing was never right. For that segue alone, I find myself liking her a little bit more.

After a decadent dinner filled with all the things I'm too lazy and too ill equipped to cook for myself, the time to have dessert has finally arrived.

"Dessert is my weakness," I tell Aubrey. "Don't judge me if I order more than one."

She raises her hands. "No judgment here. I love a woman who loves her food."

True to my word, I order three different desserts, and justify it by making Aubrey share them with me.

By the time we've cleared our plates, we've been sitting, eating, drinking, and talking for almost two and a half hours. That's a success by anybody's standards, and yet, I can't pinpoint exactly what's missing.

"Did you drive here?" Aubrey asks just as the waiter drops off some after dinner mints along with the check.

"No," I reply, reaching for the leather folder that holds our bill. "If I've never been somewhere and I don't know what the parking situation is, my anxiety about being late has me always opting for an Uber."

Aubrey plucks the folder out of my fingers. "I don't want to fight with you about who's paying. I asked, so it's my treat. Next time, you pick the place and you can pay."

There was no missing that Aubrey is already making plans for our second date. Do I hate it? No. Do I love it? Also no. But I'm in my I'm-going-to-try-anything-once era, and I vow to myself to see where this thing with Aubrey leads.

I have nothing to lose and everything to gain; at the very least, we could be friends.

"Fine," I concede. "Next time's definitely on me."

She finalizes the bill and then we make our way outside the restaurant onto the illuminated streets of Beverly Hills.

Her hand rests on the small of my back, and I immediately recognize what's missing.

"In case I haven't already said it," she starts. "You look beautiful tonight."

She turns us till we're face-to-face, holding my hips, and I return the sentiment. "As do you."

My words are weak, my voice unconvincing, but my

mind is too hung up on the fact that her hands are on me and I feel nothing. There is no spark, no heat, no desire.

That desperate need I've been chasing... missing.

Not wanting to reject her, I choose to take matters into my own hands and end the night with as little damage as possible. Placing my hands on her shoulders, I hold her gaze, then lean in and kiss her on the cheek.

Thankful.

Polite.

Platonic.

6

CLEM

I struggle to breathe; short shallow puffs of air all I can manage. My body sags to the floor, my knees hitting the concrete with a thud.

"Clem." I know it's Raine's voice, but I can't move. I can't talk. I just... can't.

"Clem," she repeats, and I don't miss the urgency in her voice. "Clem, what happened?" She holds my cell up between us, the screen completely shattered. "Who was on the phone?"

The words are heavy on my tongue, but I can't seem to make my mouth move to release them.

"Clem. Who was on the phone?"

"Lennox," I manage to spit out. "It's about Lennox."

Instead of asking me any more questions, she carefully drags her finger over the cracked screen and then raises it to her ear. Holding my hand in hers, she keeps her gaze on mine as she waits for someone to answer.

"Hey," she says. "It's Raine. Can you tell me what's going on? Because I can't get Clem to speak."

Frown lines appear on her forehead as she processes

each morsel of information. "Okay, I'll bring her to you. Do either of you need me to bring anything?" Only knowing her side of the conversation, I wait for more clues on what the hell I'm supposed to do next.

When she hangs up, I see the worry in her eyes, the crack in her stoic facade.

"Okay. Clem, listen to me." I nod. "I'm going to bring you some water, then I'm going to call Billy and work out who can cover us. Samuel will call if anything changes."

"I have to call Arlo and Remy," I blurt out. "And Frankie."

"Just one thing at a time." Raine picks herself up off the floor and then extends her hand out to me. "Lennox is in good hands, and I'm not letting you out of my sight until I know you've calmed down."

Doing as Raine says, I sit down in the staffroom and drink a whole bottle of cold water. My pulse has slowed down significantly, and now that the shock has somewhat worn off, I'm trying to remember every single detail of Samuel's phone call as I reiterate it to Arlo.

"He got injured in the game and was unconscious for a little bit. When he came to, they said he broke his collarbone and he lost his hearing."

"Can you repeat that," Arlo says. "Did you just say Lennox lost his hearing?"

"That's what Samuel told me. He said the coaches and medical staff were trying to give him instructions and he panicked, called for Samuel, and told him he couldn't hear anything."

The line goes silent, and just like Raine did for me, I give Arlo the time he needs to take everything in.

"Are you going to call Frankie?" he asks.

I know how much strength it takes for Arlo to ask,

considering when Frankie left us four years ago, he hurt Arlo and Lennox the most. None of us have seen him since, and as far as I know, I'm the only one who checks in with him whenever I can.

"Samuel said he specifically asked me not to," I confess. "But I can't just not call his brother, Arlo."

He doesn't agree or disagree with my statement, choosing to bypass the reality of the situation and talk about things we can make sense of.

"And you? How are you?" he asks.

"Well, Raine won't let me leave here until I've drunk enough water and eaten at least a sandwich—"

He interrupts. "That's not what I'm asking, Clem."

"Why the hell didn't I go to his game?" It's the same thought that's been plaguing me for the past forty-five minutes. "I should've been there."

"And done what? It still would've happened."

Huffing, I pinch the bridge of my nose, willing myself not to cry. He's right. I know he's right, but there is nothing I hate more than not being there for the people I love. It feels like I let him down, and for what? The double shift I'm leaving early now anyway.

"Will I see you at the hospital?" I ask him.

The silence between us stretches, and I already know I'm not going to like his answer.

"If Frankie comes, I don't think I can."

Unshed tears fill my eyes, anger at both Frankie and Arlo for making such a mess of things all those years ago.

"Keep me posted on Lennox." When I can't find the words to fill the silence, he continues. "I'm sorry, Clem. I really, really am."

Unable to muster up another word, I hang up, already too exhausted to do this all over again.

Like the perfect friend she is, Raine comes into the staffroom from the café floor, concern etched into all her features.

"I've got ten minutes. Tell me what you need me to do."

I hand her my phone. "Can you call Remy and tell him to meet me here so we can go to the hospital together?"

She grabs the cell, her face scrunching up at the screen. "We're going to have to do something about this screen before you cut up your fingers."

"I can't afford to fix it right now," I admit. "And if I could, I don't even have the time."

"Okay, fine. We'll put this on the back burner," she says cautiously. "I'll call Remy, and it'll be one less thing you have to worry about."

Quickly, I take myself to the bathroom and wash my face. When I return, my cell is sitting neatly on the table, and I know I can't put off that last phone call any longer.

Anger and sadness churn in my stomach, and I wonder at what point life stops being unfair. At what point do any of us get some reprieve from the constant hurdles and heartache?

Pacing around the room, I search for Frankie's number, and press call before I can even change my mind. It rings once, twice, three times, and I imagine him staring at the phone, confused as to whether or not it's a prank call.

"Hello."

As if time stood still, his voice is still recognizable, and my chest feels as if it's about to collapse in on itself at the sound of it.

"Frankie," I manage to say. "Frankie, you there?"

"Clem." He sounds cautious, and there's no doubt he's on high alert. "What is it?"

"It's Lennox," I breathe out, ripping the Band-Aid off. "He's hurt. You need to come home."

I expect his shock and his silence, but I don't have the time to coddle one brother and be away from the other.

"Frankie," I scold. "Did you hear me? You can't stay away from this. You need to come home."

"I-is he d-dying?" he stutters "Is he dead?"

"No," I say quickly, guilt consuming me that I didn't anticipate his question. "I'm sorry. I didn't mean to scare you. He's hurt and it's bad, but nobody is dying or dead."

"What happened?" he finally asks.

"He got hurt during a game. He blacked out, and when he came to..." I let out a resigned sigh, knowing I just need to get to the point. "He can't hear, Frankie." My voice cracks. "He can't fucking hear."

Just like Arlo, and I'm sure it was the same for Remy, the news needs time to sink in.

"Will his hearing come back?" he eventually manages to ask.

"Nobody seems to know for sure yet." I pause, inhaling a lungful of air, needing it to get Frankie to understand we don't have time for his indecision. "He doesn't want us around him, Frankie. And I refuse to watch him retreat into himself. Not after he's finally found his footing."

The road from childhood to adulthood was a hard one for Lennox. He'd gone from malnourished and skittish to silent and tense. Lennox and Frankie had found each other later in life—and by extension, Arlo, Remy and me— despite their biological connection. I know guilt eats at Frankie daily for failing him, then and now, but this is the time to make it right.

"Frankie," I plead. "I know you can't stand the thought

of coming back to L.A., but he needs you." Hitting him where it hurts, I add, "Your family needs you."

If you asked Arlo and Lennox, they would both tell you there are times when they've questioned Frankie's love for them—Frankie's love for all of us; his departure was such a bitter pill for them to swallow. But deep down, I know the truth. I know his demons are as big and scary as the rest of ours, and his choice to move to Seattle was a sacrifice, not an act of selfishness. But no matter what your intentions are, sometimes you hurt the people you love, and sometimes you're given a chance to heal the people you hurt.

"I'll be there as soon as I can," he eventually says, and my body sags in relief. "I have to ask my boss for the time off and tie up some loose ends."

"Do what you have to, Frankie, but make sure it's an open-ended visit, because I'm not letting you fly back to Seattle until I know he's one hundred percent okay." The tone in my voice doesn't leave much room for arguing, and I think maybe for once he won't. He knows Lennox is just as much my family as he is his, and I didn't spend years raising him and Remy and making excuses for Frankie and Arlo, just for our lives to fall apart as adults.

"I get it, Clem," he reassures me. "I'll text you my flight details as soon as I have them."

"Good."

"And, Clem," he hedges. "If anything changes, call me."

"Of course."

The staffroom door swings open just as I end the call, Billy the café owner standing in front of me. "I came as quickly as I could. I'm sorry to hear about Lennox," he says empathetically. "Take as much time off as you need, and Shannon and I will work it out."

Shannon is Wonderwood's other café manager, and I

use that term lightly, because when I'm not working an exorbitant number of hours, and it's her days on, she barely lifts a finger. And Billy isn't much different. He's a man who knows how to own a business, he just doesn't know how to run it. Either way, I'm grateful for his urgency, certain that if it wasn't for Raine, I wouldn't be able to leave here a minute earlier than closing time.

"Thanks, Billy." I offer him a sad smile. "I'm going to leave for the hospital now, but if you have any questions, please just call me."

He nods. "Hopefully, we won't have to."

A loud knock on the door interrupts us, and when Remy pops his head in, my eyes immediately start filling with unshed tears.

Shooting up from my chair, I run over to him and throw my arms around his neck. "Thank you for getting here so quickly."

"Are you kidding? There's nowhere else I need to be right now."

Grateful to have someone who understands my exact fears and knows my exact worries, I quickly round up my cross-body bag and my sweatshirt so we can get to the hospital sooner rather than later.

Giving Raine a quick hug and waving goodbye to Billy, I step out onto the curb to see Remy climbing into a pearl-white Range Rover.

"Um, Remy," I say, more to myself than him, as I walk up to the driver's side and knock on the window. He rolls it down, his expression expectant, clearly anticipating my question. "Whose car is this?"

"I borrowed a friend's car so we wouldn't have to catch the bus."

I know it isn't the time to ask questions, but I have so many. "We will come back to this," I warn.

He chuckles. "I don't doubt it."

Trusting Remy to get us where we need to be, I let myself sink into the comfortable leather seat and send a quick thank you text to Raine and a "we're on our way" to Samuel.

Lastly, I send a message to Arlo, and hope both he and Lennox can forgive me.

Frankie's on his way.

7
ZARA

"Thank you for dinner," Aubrey says as she turns onto my street. "I can't believe I've lived in L.A. for almost half my life and never been to a food and wine festival."

"I'm happy to have introduced you to something new," I say. "But I can't take all the credit. If it wasn't for one of my favorite Instagram accounts, Meals and Melodies, posting about it, I wouldn't have had a clue it was going on."

"They had that stall, right?" She clicks her fingers as she tries to remember. "The man who looked like he stepped off the set of *Vikings* and his cute boyfriend?"

"Yes. Oz and Reeve," I confirm. "Oz pairs his favorite food and beverages with his favorite songs and bands. It's like he creates the perfect date in one Instagram post."

I inwardly cringe at my date reference, knowing full well I've firmly placed her in the friend zone. It probably isn't fair that I've agreed to keep seeing her, but I genuinely enjoy her company. And since she hasn't even tried to move to first base, I think we both might actually be on the same page.

"I can't believe how much we ate," Aubrey says as she turns into my driveway. "The bite-sized pieces of everything make you feel like you're not eating a lot, and before you know it, you can barely breathe."

"Oh my gosh, tell me about it." I place a hand over my full stomach. "By the end of it I just wanted someone to roll me out to the car."

Laughing, I find myself not wanting the night to end just yet. The little bit of wine taste testing we did at the festival has me feeling lightheaded and enjoying the company of others.

"Do you want to come in?"

If Aubrey is surprised by my offer, her features give nothing away. She turns off her car, and I feel my lips curl into a smile.

"Is Raine home?" she asks, and I'm pretty sure my answer will determine exactly where her mind is at.

"She might be," I answer truthfully. "I kind of give her free rein at this age and tell her to keep me in the loop when she can."

With Aubrey hot on my heels, we reach the front door, and I slide my key in only to find it already unlocked.

"Well, that answers your question." I glance over my shoulder. "Is that okay?"

Aubrey smiles at me softly. "I think we both know this isn't more than friendship."

"Oh, thank goodness." I exhale, as we walk through the front door. "I was trying not to send mixed signals, but I've really enjoyed the few times we've been out together."

"Oh, don't get me wrong." Her fingers circle around my wrist, turning me to face her. She cups my cheek with her free hand. "If you change your mind, I'm definitely still interested. But you also can't have too many friends."

I don't know if her admission makes me feel better or worse, but the relief at being able to be honest with her, and at least make it clear where I stand, lifts the weight off my shoulders almost immediately.

"Mom."

Raine's voice interrupts the moment, and with Aubrey's hands still on me, I turn my head toward her voice, only to be met with wide, incredulous, emerald-green eyes I thought for certain I'd never see again. Blood-shot, red-rimmed, and filled with tears, they stare back at me with heartbreaking confusion. The light that shone so bright the night I met her, nothing more than a dim glow.

God, she's beautiful.

Even in her sadness she's *still* as breathtaking as I remember.

"Mom," Raine repeats, and the moniker is enough to bring my gaze back to hers. "This is my friend Clem, we work together at Wonderwood."

Clem.

Clem.

Clementine.

Thankfully, Aubrey chooses this moment to relinquish her hold on me, and I don't miss the clench in Clementine's jaw.

"Clem," I say, as I take a subtle step back from Aubrey. "It's so nice to meet you."

She quickly wipes at her eyes, and the need to ask her what's wrong sits at the tip of my tongue. "I'm actually going to go," she says as her eyes dart between Raine and me. "I forgot I had to pick something up for Lennox, and the shop closes soon."

"What? No." Raine shakes her head, my extremely stubborn daughter coming out in full force. "You need to eat, and you can message someone else to do it."

Raine's word seems to be final, and Clem nods, probably aware that arguing with Raine is usually futile. I also don't miss how she didn't respond to my greeting, and her dismissal of me stings more than it has any right to.

Raine looks at me. "Mom, I'm going to cook for us, is that okay?"

"Of course."

"Um, should I go?" Aubrey's interruption reminds me that she's still here, and a nice afternoon with my friend has turned into a six-degrees-of-separation revelation that I'm not sure I can come back from.

"No," I say, because the people pleaser in me will not kick her out after I specifically invited her in. "Aubrey, this is my daughter Raine and her friend Clem. And there's plenty of room in this house for the four of us, right?"

Completely oblivious, Raine smiles at Aubrey and nudges Clem, who has been staring at the ground since I walked in. "See? Now, just relax for a little bit before you have to go back home."

Raine drags Clem to the kitchen, and I'm left staring at the back of her, wanting to drag her back to *me*. My mind compiling a list of questions, praying that I can live with what we've done and every single one of her answers.

"Are you okay?" Aubrey looks at me with narrowed eyes, and I offer her a tight smile, hoping it's convincing.

"I'm good." I clap my hands together. "Now. Do you prefer white wine or red?"

———

Aubrey and I are sitting cross-legged on the couch, and I'm on my third glass of white wine, willing my eyes to stay focused on the woman in front of me instead of following my daughter's friend and every step she makes.

"Earth to Zara," Aubrey says, waving her hand in front of my face. "Are you going to tell me what's going on, or do I have to assume you have a problem with your daughter's friend?"

She says the last part of the sentence on a whisper, but my head still whips between her and where Raine and Clem are sitting in the kitchen.

"What are you talking about?" I ask, my voice as quiet as possible. "I don't have a problem with her."

"Do you not trust her with Raine? Or in your house? What is it?"

Her assumptions make me sick to my stomach, because that isn't at all what this is, and even if I can't tell her, I can't in good conscience let her assume the worst about someone I don't truly know.

"No." I shake my head vehemently. "She just has a familiar face, is all."

"Mom," Raine calls out. "Can you come and check this, please?"

Before I can get up, Aubrey places her hand on my forearm. "I'm going to leave."

"I'm sorry," I say sincerely. "This is not how I thought the rest of our afternoon would go."

"Oh my goodness, please, you have nothing to apologize for," she assures me. "Things pop up, and we'll see each other soon."

Her certainty eases away my guilt as she follows me into the kitchen before I walk her out.

"What am I checking?" I ask as a way to announce our presence.

"Oh, it's okay." Raine waves me off. "Clem was happy to taste test the pasta sauce."

"Clem saves the day," I say with a smile that she doesn't return.

Tough crowd.

"It's kind of ridiculous you won't taste the food you're cooking," I add.

"Because I always burn my tongue," she whines. "And there's truly nothing worse."

A huff slips from Clem's mouth and it surprises me. Her eyes are now intentionally on me. "I can think of a few things that are probably worse."

Does she mean our night together? Or is it the shock of finding out she knew my daughter all along? Neither one of us could've seen either of those things coming.

"Anyway," I say, trying to politely steer the conversation. "Aubrey's leaving and wanted to say bye."

"It was so great to meet you both." Aubrey smiles, then shifts her gaze to Raine. "And hopefully I'll get to see you again too."

"It was great to meet you too," Raine says, returning the sentiment. "I'm sorry if we ruined your date by being home. Mom usually tells me if she's bringing someone back here."

"Raine," I scold. "I do no such thing."

The grin on her face is filled with pure delight. "Well, maybe you should."

She winks, actually winks, at Aubrey, who laughs at her and her antics, while my attention gives in to the magnetic pull between Clem and me, wincing at her having to witness this banter between Aubrey and Raine, innocent as it may be. I don't want her to feel insignificant or unre-markable.

Because what we shared was anything but that.

It was memorable.

She was memorable.

Reluctantly, I tear my eyes off of her and look back at Aubrey, now wishing she left sooner rather than later, because Clementine is here, in my kitchen, friends with my daughter, and visibly itching to get out of here. And I need to work out how to make her stay.

"Okay, I better get going," Aubrey announces.

Thankful, I place a hand on the small of her back. "Let me walk you out."

The goodbye is cold and rushed, and I know I'll hate myself for it tomorrow, but for now, my only thoughts are of Clementine.

Straightening my dress, I walk back into the kitchen, feigning confidence and filled with determination. I somehow need to find the balance between the mother I am in this house and the woman I was that night in the club.

Grabbing plates, bowls, and glasses, I start to set up the table for the three of us to, even though I have no plans to eat.

"Clem," I call out, keeping my gaze off of her. "Would you be able to grab silverware for us? It's in the first drawer by the stove."

I don't wait for her answer, and I'm not surprised when I notice her in my periphery, placing a fork and knife on either side of each plate.

"So," I hedge, pretending to fiddle with the positioning of the plates. "You and Raine work together?"

"You don't have to do this," she says quietly.

Confused, I check that Raine still has her back to us as she stands at the stove, and quickly eat up the distance between us. "Do what?"

"Make conversation. You don't have to worry; I'm not going to tell her."

Irritated, I step even closer to her. "You think I'm worried you're going to tell Raine?"

She turns to look at me. "Well, aren't you?"

Her face is so close, her eyes tired, her nose still red from crying. She looks like the world is on her shoulders, and I hate that I have no business asking her why.

"No," I say firmly, sticking to the conversation. "We were two consenting adults."

She remains silent.

"Clementine."

"That's not my name," she says. "Not here."

Her words have me asking more questions I won't get the answers to.

"Please tell me it wasn't your eighteenth birthday."

When words fail her, I grab her chin and make her look at me. "Clem, please."

Her eyes soften, and for the first time tonight, she's right back there with me. Dancing, laughing... touching.

"I'm twenty-four," she answers, her voice soft. "It was my twenty-fourth birthday."

8

CLEM

When Raine invited me for dinner, it felt like a lifeline. That small break from reality that would allow me to gather my thoughts and feelings after learning Lennox's hearing loss is permanent, and the week that followed.

She mentioned her mom might be home, and I never thought anything of it. She spoke of her so often, I was actually eager to meet her, eager to meet the woman who had given birth to and raised such a caring and compassionate human.

I just didn't expect that woman to be Zara.

My Zara.

I spent months conjuring up scenarios where she and I bumped into one another, imagining all the things I would say, feeling giddy about all the things she would say.

Would the air still crackle? Would her touch still sear my skin? Would she remember me?

But this feels like some cruel twisted joke, life once again giving me a taste of what could be and then reminding me it never would. To make matters worse, she's just as gorgeous as I remember, and from the way her friend Aubrey kept eyeing her when she wasn't looking, I'm not the only one who's noticed.

Jealousy I have no right feeling, burns through me. I hate the freedom they have to date and laugh and live, wanting that so badly for myself. Wanting to be able to prioritize my needs without the guilt of everything else coming second.

I move the food around my plate, my stomach too tangled up in knots to enjoy Raine's cooking. When the struggle becomes too real, I move my cell closer to me on the table and quickly type out a message to Nina.

> Can you please pick me up?

Where are you?

> Raine's house.

Okay, when?

> Now.

Just call me now first. Pretend you have an emergency.

heart emoji

The thing about friends like Nina and Raine is they're there for you no matter what. No questions and no conditions. So, I'm not surprised when Nina's name lights up my screen, my cell vibrating against the wood of the dining table, not even a minute later.

"Hello," I greet.

"Hey," Nina says. "I don't know what you want me to say, but I can be there in twenty minutes."

"Oh no," I say dramatically. "Are you okay?"

"I don't know," she replies. "Am I? Probably not. I got my period today. Obviously, I'm always grateful I'm not pregnant, but does the pain have to be so bad? I almost wish I was."

I try so hard not to roll my eyes as Nina babbles on, inserting enough responses to make the conversation believable.

"Of course I'll come," I tell her. "I'm just at Raine's, but I'll call for an Uber as soon as I finish my dinner. I'll be there as soon as possible."

"Am I your Uber?" Nina asks.

"Absolutely."

"Okay, pin drop me the location. I'm leaving now."

"Perfect," I say, relief coursing through me. "I'll see you soon."

I quickly follow up the call with the pin she needs to pick me up, and put my cell back on the dining table, feeling both Zara's and Raine's eyes on me.

Swallowing past the lie, I raise my head, and it's uncanny how much they look alike when staring at me.

"I've got to go," I announce. "Nina's having a bit of a crisis, and I want to check in on her before I go home tonight."

"Is she okay?" The concern on Raine's face fills me with guilt. "Let me text her, she knows she's welcome here any time."

Certain panic is written all over my face.

Zara pushes her chair back, rising off the seat, clearly reading me like a book. "Why don't I pack you and Nina a container of pasta each."

It's not at all what I expect her to say, but considering she gives me an out, I run with it.

"Thanks, that'll be great," I say through a tight smile.

When Zara is out of earshot in the kitchen, Raine looks over at me, full of concern. "Are you sure you're okay to go to Nina's? I can go instead."

The thing about working with your friends is you're all up in each other's business, and for the first time ever, I hate it. I don't want to lie to Raine, and I don't want to put Nina in the middle, but I don't think I have any other choice.

I can't sit here with Zara's eyes on me, the things she knows and the things we'd done floating between us. It's too much, and I feel too naked and exposed, in a way the night with her never made me feel.

"I'll be fine," I assure her. "It'll be a good distraction. We have a shift, all three of us, this week anyway. And we'll all be able to catch up."

This seems to appease her, and my guilt, but before she can say more, her phone must vibrate in her pocket. Holding up a finger, she drags it out of her pocket and looks up at me apologetically.

"I'm sorry, it's my dad. I'll be quick."

I shake my head. "Don't be silly, take your time. I'm good cleaning up."

Rising up off my chair, I pile all the dirty dishes together and take them to the kitchen where Zara is meticulously preparing me leftovers. I have no idea why it makes me want to cry, but the reminder of just how gentle and caring she can be is too much for me to bear; the fact that for all intents and purposes, this stranger—because that's what she is—has made me feel more secure than anyone else has in my twenty-four years of existence, is a problem.

With my strides slow, I place the dishes in the sink. I

open my mouth to say something, but she beats me to it. "You don't have to leave."

A humorless laugh leaves my mouth. "Yeah, I do."

She hands me my leftovers. "I don't want to make things awkward between you and Raine."

I shake my head. "It's not that. We'll be fine."

When the silence stretches too long, I know I've over-stayed my welcome. "Thanks for dinner."

She doesn't follow me when I walk away, and for that I'm grateful. Quickly, I make sure there are no dishes left on the table and then make my way upstairs to Raine's room. She's sitting on her bed, still on the phone, and it's the perfect way for me to slip outside without any fuss.

Grabbing my backpack, I kiss her on the forehead and then bring my hand to my ear, the universal sign that I'll call her later.

"Hey, Papa," she says into the phone. "Can you give me a sec?" Then to me she says, "I can walk you out."

"No." I push her lightly back onto the bed. "I'll be fine. I'm fine. I promise. Thank you for tonight."

"Okay. Call me if you need me," she says.

"I will."

A text message shows up on my screen as I'm walking down the stairs.

I'm here.

Without any fuss or fanfare, I open the front door and slip out of my best friend's house. I launch myself into Nina's passenger seat, her eyes darting between me and the front door.

"Okay, but where's the fire? And where's Raine? What happened?"

I look back at the front door, expecting Zara to walk outside once she notices I left without saying goodbye.

"Drive first," I blurt out. "I'll explain later."

"Okay, you're actually scaring me now."

Nina reverses out of the driveway, and my pulse pounds until I can no longer see the house. I bury my head in my hands and groan.

"What the fuck, Clem?"

"Do you remember the night we went out for my birthday?" I ask, my head still lowered, my voice a little muffled.

"Yeah," she drawls. "I left and you stayed."

"That woman I stayed with..."

"And?" She huffs. "That woman you stayed with what? You're killing me here."

I turn my head to face her, and she alternates between concentrating on the road in front of her and looking at me expectantly.

"She's Raine's mom," I deadpan.

The car is silent, and after all that build up, her reaction is somewhat disappointing. "Are you going to say anything?"

She uncurls a lone finger from the steering wheel and holds it up. "Please wait."

Seconds roll into minutes, and just before I open my mouth to question her, she pulls the car over and puts it into park. Sitting up, I look outside, noting there's absolutely nothing recognizable about the house we're parked in front of.

"Where are we?" I ask.

"I don't know," Nina screeches before backhanding my shoulder. "How dare you drop a bomb like that while I'm driving?" She gestures to the random house. "I had to find a place to stop so I could freak the fuck out."

"Okay then," I say on an exhale. "Let's do this again."

I clear my throat. "Do you remember the woman from the club, when we went out for my birthday?"

She nods. "Yes."

"She's Raine's mom," I say again.

I brace myself for her reaction, but she's just staring at me, not a single sound coming out of her mouth.

"Nina," I whine. "Say something."

"There are no words, Clem." She just stares at me in disbelief. "Like how in the fuck did this happen? What are the chances? I mean, Raine's mom? Really? Does Raine know? What did she say when she saw you in her house?"

"I can't." I shake my head from side to side, my chest heavy. "I can't do this, Nina," I say, completely bypassing her questions. "Not with everything else going on."

Nina unfastens her seat belt and stretches herself over the middle console till her arms are wrapped around my neck. I lean into her and she kisses my cheek before our heads are resting against one another. "Let's just do one day at a time, okay? The thing with Raine's mom happened. You can't turn back the clock, and it's not like it's going to happen again."

If she's waiting for my confirmation or a rebuttal of any kind, she isn't going to get it. Because while tonight was filled with too much shock to think straight, I don't know if being Raine's mother is enough for me to turn down a repeat.

I press my hand over the necklace that secretly sits tucked under my shirt, maybe I was mesmerized by the woman or the act of being *with* a woman, but either way, it unlocked a piece of me that I don't want to ignore. I *can't* ignore.

And now that she's no longer a memory I occasionally

conjure up, I don't know how I can resist that either. Of course, there's the precarious issue of Raine being her daughter and one of my closest friends.

Raine is mature; she's unconventional and progressive. She's unique, empathetic, and wise beyond her years, but she is still also only human. A human with feelings, feelings that hold weight, feelings that are valid and important, feelings that I'm certain neither Zara nor I want to be the one to hurt.

"Clem," Nina says, grabbing my hand and squeezing my fingers. "Tell me you know it can't happen again."

"I know it can't happen again," I repeat.

Nina's voice is gentle now, almost a whisper, almost like she's anxious to voice her next thought. "Clem."

"Mhm."

"Do you *want* it to happen again?"

9
ZARA

A bell rings as I push the heavy glass door of Wonderwood open. The café is fairly busy, a few tables occupied and the line to order about five people deep. My eyes scan the shop from wall to wall, searching for Clementine.

Besides knowing that Raine isn't working today, I took the gamble that with Clementine being a manager she would be here this morning. It's been four days since she left my house, and my mind has known no rest since.

"Excuse me," a voice from behind me says.

Realizing I'm still standing in the doorway, I quickly cross the threshold and turn to apologize to the person.

"I'm so—" The words trickle back down my throat as I take in a flustered-looking Clementine, with her flyaway hairs, red cheeks, and curious green eyes.

"Good morning," I finally manage to say.

Her spine straightens at my greeting, her reaction either shock or defense, neither of which I like. "What are you doing here? Raine doesn't work today."

I nod, anxiously hiking my tote bag up my shoulder. "I know that. I came to see you."

She places her hands on her hips. "Why would you do that?"

"Because you left without saying goodbye."

Whatever she thought I was going to say, the words that slip past my lips aren't it. She opens and closes her mouth, words failing her, as if she's stunned into silence.

"Can we talk?" I ask her.

She flips her wrist, checking the time on her watch, and shifts her gaze to whatever's behind me.

"I can come back on your lunch break," I offer, a little too desperately. "I have the day off, so whenever you're free. I can wait."

I'm coming on too strong, I know it, but I don't have a lot of time to work with. Between all of our schedules, I couldn't guarantee there will be another day that I'll have off and Raine won't be here.

"You're serious, aren't you?" she says, her features softening.

"As a heartbeat."

"In that case, how do you feel about inventory?"

Filled with gratitude and relief she didn't turn me away, I practically bounce on my toes like a teenage girl. "I absolutely love inventory."

She rolls her eyes, but it's the subtle lift of her lips that gives her true feelings away. Feelings that hint maybe I'm not as crazy as standing here before her makes me feel.

I dutifully follow her into a staffroom where she takes my bag and places it with hers in a locker.

"I'll be right back," she tells me. "I just need to grab some paperwork and then we'll get started."

I watch her walk out the door, slip my hands into the

pockets of my wide-leg pants, and begin pacing the length of the room. Besides convincing her to take the time to talk to me, I don't really have a plan, I just want to see her. Have the chance to be in her presence without worrying about all the baggage we've suddenly acquired.

Her return interrupts my thoughts, and I'm naturally grateful for the intrusion. She hands me a tablet along with a stylus pen.

"Are you sure you want to do this?" she asks.

"I told you, I came to see you," I tell her. "If this is what I have to do, then I'll do it."

"We can probably get it done in half the time since I have help," she informs me. "And maybe I'll be able to squeeze in a longer lunch."

"That's motivating enough for me."

This makes her laugh, and I see an edge of the mask she wears around others slowly slip. It wasn't there when I met her, and it makes me wonder what it'll take to have her let it fall off completely.

We make our way into a storage room that is entirely too small to be called as such. It's a tight fit, and the air is warm, but not entirely uncomfortable.

"I'm sorry," she says, nervously tugging at her earlobe. "I know this isn't really ideal."

Finding a nearby box, I carefully place the tablet and stylus on top of it. My hands involuntarily reach for her shoulders, softly squeezing, hoping to release her apprehension. Her eyes fall closed and she drops her chin to her chest with a sigh. "Your hands are like magic, you know that?"

Her head snaps up and a hand flies to cover her mouth. "I did not mean to say that out loud."

"Why?" I say through a wide smile. "I don't deserve the compliment?"

Her cheeks fill with embarrassment, so I steer her body around till she's no longer looking at me, offering us both a reprieve. My hands continue to massage her shoulders, alternating between soft and firm touches, as my body instinctively moves closer to hers.

"Are you always this tense?" I ask.

She relaxes under my ministrations, so I continue kneading her neck and shoulder muscles.

"I've got a lot going on," she reveals. "And..."

"And," I coax.

"And I'm in knots around you," she confesses. "I'm not really sure how any of this is supposed to go."

"Tell me," I start. "If I walked into your coffee shop today and it was the first time you saw me since that night, what would you do?"

"Are you really asking me that while your hands are on me?"

I stop moving them. "I can stop."

"Don't," she rushes out. "Please don't."

My fingers glide up and down her neck, fingertips firm at her pressure points as I massage her nape and the bottom of her scalp. The silence between us stretches, but it's comfortable and familiar.

"If today was the first time I saw you after our night together," she says, bringing us back to my earlier question. "I would put my big girl panties on, act like Clementine instead of Clem, and ask if we could do it again."

My stomach somersaults at her honesty, my body heating up, my pulse frantic. I want to tell her I would absolutely do it again.

And again.

And again.

And again.

But part of me worries that if I breathe life into those words, she and I would find ourselves in a lot more trouble than we have time for. This is still her place of work, and the quick knock on the door is an instant reminder of that.

"Clem," a voice calls. "I need your help. A bus broke down nearby, so they've all piled in here wanting drinks while they wait for the repair service."

"Be out in a second," Clem calls back.

She then turns to face me, my hands reluctantly falling off of her body. "I think we were only supposed to be a one-night thing," she says. "And I don't want to burst that bubble with all this shit."

She waves her hand around the storeroom, but something tells me she means more than just her job. I don't know the whos and the whys and the hows of her life, but it's obvious she's carrying the weight of the world on those delicate shoulders.

Drawn to her and the seven layers of skin I'm sure she keeps her secrets buried under, I want to remind her of the woman she was the night we first met. That woman was air. Light. Free. And I couldn't walk away from her knowing she was anything else.

"Listen," I say, and she tilts her head up to look at me. "Let me do your inventory for you."

"What?" she asks incredulously. "Zara, there's no way."

Ignoring her, I pick up the tablet and the stylus pen, holding them up in my hands. "Show me what to do, and I'll do it."

"Absolutely not." She shakes her head vehemently. "I'll take care of it when it slows down outside."

"I remember you saying something about an extended lunch break."

I watch her put her hands on her hips, exasperated with me. "Teamwork makes the dream work, does it not?"

"Clem!" a voice outside the storage room shouts. "Hurry up."

"This is absurd," Clementine mutters under her breath. "I'm not telling you what to do. I'll do it later. Just leave the stuff in my locker before you leave."

She reaches the door, but before exiting, she surprises me by turning back and kissing me on the cheek.

"Thank you," she breathes out.

"For what?"

"One day I'll tell you." She steps back, smiling at me. Air. Light. Free. "But today is not that day."

———

True to my word, I hang back, snoop around the storeroom, and flick through the tablet to work out how to at least do half of what Clementine has on her to-do list. It's not what I anticipated when I set out to come here and see her, but there's something about reducing even a little bit of her workload that puts me on cloud nine.

Opening the locker, I switch the tablet for my bag and rummage through it for the little notebook I often keep buried in here. Ripping out a piece of paper and finding a pen, I scribble my cell number and drop it into Clementine's backpack, this way there's no pressure.

The café is still bustling, which means that her lunch break will be short, if she's even able to have one at all. And because I don't want to frazzle her any more than my presence this morning already has, I quickly exit the café with my fingers crossed, hoping she calls me.

My stomach is filled with butterflies at the idea of her calling, every part of me feeling school-girl-crush giddy. It's new, and probably a very bad idea, but I'm not in the business of pretending I don't want this to be a thing. At the very least to try.

I just wish I knew what to do about Raine.

As if she's got a sixth sense and knows I'm thinking about her, my phone rings and her name moves across the screen.

"Hey, babe," I answer.

"Hey," she sing-songs.

"How are you?"

"Good. I just needed someone to keep me company while I walk to my next class."

"Should I be flattered you called or offended you're using me?"

Raine laughs. "Either or works. How was your day?" I sit on my answer for a few seconds too long. "Mom, are you there?"

"I'm here," I say. "Actually, I went to Wonderwood today."

"Wonderwood?" she questions. "Where I work, Wonderwood?"

"The one and only."

"Why?"

"I met up with a friend from work, and they suggested it," I tell her, giving her a half lie.

"Did you see Clem?"

"I did, actually." It isn't the whole truth, but being able to share some of it with Raine makes me feel less guilty about my intentions with her friend. It isn't ideal, but it's all I have for now. "We talked for a bit, in between her working. The café was very busy today."

"Did she seem okay?" Raine asks, the concern in her voice unmissable.

"Yeah," I lie. "She seemed fine."

I know she isn't okay, and it goes against every curious bone in my body not to ask Raine why, but I also don't want to hear about Clementine's life from anyone else but Clementine. I want the words to come off *her* tongue, the secrets to slip from *her* lips. I want to earn the privilege to know the woman underneath and what it is that's weighing her down.

But all of that takes time. And it takes patience. It'll take her finding my number on a scrap piece of paper at the bottom of her bag and finding the courage to use it.

And when she does, I'll be here, waiting, because *our* Clementine is worth the wait.

Air. Light. Free.

10

CLEM

Showered and dressed, lying down in my freshly washed sheets, the night is ending way better than the day started. I stare at the ripped piece of paper, Zara's name and number scrawled in handwriting that's as pretty as she is.

It's the third night in a row that I'm going to bed holding the reminder of her. And every morning, I'm that little bit more mad at myself for not using it.

"Knock, knock, knock." Remy's voice travels through my bedroom door. "Can I come in?"

Folding the piece of paper, I tuck it underneath my pillow and call out to him. "Yeah, of course."

Wearing sweatpants and an oversized t-shirt, he ambles into my room and parks himself beside me on my bed. This isn't unusual for us—late night conversations, catching up on all the things we'd missed during the week —but with everything going on with Lennox and him losing his hearing, we haven't done it in a very long time.

"The house is so quiet," he muses. "I'm kind of having trouble sleeping."

"The house actually feels too big," I say in agreement. "And I never thought that would happen."

Like a big teddy bear, he wraps me in his arms, pulling me in for a hug. "Are you okay?" I ask, leaning against his chest.

"I just have a lot of feelings," he reveals. "But I'm not sure what to do with them all."

"You could talk about them," I suggest, a hint of humor in my voice. "I promise to listen."

I feel him shake his head. "Tell me what's going on with you instead."

I think of the paper underneath my pillow and the conversations I would usually have with Raine and Nina as I agonized over whether or not to call, and decide that if I want Remy to open up to me, I have to lead by example.

"I met someone," I blurt out. "Well, I don't know if 'met' is the right word, but I'm interested in someone."

A man of few words, he gives my whole body a tight squeeze, confirmation he's listening and encouragement for more.

"I have their number under my pillow, and I can't decide whether to text them or not."

"Well, why don't you want to text them?" he asks.

My only reason is Raine, and even that has a solution if I contemplate coming clean about it to her. But I don't tell him that, the silence answering his question better than I ever could with words.

"How about I leave you to text them?"

"No." I raise my head, resting my chin on his chest. "Not before you tell me what's bothering you. Or better yet..." I give his chest a light smack. "Whose Range Rover was that when you drove us to the hospital?"

"Ughhh," he groans. "I thought you'd forgotten about that."

"Ha. You wish," I tease. "Now, spill."

"It's my car."

I narrow my eyes at him in confusion. "Come again?"

"It's my car," he repeats.

Pushing up off him, I find myself sitting on the bed, legs crossed, staring at him, extremely unsure as to whether or not he's fucking with me. "I'm sorry, did you just say you own a hundred thousand dollar car?"

His Adam's apple bobs in his throat and his eyes are brown pools of worry and fear.

"Remy," I breathe out, my heart racing. "Please tell me you're not into dealing drugs."

"I'm not dealing drugs," he assures me. "But I take pictures."

"Okay." My brain tries to keep up, trying to work out what kind of pictur— *Oh*. I cock my head from side to side. "A-are y-you...?" I stammer. "Do you...?" I wave a hand up and down his body. "You. Pictures. For cash?"

At this, Remy bursts into laughter, his whole body shaking on my bed. "What?" I ask through a smile, laughter slowly bubbling up my chest. "Am I wrong? You said you take photos."

I grab my pillow and smack him over the head with it. "Tell me," I whine.

"Okay. Okay." Still laughing, he puts his hands up in surrender. "I'll tell you."

Pulling my knees up to my chest, I patiently wait for him to confirm what I think I've guessed correctly, giving him the time and space he needs to feel comfortable enough to continue.

When his laughter finally subsides, he sighs, loudly. "You're right. I take pictures for money."

As if I'm at school, I put my hand up in the air, seeking permission to ask a question.

Remy smacks it down. "Just ask already."

"Are they pictures of you or pictures of other people?"

"Both," he answers. "Anything else?"

"Do you want to talk about it?"

He shakes his head. "There's nothing to talk about."

I beg to differ, but I don't argue with him. "Do I need to keep it a secret?"

"Yes," he says, his tone a little more urgent and serious. "If you can, I would truly appreciate it."

"I can do that." I nod. "But I'm still stuck on you owning a Range Rover. Where the hell do you keep it? How did you keep it a secret?"

He taps my nose. "You know I'm not going to give you all the answers in one go."

"Is that what your photography course is all about?" I ask, trying and failing for more information.

Ignoring me, he climbs out of bed and then reaches for the small folded piece of paper that's sitting by its lonesome on my mattress. He unfolds and folds it.

"They have a pretty name," he says, flicking the paper in my direction. "Call them."

"Remy," I call out as he reaches my bedroom door.

He glances over his shoulder at me. "Yeah?"

"Thanks for telling me."

He winks. "Thanks for listening."

Closing my door, he leaves me alone with my apprehension and indecisiveness. It's close to midnight, and I finally enter Zara's number into my cell and save it. I'm three days too late, but if I don't send her a text now, I'm going to talk myself into doing the complete opposite of what I actually want to do.

I type and delete. Over and over and over again, eventually settling on something short and straight to the point.

> Me: Thank you for all your help the other day.

Because of the time, I don't expect a reply, but when a message from Zara appears on my screen only minutes later, my face splits into an embarrassingly wide grin, and I almost want to scold myself for taking too long to message her *and* being this excited when she messages me back.

> Oh, there you are. I was starting to lose hope that you were going to text.

> I almost didn't.

> What changed your mind?

The truth is easier to divulge when she's a whole house and phone screen away.

> My foster brother.

> You have a foster brother?

> I have four of them.

> Wow. I didn't know that.

I like that I can surprise her, that she doesn't know everything about me yet, even if Raine does.

> Any foster sisters?

> Nope. I'm the only girl.

When the bubbles on the screen dance around for too long, I take it upon myself to send her another message.

> Why are you still up? Did my message wake you?

No.

I haven't slept a full night since we moved to L.A.

> Don't you like it here?

I'm liking it more lately.

My cheeks heat at her insinuation.

> Are you hitting on me?

My words are an echo of the night we spent together.

I'm seeing where the night takes me.

It gives me confidence that she knows exactly what I'm referencing, that like for me, it isn't just a night that happened where the details are sketchy and the memories non-existent. I don't know how much she remembers, but it's enough to make me feel significant. Enough to make me not regret listening to Remy and texting her.

Are you working tomorrow?

> I'm always working. You?

I am. I have Sundays and every other Monday off.

I know what Zara does for work, as Raine has casually slipped some pieces of information into our conversations.

> That explains the impromptu visit. Maybe I'll return the favor one day. You're a hairdresser, right?

So my daughter does talk about me.

At this, I smile, because Raine doesn't just simply talk about her mother, she brags about her.

That she does.

> She's kind of obsessed with you.

smiley face emoji It's a good thing I'm obsessed with her too.

My chest squeezes at their blatant familial affection for one another, the type of mother-daughter relationship I'll never have. It's beautiful to witness, because they don't even need to be in the same room for me to know just how much they love and sacrifice for one another.

When I don't text back immediately, Zara fills the proverbial silence.

You should visit me at work.

I could do your hair for you.

My hand reaches for my hair, the thought of doing anything different with it never occurring to me. I usually cut and color it myself when it needs it, because it's easier and cheaper and I've never truly cared enough. I'm sure this information would horrify Zara, but we live two very different lives, and at more than one point, things aren't going to match up.

> Maybe one day.

My message is noncommittal and a little vague, but it doesn't seem to hinder the rest of our conversation. In fact, nothing does except my continuous yawning and the heavy droop of my tired eyes. I don't want this to stop, though, now that I've ripped the Band-Aid off and faced my fear. This place with Zara, where we aren't really anything, yet there is something between us, is a place I want to live in, a bubble I don't want to burst.

But because life is a cliché, and all things come to an end, I wake up at six a.m., my cell buried between my blankets, four unopened messages from Zara on my screen, the last one at three a.m.

> It's late, you should sleep.
>
> Okay, maybe you're already asleep.
>
> Definitely asleep.
>
> Goodnight, sweetheart.

My cheeks are getting a nice workout in the art of smiling, and to think, I thought I smiled plenty before this. My fingers move quickly, yet carefully over my cracked screen, hoping she's still asleep, but not wanting to leave her last messages unacknowledged and unanswered.

> Good morning.

> I hope you slept well.

> Have a good day.

11

ZARA

"Okay, does everyone have their calendars open?" I ask.

It's a Friday night, and Jesse, Leo, Raine, and I are on a family FaceTime call. With holidays and anniversaries and birthdays coming up, it's always a good time to just sit down and plan where everyone is going to be and when.

It isn't a shared custody situation with strict rules of who has to be where and for how long. It had never been like that, and now that Raine is eighteen it's a moot point anyway, because what she says goes. But we're a close family, and we have every intention of it staying that way regardless of Raine's age.

"I've got Leo here and he's my calendar," Jesse says, causing both Leo and Raine to roll their eyes lovingly at him.

"Are you two still coming down in a few weeks?" I ask them.

"Actually," Raine interrupts. "If you two haven't bought your tickets already, can I come to Seattle instead?"

The four of us are on the call, everybody's face visible, nobody sharing screens. So when my eyes dart to Jesse's in worry, nobody misses it.

"I'm fine," Raine says, attempting to reassure me. "I just miss it there, that's all. And I remembered it's Jamie's birthday that weekend, and a few people from high school will be there, so I wanted to at least try."

"Oh, so you're coming up for Jamie's birthday, not to see your dads?" Jesse teases.

She shrugs, a smug smile on her face. "Two birds, one stone."

"We've got our tickets," Leo informs her, "but I think we might be able to just change them for another weekend."

It's a nonissue, her going and leaving me here, but I'd been excited to see Jesse and Leo and to have them in our space for a few days.

"Zara, why don't you come up too?" Jesse says.

I haven't been to Seattle since we left, and if any of them have noticed, they haven't said a word about it to me. But I'm in a strained relationship with the place I used to call home, only going back when I absolutely want to.

"I'm good," I answer casually. "Just tell me the new dates for your visit when you have them. And, Raine, let's not forget to book those flights as soon as we get off the phone."

"I can pay for them," Jesse offers.

"No. No." I shake my head. "You're paying for that week-long trip to Florida for the three of you. I can do this."

When Raine started college, the deal was Jesse, Leo, and I would share expenses relating to food, housing, and whatever it cost for her to fly between the two states whenever she wanted to. Her income from the café covered the things she did for herself—her cell phone, going out with her friends, public transport, and the ridiculous amount of fast food eighteen-year-olds feel compelled to eat.

"And you're sure you don't want to come with us to Florida?" Jesse asks for the hundredth time.

"I know you all don't think so, but I'll be fine here by myself."

"Mom's dating now anyway," Raine blurts out. "Maybe she'll have someone spend the night."

"Raine," I say on a groan. "Why are you like this?"

She shrugs. "I don't know. You made me, why am I like this?"

"Dating?" Leo pipes in. "Do I need to grow my hair out and come to L.A. for a haircut so you can spill all the details?"

"At this stage, there's nothing to tell." I turn to look at Raine. "But I'm sure if you ask your daughter, she'll be able to give you the lowdown whenever there's news."

She pokes her tongue out at me, completely unperturbed, and like a kid, I mirror the action back at her. When I turn back to the screen, Leo's and Jesse's expressions have turned somber, anxiety etched in their laugh lines.

"What is it?" I ask. "What did I miss?"

"Nothing," Jesse says. "We wanted to make plans for Lola's birthday."

I hate that they both look at me with guilt when wanting to celebrate their daughter's life. We all hold so many different feelings about Lola, that our thoughts and emotions sometimes struggle to coexist.

But she was loved... *is* loved, and celebrating her short yet significant life is not up for discussion. It isn't punishment or a penance, but it would hurt all the same. And I would sit with that hurt, for them and for Raine, for the rest of my days.

Swallowing past the wedge of emotion in my throat, I straighten my posture, giving them all my complete attention. I subconsciously reach for my necklace, needing the strength, even though I know it isn't there. "Tell me what you want to do, and of course I'll be there."

"We can do it anywhere. We can come to you," Jesse adds, and I'll forever be grateful for this man. "But we just want to be together."

"I can come to you," I say, realizing that moment of dread has arrived sooner than I expected. "Lola's there, in Seattle; there's no need for us to be anywhere else."

Unshed tears fill all of our eyes, the screen becoming blurry, everybody's faces hard to see. As a family, we try to share our grief as much as possible, but sometimes it's just too hard to watch everyone crack and break while you're cracked and broken too.

———

"Mom," Raine calls out from the bathroom. "Can you drive me to work? I slept in and I'm going to miss the bus."

"Of course," I shout back from my bedroom. "I don't have plans of my own, I've just been waiting here with bated breath for you to need me."

A few minutes of silence pass and then Raine appears in my doorway. "But seriously, is it okay if you take me?"

"Of course, babe," I say reassuringly. "You know I'll take any reason to skip a workout. Let me just change, though, because I'll go straight to work from there."

After I take off my gym gear, I have a shower, choosing not to wash my hair and get ready for work. I don't love that I need a full face of makeup to work at The Hills, and because I have to get Raine to Wonderwood sooner rather than later, I'll end up having to do it in the car.

Tipping my head upside down, I cover my roots with dry shampoo before styling the loose curls to fall around my face and down my back. Grabbing my fitted tank knit dress from my closet, I slide it down my body, make sure all the seams and zippers are in the right place, and call it a day.

"Raine, I'm ready," I say as I pass her room and walk down the stairs. "Do you want me to make you something to eat? Grab you a granola bar?"

"A granola bar will do." She barrels down the stairs wearing skinny jeans and a black tee, her hair in a perfectly styled fish braid. "Actually, make that two."

I grab them out of the pantry and throw them her way before I lock up the house and we both make our way to the car.

The traffic is pretty shitty, but I'm learning that it's par for the course here in L.A., and I'm grateful that it's so bad, as it puts Raine off from wanting her own car. When we arrive at the café, I feel almost blessed from the heavens that there's a parking spot right out front.

"Thank you so much, Mom." Raine leans over, kissing me on the cheek. "I'll text you what time I'll be home, because I might attend a study group later."

"All good. There are leftovers in the fridge if you decide to eat at home," I inform her. "And I won't be home till about nine since I'm closing up tonight."

"Got it. Love you."

As she hops out of the car and closes the door behind her, a gorgeous-looking Clementine steps into my line of sight, meeting Raine on the sidewalk and throwing an affectionate arm over her shoulders before running a hand over her braid, clearly appreciating it.

The closed window and distance from the car, means I can't hear anything either of them are saying, relying solely on their mannerisms. Clementine doesn't notice the car, or me, until Raine says something that has her looking back.

She glances between me and Raine and then points at her hair. Raine nods and then turns and walks into Wonderwood on her own.

I feel myself fidget in my seat as Clementine approaches the car, our communication lately completely reliant on text. It's been a little over a week, and I've been enjoying the slow crawl of it all. The night with her was explosive and unparalleled with anything I've ever done before. But there's something to be said about living in a constant state of anticipation.

Will she text? Won't she?

What will she tell me? What won't she tell me?

I don't know which one of us is using willpower and which one of us is being indulgent, but either way, we're always meeting in the middle, our texts full of give and take, less is more, now or maybe later.

Usually shy in public, I'm surprised when Clementine has no issue rounding the car, opening the passenger door, and climbing right in.

"Hey, you," I greet, always so surprised by how under-stated her beauty is. "To what do I owe this pleasure?"

"I told Raine I was going to ask you some questions about coloring my hair, but I really just wanted to say hi." She shifts in the seat till she's facing me. "Hi."

We stare at each other, our mouths tipping up in subtle smiles, the air around us comfortable and content.

"Can I take you out on a date?" I blurt out.

Her head turns to the café entrance, and my thoughts immediately follow hers. "I have no issues with telling her," I say.

"Telling her what exactly?" Clementine snaps, her gaze still locked onto Wonderwood, her tone full of attitude. "That you fucked her friend?" A humorless laugh leaves her mouth as she turns to face me, that Clem mask slipping right back on with way too much ease. "You'll tell her you fucked her friend and then what?"

If I'd known asking her out on a date would make her skittish and have her reduce what we did together to a simple fuck, I would've waited. But the words fell from my mouth so easily, because I want it so badly.

Hating the distance between us, I lean over the center console, curl my hand around her neck, and bring her close enough to me that she's inhaling my exhale.

"We are not obligated to tell her anything about that night," I say. "I didn't know you and you didn't know me. So no, I'm not telling her I fucked her friend, just to tell her." I keep my voice steady, my eyes fixed on hers, using her own crass words to get my point across. "I'm telling her I fucked her friend because I'd like to do it again."

12

CLEM

"Earth to Clem." Remy nudges me.

We're lazing about at Frankie's rental, something we all do now that Lennox has moved in with him after his accident. Like Remy said the other night in my bed, our house is quiet now that this place has become the epicenter of our family. But I have to keep telling myself, it doesn't matter where we congregate, just that we all, at some point, are together.

"Where are you right now?" he asks.

"I'm right here," I lie, staring at my cell.

Truthfully, I'm on day five of imagining what a repeat with Zara would feel like, her words from the car making me *ache*. But I'm also on day five of giving her complete radio silence because I'm stupid and stubborn and maybe a little bit scared.

She was so willing to tell Raine, that it freaked me out a little. She was so certain and so sure of herself and whatever it is between us, I'd be lying if it didn't unintentionally make me feel a whole lot less put together. She was my first for so many things, and I need to make sure I'm not confusing the newness of it all with my feelings for her and vice versa.

And then there's my friendship with Raine. What if she's mad or disgusted or just doesn't like it? She's not going to choose me over her mom, nor would I expect her to, but where would that leave me? I don't want to lose Raine, but I also don't want to lose whatever this is with Zara either.

"Seriously, where are you?" Remy repeats.

"What are you talking about?"

"You've been sitting here for ten minutes, completely lost in your own head. And every two minutes you're sighing. Loudly."

"Well, I've got a lot on my mind," I retort defensively.

"You mean you've got Zara on your mind," he whispers conspiratorially.

I elbow him in the ribs. "Shut up Mr. I Take Photos Now."

Nobody is paying Remy and me any mind, most of the conversation lately focused around Lennox and his adjustment to life without his hearing. He's surrounded by his friends Samuel and Rhys, the three of them texting and practicing makeshift signs, while Arlo and Frankie are in the kitchen.

Thoughts of Raine and Zara aside, it's been a tough couple of weeks for all of us; life changing before my very eyes. I thought as a child of the foster system I was very accustomed to change, adaptable, but I didn't realize how change hurt differently when you loved and cared about the things that were changing.

When my phone vibrates against my thigh, I expect it to be more messages from our family group chat, but Zara's name on the screen makes my heart skip a beat.

Surprising me, Remy snatches the cell off my leg. "Jesus, Clem, why haven't you gotten this screen repaired?" he scolds.

"We're not all rolling in Benjamin's, my love," I quip. "I'll get it done when I get it done."

"Let me just buy you a new phone," he suggests. "Or at the very least get the screen repaired."

"I'm not in the market for a sugar daddy, and unless something's changed, I don't think you bat for my team, but thank you."

He hands me my cell back. "You're ridiculous."

Carefully, I swipe at my screen, Zara's message on the display almost immediately.

> Just checking in. I hope you're well.

Guilt surges through me. I should've never ignored her. Not when a simple conversation could've made it all right. Feeling fed up and deflated, I rise up off the couch and glance back at Remy. "Do you want to go?"

"Sure."

Remy asks no questions, and it's what I love about him the most. After saying our goodbyes to everyone else, we drive home in the car he told everyone was his friend's— aka the Range Rover itself.

It's only a twenty- minute drive from house to house, but it's enough to make me feel jittery and unsettled. I feel like I'm punishing Zara for something that is completely out of our control. Determined to make it right, I opt out of responding and choose to call her once I've showered and climbed into bed.

Used to her night owl hours, I don't think twice when I slip my earbuds in and eventually make the call.

"Hello," she answers after the second ring, her voice giving me instant relief.

"I'm sorry," I blurt out.

A soft chuckle reaches my ear. "There's nothing to apologize for. I think maybe I came on too strong, so if anything—"

"No," I interrupt. "You didn't come on too strong. You were honest, and I appreciate that."

"Not too honest?" she questions.

Even though she can't see me, I shake my head. "You just said what I was thinking."

Closing my eyes, I put my cell down on my nightstand and swallow past the irrational fear of rejection, knowing she wants me just as much as I want her.

"The ball's in your court, sweetheart. You tell me what's next and I'll do it."

I love it when she calls me sweetheart. Endearments are my kryptonite, probably because for twenty-four years nobody had ever called me anything else but Clem.

"I'll go on a date with you," I say, answering her invitation, fearing it's five days too late. "I don't really know the logistics of it all, but I want to give us a chance to at least work it out."

"God," she sighs. "I am so relieved to hear you say that, because I can't stop thinking about you."

Besides the day in the car, it's the first time she's made it explicitly clear that this is where we're heading. In text messages we're always teetering on the edge, depending on only banter and light flirting, the decision to hold back an unspoken one.

But all bets seem to be off now. And after admitting we're both very much on the same page—just like our first night—I'm hanging on by a single fucking thread.

"I can't stop thinking about you either," I admit. "I haven't stopped, even before I knew who you were."

"Tell me," she says. "What is it about me you thought about the most?"

I can't answer her question any more than I could pick my favorite food or favorite color. I think about her always, the way she makes me feel, the complete disbelief that someone else has the power to make me feel so good.

It's like opening the door to a brand new world, and never wanting to leave.

"Your hands," I breathe out, knowing it's what I reminisce on the most. "All over me. It's like you seared your touch into my skin."

"Can you imagine my hands on you now?" Her voice is like a surround sound in my ears. "Which part of you would I be touching first?"

When there's nothing but the sound of us breathing, she orders, "Touch yourself, Clementine."

Her use of my full name gives me the courage and confidence to step into the shoes of the woman I was that night. To own my sexuality. To chase my pleasure.

"Slide your hands underneath your shirt," she instructs, and my fingers brush against the necklace that rests between my tits. "I want you to caress those perfect breasts of yours, play with your nipples."

I pluck and pull and roll them between my fingertips. I'm her puppet, and her voice moves my strings.

"How's that belly button piercing?" she muses. "I want you to play with it, tease yourself before I tell you to shove your underwear down your legs and fuck your fingers."

Clenching my thighs together, I bite on my bottom lip to stop the whimper that threatens to come out as I fiddle with the metal barbell, anticipating her next order.

"Do you want to touch yourself?" she asks, and my clit throbs at her question.

"Please," I breathe out.

"Do it," she coaxes. "Slide those delicate fingers between your legs."

My hands eagerly obey, traveling down my stomach, fingers dipping beneath my damp underwear before gliding up and down my slick center.

"I bet you're soaked."

Her words come out a little breathlessly, and I imagine her naked on her own bed, hair fanned around her head, nipples hard, her own fingers at the apex of her thighs.

"Wet," I manage to breathe out. "So. Wet."

"If I were there, I would spread you so wide," she promises. "Bury my face between your legs and lick every inch of you."

"Fuck, Zara," I moan as my fingers apply pressure to my clit, massaging it almost desperately.

"I want you to slide two fingers inside," she coaxes.

I push two digits inside myself, my arousal coating my fingers. My body is a live wire, every nerve ending nothing but heat and lust.

"Fuck yourself," she demands. "Imagine it's me."

My own touch would never be as good as her hands and mouth on me, but with her play-by-play directions in my ear, and the visuals of our night together, it sure as hell is a close second.

I'm close, my muscles coiling, my fingers moving at a deliciously excruciating pace, thrusting in and out, desperate for more. Moving my free hand to my clit, I rub at the bundle of nerves, heightening the rush.

"Zara," I pant. "I need to come."

"Come," she orders. "I'm right there, sweetheart. Come with me."

Her permission is my undoing, and my body arches as my orgasm barrels through me.

I moan into the empty room as pleasure consumes me, the sound of Zara reaching her own release echoing beautifully in my ears.

"Oh my God," I breathe out, words almost impossible to come by. "That was…"

"That was something else," Zara finishes. "*You're* something else."

I preen at her praise, grateful she can't see the embarrassing flush of my cheeks.

"Thank you," I say sleepily.

"For the orgasm?"

"No," I say through a laugh. "Well, yes, but also for sticking around after I practically ghosted you."

"Patience never killed anyone," she says. "And, yes, orgasms with you are a great way to pass the time. But I think we could be more than that, or at least try to be."

I always appreciate her honesty; the way she lays her cards on the table makes me feel safe. It gives me the power to opt in or out with no consequence, and I like it a whole lot.

"I don't really know what I'm doing," I admit.

"You know, you've said that to me before," she reminds me. "And that night turned out great."

"About that date," I prompt, not wanting to lose my nerve, wanting to hold on to more of Clementine before the sun rises, a brand-new day starts, and she's nowhere to be found.

"Raine goes away for the weekend in two weeks," she informs me. "That's our weekend."

Our weekend. I like the sound of that.

At the mention of Raine, I think back to the conversation that pushed us here together in the first place. "Are you going to tell her?"

Seconds of silence stretch before she answers. "I'd rather wait until you're ready to tell her too."

13
CLEM

"This is so stupid," I huff, throwing clothes everywhere. My bedroom is a mess, and if I'd just listened to Nina and agreed to have her dress me, I wouldn't be in this situation.

"Maybe it's not too late to get Nina to come over," I say to Remy, who is lying down on my bed, scrolling through his phone.

His eyes dart up from the screen to look at me. "Are you asking me or telling me?"

"Why did I agree to this? I'm not this person."

He raises a brow. "What person?"

"This." I point to all the clothes. "I don't care about this stuff. I don't go on dates."

"Knock, knock, knock," Nina says, like an apparition standing in my doorway. "I'm here to save the day."

"What are you doing here?" I ask, my whole body visibly relaxing at her impromptu visit.

"Did you think I was going to take your word for it when you said you were fine?"

"I *am* fine," I say defensively.

"So not fine," Remy interjects.

"Hey," I scold. "You're supposed to be on my side."

"There's no side." He climbs up off the bed and walks toward Nina, squeezing her shoulder when he reaches her. "Calm her down, please. I'll be in my room if you need me."

Nina walks farther into my room as Remy walks out and closes the door behind himself.

"Are you okay?" Nina asks, the sarcasm and bravado now missing from her voice.

I throw my hands in the air, frustrated. "I spent money I don't have on outfits I don't love."

Nina's face softens as she sits down on my bed and sifts through my strewn about clothes.

"You really like her, huh?"

Groaning, I tip my head up to the ceiling, not wanting Nina to be able to see how true her words are. It's not that I can't admit it, it's just that what I'm admitting feels sacred and personal, and unlike anything I've ever experienced.

I've been friends with men, slept with men, thought I liked some of them, and allowed them to overstay their welcome in situation-ships that did nothing more than pass the time. Nothing, and I mean *nothing*, has felt as significant or as important as this weekend.

Everything about it is new for me; the effort, the care, the excitement. It feels like my whole world is shifting in ways I never saw coming. But there's also the fear and the apprehension of not giving myself permission to indulge and enjoy and want something that's solely for me.

Overwhelmed and a little bit defeated, I lower myself onto the bed, sitting beside Nina, who is patiently silent as I try to process my thoughts and feelings. I fall back onto the mountain of clothes and she does the same.

"It's weird," I start, as we both stare at the ceiling. "I

thought since we'd already slept together that it would take the pressure off how perfect I want this all to be."

"Perfect for you or perfect for her?" Nina asks.

I contemplate her question. "Both, I think," I hedge. "But mainly her. I guess I'm feeling a little insecure about who she could have and what else she could be doing instead of whatever this, with me, is."

"I don't like hearing you underestimate yourself," she scolds lightly. "If I've understood everything that's happened between you two correctly, she *wants* you. So, yeah, maybe she could be doing whatever with whoever, but she really wants this with you."

Logically, I know she's right, but I can't help but feel like Zara's a little bit out of my league.

"So, what's the plan tonight? What kind of date is it?" Nina asks.

"I agreed to dinner out, and she said she would let me know the details later tonight, but I really don't want to," I admit. "As nice as it is, that's not me. Not with how anxious I'm feeling now anyway."

"Tell her," Nina suggests. "If you want it to be perfect, you have to be comfortable."

"So, what, just text her and say 'hey, do you mind if we order in and I just dress in my pajamas'?"

"If that's how you want the night to go, then yes, tell her."

It sounds so easy. Ask and you shall receive, a concept that is so beyond foreign to me. A world that exists where you can want something and it could actually be yours— what's that?

Nina sits up and rummages through my bed until she finds my cell and hands it to me. "Text her."

"I'm sorry, what?"

She pushes the cell into my chest. "Text her. I have a point to prove, and if I'm right, and Zara is the type of woman I think she is, she'll prove it for me."

"What am I supposed to say to her?"

Nina snatches the phone back off me and types in my passcode.

"So much for privacy," I mutter underneath my breath.

As soon as she opens the text thread, I cover the screen with my hand. "Absolutely not."

"Oh my God," she gasps excitedly. "Have you been sexting? Who are you and what have you done with my friend? I like this Clem."

"Please stop," I say, my face reddening as I take my phone back.

"Okay, but text her," she repeats. "Tell her you don't want to do dinner out and you would rather just keep it low-key at her place. What's the worst that's going to happen?"

"She's going to say yes."

This silences Nina, her brows scrunching together. "But isn't that the point?"

"Yes, but no. What if she's a people pleaser and just says yes?"

"You mean, what if she's like you."

Annoyed, I push her shoulder so she falls back onto the bed, and she squeals. "Why are we even friends?"

"I'm sorry," she says through a laugh. "But you know there are people out there who like to people please, it's their love language. It's called acts of service."

I raise an eyebrow. "But it's not that when I do it?"

"Not if it's not for people you don't love or care about."

I put this information to the back burner, not really wanting to dive into the nitty gritty reasons of all my people pleasing behavior, and throw my phone back on the bed. "Can you just help me find something to wear?"

"Fine," she says. "But for the record—"

I glare at her, cutting her sentence short. "Clothes, Nina. That's it."

It takes two hours of me trying on different versions of the same outfit to find exactly what look I'm going for. I could say that my access and affordability to expensive clothes hindered my selections, but I wasn't really that girl to start with. I prefer comfort: jeans, boots, tanks.

I don't really eat in restaurants or dress up, but if anyone could help me find that middle ground of dressing up and still dressing as me, it's Nina.

"Neen's," I say as I look for my duffle.

"Hmmm?"

"Is it presumptuous to pack a bag?"

"Text her," she groans. When I don't answer, she adds, "My therapist says communication is key."

I whip my head up. "You don't see a therapist."

"I don't, but I bet you if I did, she would say that."

"You know what I need?" I say, ignoring her. "I need a car."

"Actually, that's not a bad idea." I watch her search for her handbag and then pluck out her car keys and lob them at me. "Take mine."

I throw them back. "I've got a better idea."

Grabbing my phone, I pull up my text thread with Remy.

> I have a favor to ask.

> And you didn't just want to make the short trip to my room to ask?

I ignore him and keep texting.

> Can I borrow your car?

I guess. What for?

> I'm going somewhere and I need to have an escape plan in case I'm uncomfortable.

When do you need it?"

> Tomorrow.

Okay. Done.

> Really?

Yes. Just tell me the time and I'll work out the rest.

"Okay," I say, looking back up at Nina and feeling much more hopeful and put together. "I have a car and I can put the bag in there and pull it out if I need it."

"Yay," she cheers, clapping excitedly. "It's ridiculous how excited I am by this."

"Same," I admit with an unmissable grin. I lean forward and grab a random piece of clothing and toss it at her face. "Now, help me put all this shit away."

She glances around the room. "Considering I never see you in anything but black skinny-leg jeans and Wonder-wood shirts, you sure do have a lot of clothes."

"I also may have an issue with throwing things out that I no longer need," I say. "Foster kid trauma—you never know just when you might need something, and if you keep it, you don't have to ask anyone to buy you anything later."

Nina's expression falters. "I never thought of it that way."

"Why should you?" And I mean the question genuinely. If you're not experiencing things firsthand, it's not always your default thinking to be conscientious or understand things you don't need to. "One day I'll let you throw out the things I don't really need. I just can't be here when you do it."

"Let me do it now," she offers.

"What?" I ask, a little startled.

"We can start and just go through them and sort them into piles," she explains. "And then I'll take them when I know you won't notice."

"That's completely unnecessary."

"I want to," she says, her voice full of nothing but sincerity. "If I had a therapist, she would say this feels like the next chapter of your life and you need to embrace it."

"Okay, hold up. Let's back up here for a second," I say. "What am I missing? Are you trying to tell me you started therapy? Or do I need a therapist?"

This has her laughing. "I may have started a self-help audiobook last night and it's got me thinking."

I frown. "What happened to romance audiobooks?"

"I just needed a palate cleanser."

I gag to be dramatic before asking, "What did it make you think about?"

"Just how sometimes we get stuck in a cycle and we think that's all it's ever going to be."

The accuracy of her words has me running a hand over my face, unable to look at her.

"And I know," she continues, "that sometimes you don't give enough attention to your own life, thinking there's no point because nothing's going to change."

"I'm not unhappy with my life," I interrupt.

She shakes her head. "I never said that. I'm just

thinking of how complacent I can be sometimes, not pushing myself, not wanting more, not fighting for something different." She picks at her cuticles. "Could you imagine me actually putting my money where my mouth is and actually stepping out of my parents' shadow?"

The question is rhetorical, because we both know where she's trying to go with this.

"Okay," I say, surrendering. "Hurry up and get it off your chest."

"I'm just saying, you're changing. I can see it every day. Turning those pages till you reach a new chapter, and I can't wait till you do."

Emotion lodges itself in my throat, my eyes stinging. I've been doing a lot of this lately, my hard exterior cracking, the life I seemed to be content living, suddenly not enough. I try to avert my gaze from hers, picking up pieces of clothing and sorting them into piles as she asked.

"Don't overthink this thing with Zara." The warning is clear, even though her voice is soft, and when I cock my head to the side, she adds, "Not any more than you have to. Don't let it fall apart before it can start, just because you're too scared to be honest and claim what you want."

Nina has unknowingly hit the nail on the head, pointing out the exact distinction between Clem and Clementine. The woman I am with everyone else and the woman I am with Zara.

I know I'm changing and shifting, evolving even, but it feels risky, and yet I don't know why. Nobody has ever said my only purpose in this life is to live for everyone else, and yet that's the role I've pigeonholed myself in, so much so, it's my only comfort.

Because I don't know who I am without the foster family, the outdated and unnecessary clothes, and the laundry list of insecurities. This new version of me is still a stranger. One I like, one I want to become familiar with, but one who means letting go of things I didn't think I ever could.

I know Nina is right, but this is already too much for me. Too much thinking, too much introspection, just... too much.

"While I appreciate the free therapy"—I throw the t-shirt in my hand at her, hoping to derail her focus—"let's bring back Nina the romance audiobook listener, yeah?"

"You're going to regret you ever said that," she warns, resting the shirt in her lap. "Because Nina the romance audiobook listener and self-help Nina are both all about that happy ever after."

14

ZARA

"Why do you always wait until the last minute to pack?" I ask Raine.

"Because it's truly so much better when you do it for me," she retorts smugly.

"The only reason I'm even entertaining this idea is because I want to talk to you about something before you go."

This has her whole demeanor changing, and my stomach twists at her assumption that it's bad. I reach for her shoulder, squeezing it in reassurance. "It's nothing for you to worry about. I just wanted to tell you what I'm doing this weekend while you're gone."

At this she perks up. "Is Aubrey sleeping over?"

I sigh and lower myself onto her nearby desk chair. "Why are you so fixated on Aubrey sleeping over?"

Her shoulders quickly rise and fall in a shrug. "I don't know, I guess it makes me feel less guilty for leaving you alone."

"Raine, how many times have we been over this?" I chastise, albeit lightly. "I appreciate it and you, but you don't need to worry about me, and I don't need to fill my bed with people I don't actually want to be with."

What we have is unique when it comes to mother–daughter relationships. We share in excess, all the time, and people often think we're strange, but I'd been a child raising a child, and we grew up and learned life lessons together. Traditional and conventional roles and relationships fell by the wayside.

As Raine entered adulthood, the small amount of authority that I wielded became less and less, and now we very much exist as best friends ninety-five percent of the time. We cry together, we laugh together, and, more often than not, we overshare, way too much; case in point.

"But I thought you liked Aubrey."

"I do like Aubrey," I confirm. "I just think we're better suited as friends."

"Is that what you wanted to tell me?" she asks.

"Not exactly." She raises her eyebrows at me expectantly. "I met someone a few months ago," I disclose. "Our paths crossed again recently, and I'm going to go out with her this weekend."

This is where I straddle the line between telling my daughter as much as I can without outright lying to her and keeping my word to Clementine. People would tell me, I'm the adult and I don't really owe Raine an explanation at this stage, and they'd be right. But maybe if she knows how invested I am beforehand, it will reduce the shock factor if and when she finds out it's Clementine.

"And you really like her?"

"I do," I admit, my whole body lighting up at the simple thought of Clementine. "I really like her."

"Mom," she drawls. "Are you blushing?"

Laughing, I shake my head and hide my cheeks. "I don't

know what you're talking about. I've never blushed a single day in my life."

With a huge smile on her face, Raine drops the clothes she's holding into her carry-on suitcase and makes her way toward me. She grabs the back of her office chair and pushes it, with me on it.

"What are you doing?" I squeal.

She stops us in front of the full-length mirror she has hanging inside her closet.

"Look," she instructs. We both stare at my reflection, the pink in my cheeks unmissable. "Pink suits you."

Spinning the chair, I wrap my arms around her waist in a rush and then run with her toward her bed, until we're close enough I can push her on it.

"Mom," she shouts in between laughs as she turns herself and looks up at me.

My cheeks now hurting from smiling with her, I place my hands on my hips. "Now, are you going to finish packing or not?"

"Ughhhh," she groans. "I can't decide what to wear for Jamie's party."

"Something warm," I say firmly. "I checked the weather in Seattle, and let me tell you, I do not miss it a bit."

"Right?" She leans up on her elbows. "And everybody is wearing crop tops or dresses with cutouts. And I refuse to freeze for fashion."

"That's my girl," I say proudly. "You can do wonders with boots and stockings."

"But I don't have boots and stockings," she whines.

"I guess it's time to go shopping and put that hard earned money to use."

She raises an eyebrow, her eyes full of mischief. "Your hard earned money or mine?"

———

"Hey, her plane hasn't landed yet," Jesse says into the phone, assuming I'm calling about Raine.

"Yeah, I know, I get the notifications," I retort. "That's not the reason I called."

"Oh." He sounds perplexed, like we don't often talk about anything but Raine. "Okay, what's up?"

"So I'm gonna tell you something," I start. "And I need you to just listen, okay? No interruptions, because if I don't get this out now, I never will."

"Jesus, Zara, did you kill someone?"

His question leaves me stumped. "No, but also, how is that your first thought?"

"I don't know, Leo is into crime podcasts lately. Blame him."

Pinching the bridge of my nose, I ignore Jesse's detour and focus back on the issue at hand.

"I met someone," I blurt out. "She's ten years younger than me, but the age difference feels like a non-issue, so I don't even know why I mentioned it."

"You're rambling," Jesse informs me, and maybe his interruptions aren't such a terrible idea. "Where did you meet her?"

"I said no questions," I argue.

"I'm keeping you on track. Now, tell me, where did you meet her?"

"That weekend I flew to L.A. and you, Leo, and Raine drove up with all the furniture," I explain.

"Oh, I remember that weekend," he says. "Have you been seeing someone for that long and you're only just telling me now?"

"Focus, Jesse, please."

"Okay. Okay. I'm sorry,"

"We met that night, spent the night together—a *great* night together—but that was supposed to be the end of it."

"But," he hedges.

"I didn't think I was going to see her again, and I regretted it almost immediately because I've thought about her on and off for months."

"Why didn't you get her number?"

"Fucking hell, Jesse, why are you so bad at listening to instructions," I shout. "And I didn't get her number because when I moved here I thought I wanted to be alone, and the one-night stand would be enough." Lowering my voice, I confess to Jesse what feels like my biggest secret. "Turns out maybe I want what you and Leo have."

"There's nothing wrong with that, Zara," Jesse assures me. "And you think you could have that with this woman?"

"Clementine," I correct him. "Yes. No. Maybe?"

I run a hand over my face as I try to collect the right words to explain exactly what I want to say.

"I like her enough to want to try," I confess. "And nobody has ever come close to that."

"So, what am I missing?" he asks. "What's the problem?"

"The other week, Raine brought her friend over," I say. "She works with her. And, of course, I walk through the front door of my house and who do I come face-to-face with?"

"Fuck me, Zara," he breathes out, realization dawning on him. "Really?"

"I know," I whine. "Like, what are the chances?"

"So, what happened?"

I shrug, even though he can't see me. "I like to believe Raine won't have an issue with it, and I'm doing my very best not to angst over it. But, obviously, I don't want tension with Raine, and I don't want Clementine to have tension with her friend either.

"I may have organized to go on an official first date with her this weekend," I say. "Just to test the waters. And I told Raine I was going out with someone this weekend. Kind of letting her know I'm invested in someone," I ramble. "Geez, I hate lying to her."

"Hey, listen," Jesse says. "Stop stressing for a minute." The tone of his voice turns more somber and serious. "You and I got lucky when it comes to Raine. Most of the time she's the parent, and she has empathy like no other," he explains. "If she and Leo could work through the last two years, I'm sure whatever happens if and when you tell her, will work out exactly how it's supposed to."

His confidence gives me confidence, because not only does he know Raine as well as I do, he and Raine are also so similar. The empathy he boasts about so proudly, was passed on directly from his DNA to hers.

"I feel good about this, Jesse," I admit.

"Then I do too."

"You're the best, you know that?"

"Hardly," he objects. "It's been hard. With Leo and me," he pauses, and I know even a simple mention of the last two years can be almost too much to handle. "Love isn't in the business of being easy, but damn, it's so fucking worth it."

My eyes sting at the absolute love and reverence in his voice when talking about his husband and his marriage. Not in envy or jealousy, but with absolute respect and adoration for Raine's fathers and their commitment to one another.

"Okay, let's be done with the sappiness," I joke. "I have an evening to plan."

"I would say be sure to go all out," he says. "But I married my one-night stand, so at this point, it's already a sure thing."

"Goodbye, Jesse."

"Goodbye, Zara."

15
CLEM

"Okay, but why is this car so excessive?"

"None of those words resemble a thank you," Remy says as his voice comes through the speaker of the obnoxiously comfortable car.

"I called you to say thank you," I counter. "But if I knew you were going to stay on the phone with me for the whole car ride, I would've reconsidered."

He pretends to gasp in outrage. "Don't you want to talk to me?"

"Oh, this isn't talking," I tell him. "You're making sure I'm being careful with your precious car."

When he doesn't respond, I smack the steering wheel. "I knew it."

"Hey," he chides. "Did you just hit my steering wheel?"

"What are you going to do about it?" I smart. "I already have the car."

Remy responds, but I drown him out as my eyes land on the upcoming street name. I flick my turn signal and search out the name of the Lebanese restaurant Zara texted me to meet her at. It's a hole in the wall, and I'm relieved it's this nice tucked-away place in the suburbs. Not because I'm hiding, but because a place like this screams comfort, and comfort right now is exactly what I need.

After trying to talk myself out of this—several times today—Nina had to practically throw me into Remy's car. Now that I've had time alone to think about it, I've allowed myself to acknowledge that I look and feel great. I'm excited to see her, and there really is no reason tonight isn't going to go well. As Nina so kindly pointed out, Zara and I have been speaking through text messages and phone calls for about a month. She's already seen me naked, and she's already made me come.

What is the worst thing that could happen?

"Okay, I'm here," I announce to Remy as I reverse into a parking spot. "And your stupid car is in one piece."

He chuckles. "Thank you. I'm glad you got there safely."

I grumble, "Glad *I* did? Or the car?"

Getting confused on which side the power button of the car is on, I eventually press it, and Remy's voice is no longer loud in the car but a murmur coming from my cell. I reach for it and put it between my shoulder and ear as I grab my bag.

"Okay," I say, cutting him off, having no idea what he's been saying for the last few seconds. "I'm going in before I chicken out."

"You've got this," he encourages, completely following along. "Enjoy yourself. I don't want to see that car till Sunday night."

"Remy," I admonish, my cheeks heating. "I'll message you later."

"Bye," he sing-songs, and we both hang up at the same time.

Climbing out of the car, I straighten my outfit. The sun is just about to set, and I have just enough of a glow to be able to see my reflection in the window.

Nina convinced me to wear a white baby doll dress that's shirred across my chest and the full length of the sleeves. It's different for me, but it's not too tight or uncomfortable, and we compromised with my worn-in, knee-high black biker boots and matching cross-body bag. My hair falls loosely over my shoulders, and I'm grateful it cooperates with almost no effort from me ninety-nine percent of the time.

Before grabbing my clear lip gloss, my fingers detour deeper into the bag, touching the silver necklace that's quickly become my talisman, my reminder of Zara before I truly knew what we could be. Quickly applying my lip gloss, I smack my lips together and lock up the car, slipping my cell and key fob into my bag.

Butterflies fill my stomach. I'm buzzing with energy, finally feeling excited rather than anxious. As I take a step up the short set of stairs, a voice I've come to recognize stops me.

"Hey, you."

Turning, I glance down at a strikingly beautiful Zara. She's smiling up at me, her hair tied in a low ponytail, the last bit of the evening sun shining an ethereal glow around her. She's wearing a high-waisted, full-length khaki skirt with large black flowers printed all over it, with a half-sleeve, black crop top that leaves a tiny sliver of skin exposed between the two pieces of clothing.

Beautiful is an understatement.

She is refined and elegant, and in every lifetime I'm sure I've ever lived, a woman like her would be unattainable to a woman like me. But she's looking at me with stars in her eyes, and I'm not about to give that up for anything.

"Hey." I feel my smile split my face in two as the word leaves my mouth. "Great timing."

She walks up the two steps until she's beside me and then slides a hand around my waist before kissing me on the cheek. "How are you?"

I can't help the cheesy line that comes out of my mouth. "Better now. You?"

She leans closer, kissing me on the cheek again, almost like she can't help herself. "Same."

"This place looks nice," I tell her.

"I've never eaten here before," she admits as we walk inside. "But a client told me about it at work, and it sounded so much better than an upscale restaurant with menu items I have no idea how to pronounce."

We wait till one of the servers is available to lead us to our reserved table. It's situated in the back of the restaurant, tucked away in a cute little alcove, tea candles in the center of the wooden square table, the chairs opposite one another.

It's quiet and intimate and so very different.

Taking a seat, the server is quick to hand us our food and drink menus, along with some water for us both. I reach for the glass, taking a quick sip, and enjoy the cool glide of liquid down my throat.

Zara is looking at the menu, and I use that moment to sweep my eyes over her one more time. Her tongue is absentmindedly pinched between her lips as she scans the menu. I notice the moment she's decided what she wants to eat because she straightens her posture and raises her eyes to meet mine.

"What?" she asks with a shy smile.

"Nothing." I pick my menu up off the table. "Anything look good?"

"I'm so hungry, everything looks good."

I shrug. "So let's order everything."

She tilts her head. "And who's going to eat it all?"

"You just said you're hungry, didn't you?"

"Yes," she says slowly. "But I've got eyes bigger than my stomach."

Chuckling, I look through the food options. "What about a set menu? They've got a little bit of everything included on here."

"Yes. That sounds great, actually." She swaps out her food menu for the drink one. "Do you want a cocktail or to share a bottle of wine?"

"I'm good. I actually rarely drink alcohol," I reveal, almost bracing myself for the shocked reaction that everyone always has. "I think that night at the club was the first and last time this year."

She casually waves her hand in the air. "That's fine. I don't have to drink."

"I didn't say that." I look around, catching the eye of the server and nodding. "I have no issue with you ordering alcohol."

"Hi," the young lady says. "Ready to order?"

I point at the option Zara and I agreed on. "Can we please order this?"

"And drinks?"

"I'll have a Coke, please, and..." I look at Zara expectantly.

"I'll have one too."

"Perfect." The server tucks her tablet underneath her

arm and collects the menus. "I'll be out with your drinks and your appetizers soon."

When she's out of earshot, I look back at Zara. "You didn't need to do that."

"I know," she assures me. "I did it because I wanted to."

Her choice to just blindly do something for me without asking any questions has me eager to explain myself. "My oldest foster brother is a recovering addict. Drugs, not alcohol. And I kind of made the decision to make his journey mine and not really indulge in any of that stuff."

"How's he doing?" she asks, surprising me. "Your foster brother."

"Arlo," I say with a smile. "He's doing really well."

"Ah. Leo, one of Raine's dads, is also on his recovery journey," she says.

"Really?" My interest is piqued, loving that there are things about her and the people in her life I don't know.

"I thought Raine might've told you."

"No." I shake my head. "I know you had her at sixteen and she has two dads. All the other stuff is the little details of information you collect along the way."

Her expression turns pensive, and it looks like there's something she wants to say, but she holds it back, and I don't press.

"You know, come to think of it..." She taps her manicured finger to her lips. "I think she mentioned a Clem once or twice. And I never really even thought to connect the dots."

"Neither Clem or Clementine are common, so it's not really a surprise that you didn't."

"But Raine doesn't call you Clementine, does she? Because there's no way I would've missed that."

I take a sip of my water, holding her chocolate-colored gaze before admitting, "I only let you call me Clementine."

My revelation has the corner of her mouth tipping up before she asks, "What's your full name?"

"Don't make fun," I warn, and she shakes her head and purses her lips together. "It's Clementine Blake Ford."

"That's a gorgeous name," she compliments. "It's so—"

"Pretty," I blurt out, my face scrunched up. "It's so pretty."

"I have never met someone who is so offended at how pretty something sounds."

"It's just... It's just a little delicate for me. That's why Clem works. It's more..." I wave my hands around, searching for the words. "It's more rough and tumble."

She raises a brow. "And you're rough and tumble?"

"Hey," I chide playfully. "You don't know all the sides there are to me."

"Yet," she throws in nonchalantly. "I don't know them all, *yet*."

"Does that confidence of yours come with age?" I challenge.

She smiles at me smugly. "Are you saying I'm old?"

"I'm just curious if it'll kick in for me."

Her head tilts. "You don't think you're confident?"

"I can be, but no." I graze my teeth against my lip. "I don't think I am."

The server returns to the table, interrupting us, placing down our drinks and an assortment of plates filled with traditional chickpea and eggplant dips, fried and fresh Lebanese bread, fried balls of meat, falafel, and what I'm pretty sure was on the menu described as raw lamb mince.

The young lady then lowers two smaller plates, one in front of each of us, along with our cutlery.

"Is this what you meant when you said your eyes are bigger than your stomach?" I tease as we both size up the amount of food in front of us. "Because I'm sure I won't be able to fit anything else in after this."

"I told you." We both reach for the fried bread and scoop out some dip. "If I feel this way and I go grocery shopping, the whole store is in my cart."

"That tracks," I agree. "Try grocery shopping with three brothers after they've all done a gym workout. Apparently, you need a different cereal for every day of the week and every Lay's flavor to ever exist."

"I can't imagine what that's like," she says as I place the bread into my mouth, enjoying the eggplant dip more than I thought I would. "Having four brothers and feeding them. I remember what it was like for my mother to feed Jesse when he was over." She shakes her head in disbelief. "Like, where the hell does all that food go?"

We alternate between talking—asking questions and answering—and tasting all the food in front of us. I watch her as she tears off a piece of fresh Lebanese bread, picks up a piece of the raw lamb mince with it. "Are you ready to try this?"

It's the only untouched dish, and I don't know if we subconsciously did it on purpose because we're nervous to eat it. "Have you tried it before?"

She shakes her head but leans forward, arm extended like she's about to feed it to me. "When I sent you that list of restaurants and you said you've never had Lebanese food, I figured it could be a first for both of us."

This has my chest tightening; it's always the simplest of things with her. I mirror her actions, tearing off a piece of the bread and using it to pluck a piece of the raw meat. I too lean forward, hand raised in front of her mouth. We're nothing but big, goofy smiles now, her eyes full of challenge and excitement.

"Are you ready?" I ask.

"One," she says.

"Two," I follow.

And then in unison. "Three."

16

ZARA

"I'm so full I don't think I can walk out of here," Clementine says, leaning back on the chair, her hands on her stomach.

She looks relaxed and at ease, and a sliver of pride courses through me that I make her feel like that. Okay, maybe it's me and the food, but I didn't miss the hint of anxiety she was feeling when we first arrived, and the need to erase that completely when she's around me has become more of a need than a want.

"I can absolutely do that if you want," I tell her. "But where am I rolling you to?"

The question is forward, but we don't leave things to chance and insinuations, or at least I don't, and not tonight. When I said we have the weekend, I meant it, and I'm not going to let her out of my sight even a single second earlier than I have to.

She bites the corner of her mouth before feigning confusion. "To my car?"

"And then?"

"Home?" The tone of her voice is teasing, the perfect match to the glint in her gorgeous green eyes.

"Mine or yours?" I challenge.

This has her straightening in her seat. "You want to come to my place, the possibility of all my brothers being there and doing whatever it is they do to entertain themselves?"

"If it means the night doesn't have to end, yes," I answer honestly.

"The night doesn't have to end," she assures me. "But we're not going back to my place."

I don't know why, but this prompts me to ask a self-indulgent question. "Did you tell them you were on a date?"

"Remy knows," she replies. "Because I borrowed his car for the occasion." As if sensing I'm searching for an ego boost, she adds, "But he knew about you before that too."

The moment is interrupted by the server silently placing the bill on the table. I stretch to reach for it, but Clementine swipes it out from under me.

"What are you doing?" I ask.

"Paying," she answers, as if it's the most obvious thing in the world.

"But I asked you out." I almost leap up off the chair to take it out of her hand.

She maneuvers it away from me. "Is that a rule I should know about?"

"Kind of."

"Meh." She shrugs nonchalantly. "Rules are meant to be broken. And if I recall, you paid for drinks that night, did you not?"

"Doesn't change that I invited you to dinner."

She signals to the server that she's ready for her return. "You can pay next time."

Her statement shuts me up quickly, and the well-pleased look on her face tells me she knows it. "Fine," I concede. "Next time it is."

It only takes us a few more minutes to finalize the bill and then walk outside into the cool night. The sun has completely set, the crescent moon now big and bright in the sky. We're standing on the sidewalk when Clementine surprises me by turning to face me. She places her hands on my hips, in a move that's bold for her, and brings me closer to her.

"Can I take you somewhere?" she asks softly.

I raise my arms and link them around her neck. "I think I made it clear, I'll do anything to prolong the evening with you."

"So that's a yes?"

When I nod, her eyes dart between mine as she raises her hand to my cheek. Tilting her head ever so slowly, I don't anticipate the gentle press of her lips against mine. It's unexpected, but welcome, and over much too quickly. As she nervously pulls away from me, I hold her gaze expectantly, giving her the permission and encouragement she doesn't need yet wants all the same.

Our mouths move toward one another at the same time, her hand sliding around to my lower back, pressing me into her. It feels so good to be this close to her again, my body against hers, my lips reacquainting themselves with the touch and taste of her. My body hums at her increasing confidence, happy for her to lead, happy for her to take exactly what she wants.

"I've been thinking about that for so long," she murmurs against my lips. "So, so long."

My lips eagerly return to hers, echoing the sentiment, letting her know I, too, can't get enough. It isn't until we hear the voices of people passing us on the sidewalk that reality slowly starts to creep in.

"Let's go," she breathes. "Otherwise, we'll be standing here with my mouth stuck to you all night."

There are definitely worse things, but I understand her point. Releasing our hold on each other, I slide my hand in hers and let her lead me to her car. As usual, I took an Uber, only for Clementine to find out and be irritated. I didn't tell her because I didn't want her to feel obligated to drive to the restaurant together.

My body comes to a halt when we reach Remy's car. "Um, Clementine?"

"I know, I know," she says, reading my mind instantly. "Don't ask me questions I can't answer, but it's his."

I make a show of zipping my lips closed, despite the hundred and one questions I want to ask her. We climb into the Range Rover, putting our seat belts on as she starts the car. I reach across the center console, placing my hand on her exposed leg. Her skin is warm as I graze my fingertips up and down her inner thigh, loving the goosebumps that follow.

It's a comfortable quiet as she pulls out of the parking spot and drives us to whatever it is she has in mind, eventually placing her hand on mine and slotting our fingers together.

"Is Raine the reason you moved to L.A.?" she asks, breaking the silence.

The answer is yes—easy and simple. But it's not really the whole truth, and I don't think it's really what she's asking me. Licking my lips, I find myself stalling, remembering a time in my life when I made the choice to follow my daughter, because I wanted to leave where I was more than I wanted to stay.

"I always knew she would move for college," I start. "I'm not really that mom who wanted to cramp her style, but a lot of stuff happened in the eighteen months before we moved, and I kind of used her as an excuse to leave Seattle."

At this small peek into my past, she squeezes my hand, offering me some comfort. I wait for her to ask for more, because I don't know if I can bring up Lola all by myself.

"Has it helped?" she asks, completely bypassing the obvious question. "Being here?"

"Kind of felt like being a new kid at school," I admit. "Making new friends, starting a new job, finding ways to keep myself busy while watching Raine become more and more independent."

Because I'm not familiar with our surroundings, I don't know where exactly we are, but I notice she's parked us across the road from a red brick building that has a huge sign in front of it that says On The Horizon.

"I remember that feeling," she confesses, staring out the window. "It was like that when I left this place." She turns to face me, and my eyes shift from the building and back to her. "This is the group home where I grew up."

The street lights give just enough of a glow that I can see the mixed emotions swirling in her eyes and the sad smile sitting on her lips. My heart squeezes for the little girl who grew up here; what she lost, what she gained, what she endured. Grateful and privileged that she chose to share something so private and intimate with me.

"Do you visit it often?" I ask, curious for her reasoning behind bringing me here.

"I wanted to keep in the line of firsts between us," she says, referring to my earlier statement about the restaurant.

"I visit the kids here once a month. Cook dinner, watch a movie, help with homework."

"Clementine, that's am—"

She puts her other hand up between us, my words trickling back into my mouth. "I don't want the praise. I've just never told anyone before."

Shifting in my seat, I grab the hand that's still held up in mid-air and put mine flat against it, palm to palm. "I'm going to praise you whether you want me to or not, because it's amazing. I have no doubt it means everything to those children, But why haven't you told anyone else?"

Her shoulders rise and fall. "What's the point? To get praise? A pat on the back? I'm not doing it for that."

She deserved all that and every other kind of accolade that comes with her generous act of kindness, but since I know she doesn't want any of it, I ask the only other thing I do care to know. "So, why choose to tell me?"

Pink tints her cheeks, and she momentarily averts her gaze before raising her eyes to look into mine. "I don't really want to be the same person with you that I am with everyone else."

I *think* I know what she means, and yet it still stings, because I want to know all of her. I want to know every side and every version. I want to know what she thinks is wrong with the person she is with everyone else versus who she is with me.

"You know you can be both," I remind her. "Or you can ditch one and be the other. There's no hard or fast rule that says you can never change."

"I think it's more everyone's expectation that you'll never change," she confides. "That you're reliable and dependable and always there."

Her words strike a chord, so deep, it borderline hurts.

There isn't a day where I don't want to be the person Raine and Jesse and Leo can turn to about Lola, and yet, some days I want to yell and scream because I can't bear the weight of the wall my own feelings are hiding behind.

"I was a surrogate for Leo and Jesse, Raine's dads." The words tumble out of me, like her own self-awareness was the key to unlock my own. "But Lola died at birth."

She swallows hard as she takes in my words, all her attention on me, eyes full of empathy. Our palms still touching, her skin soft against mine, the current a low electric hum between us. As if the connection is the only way we can exchange truths.

"And some days..." The words sit on the edge of my tongue, second guessing whether or not I want to say the ugliest secret I have ever.

"Some days," she echoes, her voice a soft, gentle coaxing.

"Some days I wish I could just turn it all off," I reveal. "Some days I wish I could remind them that I hurt too."

It's a mix of both betrayal and freedom to have the confession slip past my lips. I both hate and love it.

"I've never told anybody that," I say, feeling a whole lot of shame. "It makes me feel so selfish to even think it."

Clementine's hands drop from mine, and she swoops in, cradling my face, bringing hers to mine, till we're only a breath apart.

"A first," Clementine says, the words ghosting over my lips, before she presses her mouth to mine. I kiss this version of her that takes what she wants. I let her absolve my guilt and trust her to keep my secrets.

17
CLEM

There are a host of questions sitting between us as we drive away from the group home, but I know in time she'll answer mine and I'll answer hers. For now, I'm caught in between admiration of her actions and sadness over her loss. I feel it as acutely as she does, that heartache that comes with loving other people so much, their pain is yours and your pain then increases tenfold because of it.

We don't need to fill the drive with meaningless words, her hand back on my thigh is enough to center us both. It wasn't my intention to bring her to On The Horizon, but the second the idea popped into my mind, I couldn't shake it. My time there is a big part of my life, and the time I spend there now even more so. And as the awkwardness on my end dissipated into nothing, I found myself wanting. Wanting to give her more of myself, wanting more *for* myself.

Zara's voice interrupts the quiet. "Thank you for taking me to see where you grew up."

"Of course." I curl my hand around Zara's and lift it up

off my thigh to brush my mouth against her knuckles. "Thank you for telling me about Lola."

I didn't know Raine had a sibling or that she had passed away at birth, and even though I wonder about all the exchanges Raine and I have had and why she hasn't yet told me, I'm grateful to the universe for allowing it so I only heard it from Zara's mouth.

It's obviously such a very big part of her, and one of the reasons she needed to leave Seattle. I could read between the lines, and even if she did only divulge a very minute amount of information, it was enough. She carried a baby for nine months, for people she loves and cares about, and their baby died. Grief isn't even an adequate enough word to what she must be feeling.

"I'll try to keep the depressing talk to a minimum," she says, but I find myself cutting her off before she adds anything else.

"If I wanted to talk about depressing stuff, you would let me."

I catch the subtle roll of her eyes from the corner of my eye, kind of like, *I hear your point but I don't like it,* and it makes me laugh because it's so unexpected and childlike.

"I saw that," I jokingly scold as I turn onto her street. "And you know I'm right."

Smiling, she dramatically slides her hand from underneath mine. "I know no such thing."

We pull up to the front of the house, and the air between us changes almost instantly, the lighthearted banter replaced by a thick, almost suffocating heat. It's not like I didn't know the possibility would present itself. Raine is out of town, and I have an overnight bag in the trunk, and we spoke about the night not ending casually at dinner. The writing is on the wall, but I could tell neither one of us wanted to assume, especially Zara.

I know her well enough to know the decision would be mine. There is never any awkwardness, pressure, or expectation—it's what singled her out from everybody else in my life, but in this small confined space, the pull between us is undeniable.

I couldn't walk away, even if I wanted to.

"Can I come inside?" I manage to ask with every ounce of confidence I can muster.

She bites on her bottom lip, but the smile still manages to stretch across her face. "I would love nothing more than that."

Choosing to leave the bag inside the car, I take Zara's hand as she leads me inside the house. Raine's absence is more significant than I expected. Only having been here once before, and with her, it takes me a few minutes to adjust to the idea of being here without her, which makes me wonder what Zara feels when she's alone.

"Do you miss her when she's not here?"

Zara takes off her shoes before she walks into her kitchen, and I do the same. We place our bags on the counter and I take a seat on one of the stools tucked beneath.

"More so since we moved here, but usually, not really. I've been sharing her with Jesse since the day she was born."

I watch her practically float around her kitchen as she grabs two of everything: glasses, soda cans, and cold bottled water.

"It never bothered you?" I ask. "Sharing her?"

She shakes her head as she places everything on the counter between us. "It's not like we were ever together, and there was no animosity or bad energy," she explains. "It's co-parenting without the failed relationship."

This made more sense, and was true to the person Raine is. She is a collection of good and honest qualities, her heart always open and untainted. It's easy to see the similarities between mother and daughter this way, the pure and honest way Zara had raised her.

"And you two never wanted more?"

The question tumbles out of my mouth, the need to know every single thing about her too damn strong. Zara rounds the counter and takes a seat beside me. It's neither uncomfortable nor comfortable, but I love her proximity to me all the same.

"Jesse and I?" she clarifies. I nod, and she sways her head from side to side. "Raine's conception was the result of two young kids who thought all it took to be a couple was being best friends, but we're very much platonic and always have been. And I'm sure I used him as my guinea pig to confirm whether or not I was really into girls."

An inside look into her sexuality piques my interest. And a small sliver of envy ripples through me at people who weren't having come-to-Jesus moments about their life, mid-orgasm, at the age of twenty-four. I feel heat rise up from my chest to my neck and settle on my cheeks as I think back to the night we met at the bar, the way we tumbled into her hotel room, her mouth stuck on mine.

"I've never done this before," I whispered against her lips.

"Done what?" she asked.

"I've never been with a woman."

"What are you thinking about?" Zara asks, bringing me back to the present.

Swallowing hard, I give my head a quick little shake. "Nothing."

"Try again, sweetheart." She looks at me with a smug smile and knowing eyes as she raises her hand to my hot cheek. "Your flushed skin is giving you away."

A shiver races down my spine, my legs pressing together, the thought of her reading my mind turning me inside out.

"Can I use your bathroom?" I say a little too quickly, forcing Zara to drop her hand from my face.

"Of course," she answers, completely unfazed by my moment of panic. "Why don't you use the one upstairs, in my bedroom."

Sliding off the stool, I practically run to the staircase, climbing up it two at a time. When I find her room, my eyes get stuck on her queen-sized bed, imagining her lying there all the times we've been on the phone, her hands on her own body, bringing herself pleasure.

Stepping into the bathroom, I close the door and catch my reflection; wide green eyes, red cheeks, pink, pouty lips. I look freshly fucked and the woman hasn't even touched me. Turning the faucet on, I stick my hands under and let the water run over them for a few seconds before I gently press my cool hands to my cheeks and behind my neck.

Sex has never been at the forefront of my mind; it's more of an itch that occasionally needs to be scratched, and even then, most of the time I could do it myself. But for eight months now, even before connecting the dots and finding out who Zara was, I have spent endless nights dreaming about soft hands, full breasts, and the single most memorable body I've ever had the pleasure of touching.

I reapply cool water a few more times, doing everything I can to bring down the heat and need that are coursing through my body. Counting down from twenty, I finally switch off the water and dry my hands.

When I open the bathroom door, Zara is sitting on the edge of her bed, legs crossed, waiting for me. She gets to her feet when she notices me.

"Are you okay?" she asks.

"I am," I breathe out. "Was just in my own head for a second there."

"Yeah?" She steps toward me, desire written on her face, the air between us crackling the closer she gets, that all-knowing smile still dancing on her lips. "Anything I can help you with?"

I shake my head as I bite the inside of my cheek. "I don't think so."

She raises an eyebrow. "Are you sure?"

"I don't know." I raise a shoulder. "What is it you think I need help with?"

She doesn't waste time with words, reaching for me and bringing me to her, our bodies flush against one another. Burying her face in the crook of my neck, she kisses and licks my collarbone before traveling up the length of my nape, her lips close to my ear.

"Are you thinking about that night?" Her voice is raw and sultry, causing goosebumps to erupt all over my body at the feel of her hot breath against my skin. "I don't know what I said that triggered your memories, but you know I'm here for a repeat."

Her lips skate across my jaw as I make the choice to answer. "You said you used Jesse to confirm you were into girls, and my mind went straight to that moment, where I too realized I was into girls."

This has her moving her head back to get a good look at me. The lust from minutes earlier is muted, just a little, as she stares at me with something akin to wonder and pride.

"What?" I ask, feeling a little self-conscious.

She shakes her head before lowering her mouth back to my neck. "Tell me about it," she says softly against my skin. "Tell me all about that exact moment."

My heart rate quickens at her request, the pulse in between my legs throbbing. "We'd made our way to the hotel room, and you were kissing me in the dark," I start, my breathing already coming out a little ragged. "And when I told you I'd never done this before, you stopped. And all I kept thinking was..."

Her mouth brushes over my collarbone as she slides the sleeves of my dress off my shoulders, disrupting my concentration. "And all you kept thinking was what?"

"*More.*" The word comes out as an embarrassing breathy whine as her hands cup my covered breasts, caressing them through the fabric.

"And then what," she presses, her eyes full of heat and mischief. "Did I give you more?"

"Fuck, Zara," I pant, completely dazed. "I can't."

"Yeah, you can, baby," she coaxes as she leads us back to the bed and guides me to sit on the edge of the mattress. Still dressed like a fucking goddess, she gets down on her knees, widens my legs, and settles herself between them. Brown eyes peer up at me. "I've got all fucking night."

She slides my dress sleeves off my body completely, the shirred material now only covering my breasts. Her hands slide up my thighs, and when she splays them across my inner thighs, her thumbs skimming both sides of my underwear, my body falls back, leaning on my elbows, and my head tilts to the ceiling, eyes fluttering closed. I'm done for.

Clit aching.

Tits heavy.

Body desperate.

I'm nothing more than putty in her hands, and I know she loves me this way.

"Now, Clementine, sweetheart," she says, the words more tease than endearment. "What was the exact moment?"

18

CLEM

THAT NIGHT: EIGHT MONTHS AGO

The hotel room door falls shut with a thud and Zara pushes me up against it, melding her mouth to mine, our tongues dancing together beautifully.

"Wait," I manage to breathe out. "I've never done this before."

Anxious energy courses through my veins as the revelation leaves my lips. Worry and anguish settling in the pit of my stomach. *Will she still want me? Will she tell me to leave?*

"Done what?" she asks in between kisses.

"I've never been with a woman."

She stops, and I miss her mouth on me almost immediately. She steps back, giving me unwanted space, her eyes taking me in. I expect anger or disgust or confusion, but she's still looking at me with the same amount of respect and desire that was in her eyes only mere minutes ago.

My shoulders deflate in relief, because this woman has encouraged me to call the shots from the very minute I laid eyes on her, but her silence unnerves me.

"Say something," I whisper into the dimly lit room.

"Right now." Her voice is gentle but firm as she runs her thumb over my bottom lip, her eyes darting between my eyes and my mouth. "What do you want?"

Years in the foster system have taught me how to be a chameleon, how to change my skin to fit in seamlessly and to not stand out from the crowd. Survival skills. Years of being whoever and whatever the world needs me to be, at the expense of my own needs and wants, every time. I can't remember a moment where someone ever asked me what it was I wanted, and now they have, I feel both fear and exhilaration at answering.

I open my mouth, but the words sit there, at the tip of my tongue, like being on the edge of a diving board and refusing to jump off.

She softly tucks my unruly hair behind my ear, waiting patiently. "If you don't want to do this, just say the—"

"I want you," I blurt out, a little too loud for the quiet room.

"Have me," she says with certainty. "Whichever way you want. You call the shots, sweetheart."

Inspired by her self-assurance, I keep my gaze locked on hers and wrap my arms around her neck. "Kiss me."

Her mouth is on mine in an instant, pushing me against the heavy hotel door. She presses her body to mine, and I don't miss the way we fit perfectly together. She curls her hand around my neck, her thumb skimming my cheek as the kiss deepens.

If the softness of her lips against mine is supposed to feel foreign, it feels anything but. Her taste is sweet, the faint hint of alcohol on her tongue, and I'm completely drunk on her.

My body hums with anticipation, wanting more but not

knowing exactly what *more* is. Fueled by nothing more than instinct, I push against her shoulders, making my intention known. Together, her mouth still sealed to mine, we walk backward, farther into the hotel room, until the back of her legs hit the edge of the mattress.

I falter for a quick moment, my eyes darting between the bed and Zara, but it's not quick enough for her not to notice.

She brushes her fingers against my cheek. "What is it?"

The concern in her voice wraps around me like a warm blanket, making me feel safe and protected enough to be vulnerable and honest. "I know the reason you're giving me total control and I appreciate it way more than you know." Swallowing back my anxiety, I meet her gaze. "But I don't want it."

Hands on either side of my face, Zara's deep brown eyes bore into mine. "Just promise to use your voice if and when you need to." I nod, and she gently presses her lips to one side of my mouth and then the other before we're kissing again, but this time there's no frenzy and desperation.

The kiss is slow and sensual, full of respect and gratitude to the consent I've given her. "Sit down," she murmurs against my lips. As I lower myself onto the bed, Zara takes a step back, putting some space between us. Surprising me, she toes off each of her high-heeled shoes and then undoes the button on her waistband before slowly dragging the zipper all the way down.

My eyes are glued to her, my heart pounding as she pushes her pants over her round hips and down her thighs. She's beautiful, and not just in the inherent ways women are, but in a way that makes her stand out from the rest. Her every move is full of poise and conviction, like she's so comfortable in her skin, she doesn't ever think twice.

I want that.

I also want her.

I find myself clenching my thighs together, trying to dull the distracting throb between them. The move doesn't go unnoticed and Zara smirks before effortlessly dragging her body suit up her torso and throwing it carelessly on the floor.

My eyes can't decide which part of her I want to stare at more. I know, hand on my heart, I have never looked at any woman the way I'm looking at her, and my body has never wanted a woman the way I want her. It's easy to get caught up in the hows and whys and why nots, but this isn't the time for that. I don't need the answers badly enough to make this moment about that.

I take in her figure wrapped in a black lace bra and matching thong, the way her breasts sit, full and heavy in each cup, the flat yet soft expanse of her stomach, and her smooth, toned thighs.

Her body is proof of life and experience, and I itch to have my hands on her, to feel her skin against mine, to become acquainted with the shape of her. These are things that are new and foreign.

When my eyes manage to find their way back to hers, I'm certain there's no hiding just how mesmerized I am by her, just how captivated I am by her every move.

"You're fucking beautiful," I breathe out.

She bites the corner of her mouth to hide her smile, but the blush blooming on her cheeks makes me want to continue to compliment her to keep it there.

Without even giving myself a second to think about it, I raise my hands in the air, wanting to be as stripped bare as she is. Wordlessly, she steps forward in understanding, hooking her fingers underneath the edge of my tight crop top and dragging it up and over my head.

If Zara is surprised by my naked chest, her face shows no signs. My top is tight enough and my boobs are small enough that a bra is unnecessary, except now that means there is nothing hiding how hard my nipples are.

Trying not to get sidetracked by how exposed I am, I channel my own version of Zara—confident and carefree—and rise up off the bed and glance down at my shorts.

"Can I?" Zara asks.

Nodding, I hold my breath as I watch her deftly undo the vertical line of buttons and then glance back up at me, her eyes asking for permission, asking for more. Wrapping my arms around her neck, I tilt my head and press my mouth to hers, giving her the permission she's seeking, and then some. Her tongue wraps around mine as her hands settle on my ribs, thumbs skimming the underside of my breasts, teasing me in the most subtle of ways.

Hands move down to my backside, pushing my shorts and stockings down to my thighs, leaving me in black lace boy shorts. She glides her fingers across the front of my underwear, and my breath hitches at just how good her feather-light touch feels.

"Do that again," I whisper against her lips.

I lower my gaze to watch as she rubs my clit through the lace, my head falling to her shoulder, my body slowly losing the ability to stand up on its own.

"I can feel how wet you are through your panties," she says into my ear. "Is that for me?"

I let out a strained chuckle before admitting, "Yeah, that's definitely for you."

"Give me your dominant hand." I immediately drop my right arm from her neck and put my hand in hers.

She guides my fingers to the apex of her thighs, the damp spot between her legs eliciting a low "Fuuuck" from my lips. "Is that for me?" I ask, echoing her question and mirroring her movements.

"Yeah, sweetheart," she pants. "That's definitely for you."

As if there's an elastic band wrapped around our restraint, and the evidence of our pleasure is all we need to let go, Zara's mouth slams onto mine and we tumble clumsily onto the mattress. We fumble with my shorts and stockings, both of us now in nothing but our underwear. We move to the center of the bed, me up on my elbows, Zara raised up on her knees, peering down at me.

She glances down at my underwear and then raises her brow at me in question. Running on lust alone, I ask her the same wordless question but keep my eyes on her tits.

She winks at me, slowly dragging each strap over her shoulders as I hook my fingers into the waistband of my panties and drag them off my legs. I'm naked and exposed, completely vulnerable, and yet I've never felt so safe and secure in my life. She lets her bra fall to the bed, along with her thong, and that slight bounce of her breasts, her necklace hanging between them, makes me want them in my mouth.

That's new.

I hold my hand out to her, and when she places her hand in mine, I pull her to me till she's on all fours on top of me, her mouth on mine, her tits lined up perfectly with mine. She has her thigh right between my legs, and I can't help the way my body rocks against her.

"You're making such a mess on my leg," she says into my ear. "I wonder what'll feel like on my face."

Every word that comes out of her mouth sets my body

ablaze. Her lips trail down my neck, kissing and sucking my skin as she makes her way to my breasts. The first swipe of her tongue across my nipple has me arching off the bed. She alternates between each breast, using her tongue and fingers, sucking and rolling, her touch making my core throb.

She moves farther down my body, and my hands replace her mouth, plucking and rolling my own nipples. When her tongue glides up my center, a loud moan leaves my mouth before I sit back up and lean on my elbows, not wanting to miss the view of her between my legs.

She manages to peer up at me, her dark-brown eyes focused as she feasts on me. I rock against her, moaning as she drags her tongue through my folds.

She pushes my thighs farther apart, stretching me wider as she slides two digits inside of me. My body sags onto the mattress, the pleasure too much to hold myself up. She thrusts her fingers, hard and deep, as she licks and sucks my clit.

My legs tremble, closing around her head as my orgasm coils around my veins, squeezing me so tight, every pulse point pounding before my inevitable release.

"Fuck, Zara," I cry out as she continues gently circling my clit, the aftershocks of my orgasm turning every nerve ending in my body sensitive and fragile. My chest rises and falls, heavy breaths filling the room, as I try to form a single coherent sentence after the best orgasm of my life.

Zara's head pops up, eyes blazing, her lips glistening with my arousal. My stomach flutters at the sight of her and how she's so proud to have my mess on her face. She crawls up my body and I curl my hand around her neck, slamming her mouth to mine, curious to taste myself. It's unhinged and completely unlike me, and yet I couldn't foresee myself ever being the same after tonight anyway.

"I don't taste too bad," I joke.

She brushes her nose against mine before kissing me again. "You taste like one of the best decisions I've ever made."

In my life, words are useless, empty, often misspoken, but Zara makes every single one of hers count, no matter what she says, and that includes words that make me feel like I'm on top of the world.

There are too many moments in my life that are memorable for all the wrong reasons, but this isn't one of them. This realization that a whole other world exists, a place where I feel both inexperienced and welcome all at the same time.

It isn't an epiphany where the veil has been lifted and suddenly everything in my world starts making complete sense, but it's the fact that I didn't see any of this coming, and yet not a single decision I have ever made before this moment ever felt this right.

It's not even about the sex.

It's the revelation that I could give *and* take.

The revelation that I could want *and* be wanted.

The revelation that I could feel sexy *and* safe.

Sex has never been anything more than just sex for me; it's transactional. I've never felt safe enough to explore my sensuality. But with Zara, the wants, the needs, the outcomes are all *mine*. And I don't know if it's because I'm having a bisexual awakening at twenty-four, or because I've finally connected with someone who happens to be a woman.

I don't have the answer right now, and I also don't know if I care enough to want it. All I know is I want to spend the rest of the night making this woman feel as good as she's made me feel.

Give *and* take.

Want *and* be wanted.

Sexy *and* safe.

19
ZARA

I've been with plenty of women, but none of them had ever turned me on the way Clementine does. I don't know if it's the way she's so responsive to my touch or if it's the way she makes me feel like a fucking god when she touches me.

I'm not going to lie, there's something that makes me feel a little unhinged and possessive that I'm the first woman she's been with. Something that makes me want to be the one and only woman for her. Something that scares and excites me all at the same time.

It's a premature thought—for so many reasons—and yet I find myself thinking it way too often, and when she's voluntarily in my space, enjoying my company, like now, it's all I think about.

We're naked in my bed, Clementine's hands roving all over my body, like I'm a shiny new toy that she's enjoying exploring.

Her hand cups my breast and she starts to slowly strum my nipple with her thumb. The motion has me wanting to gently rock my hips against her, but the expression on her face tells me to hold off, just a little.

My fingers smooth the worry lines between her forehead. "What's got you playing with my nipple and thinking so hard?"

A soft, lackluster laugh leaves her mouth as she flicks her gaze back up to meet mine.

"I really like your tits."

This has me laughing but infinitely more confused. "And you're frowning because you really like them?"

A rattling on one of my nightstands interrupts us, Clementine's phone vibrating incessantly. Groaning, she turns and reaches for it, barely glancing at who's calling. She taps the screen and I hear a man's voice come through the phone.

"Hey, where are you?"

She curls back into her original position of facing me, placing her cell, that has a completely shattered screen, on the mattress between us, her thumb back to flicking my nipple.

"Really?" I mouth, and she blows me a kiss.

"I'm out, why? What's wrong?"

"We just wanted to know if you would be here for dinner," he says. "We're all in and ordering pizza."

A myriad of emotions I can't quite catch crosses her face before she answers. "I'm good. I'm not going to be home till tomorrow."

"Monday," I whisper.

"Maybe Monday," she adds.

"Clem." The man's voice is full of concern.

"It's fine, Arlo."

The silence stretches, a wordless conversation between her and her foster brother that I don't miss.

"Can you at least pin me your location?"

"I'll do it as soon as I get off the phone."

"Okay," he says, only mildly comforted by her acquiescence. "Love you."

Clementine's hand quickly forms into a fist before she releases her thumb, forefinger, and pinky all at the same time, it looks like she's using sign language as she says the words. "Love you."

The line goes dead and the call automatically ends. When she makes no move to pick up her cell, I grab it off the bed and hold it between us. "Send him the location."

She cups my breast. "I'm kind of busy."

"Clementine," I say gently. "For whatever reason, he's worried about you. And I don't want anybody to be worried when you're with me."

Her face softens as she sighs and takes the cell out of my hand. She places it back between us and strategically moves her finger around the screen, avoiding the shattered glass.

"Are you going to get that fixed?" I ask.

"What?" Her phone vibrates against the mattress, and I internally sigh with relief knowing she's sent him her location. "My screen?"

"Yes. It looks like a death trap."

"One day." She puts the cell back on the nightstand before turning back to me.

"What's he worried about?" I blurt out, cringing at how invasive my question is.

"I thought you didn't want to talk about depressing stuff." She doesn't seem perturbed by my question, instead smiling at me smugly. "Or was that just for you?"

"Okay." I huff. "You proved your point."

She leans in to kiss me, her lips lingering, like we have all the time in the world.

I secretly love that.

Surprising me, she pushes me to my back and then straddles me. I take in her expression, knowing she's trying to distract me from my unanswered question, her smile wide and irises no longer buried under emotion. She looks so breathtaking with her disheveled blond hair, pink cheeks, and dusty-rose nipples on full display, that I indulge in her deflection.

I glide my hands up her body and cup her breasts, thumbing her nipples. She lowers her mouth to mine.

"We can talk later," she murmurs against my lips. "But for now we should get back to how much I love your tits."

She glides her lips across my jaw and down the length of my neck. She leaves open-mouthed kisses down the valley between my breasts as she gets on her knees to give herself better access to lick and suck my nipples.

Her hand slides down between us, the pads of her fingers massaging my clit, before she dips two and then three digits inside of me. It's an easy glide, two orgasms earlier and my constant state of arousal around her and she's knuckles deep.

Her lips and tongue venture away from my breasts, trailing down my stomach and joining her fingers. I groan as she gives me all her attention, tasting and teasing me, opening me wide as she fucks me with her fingers.

My hand finds the back of her head, pressing her face to me as I rock against her, loving the deliciously torturous climb to my release.

"Clementine," I gasp as she curls her fingers inside me, grazing my G-spot. "Do it again."

My wish is her command as my feet dig into the bedding, and heat coils around the base of my spine.

She pushes me to the brink right before surprising me and stopping completely.

"Clem," I whine.

"I know. I know." She gets up on her knees, straddles my thigh, and grabs my hand, placing it over her sex. "But your pussy has me in a chokehold and I need to come with you."

My fingers glide beautifully through her slick center, her arousal coating my fingers. I slip the digits between my lips and moan at the taste of her. "You're too fucking sweet, baby."

She slams her mouth to mine, and we get lost in the taste of one another just before she maneuvers my leg so our mounds are flush against each other.

"Oh, fuck," I cry out as she grinds against me, our clits furiously rubbing together.

"Zara, please come with me," she pleads.

"I'm right there, sweetheart," I pant. "Fall apart with me."

We're completely enamored, our gazes never straying from the other's. We rock back and forth, over and over, her wetness mixing with mine. It's always too much and always never enough.

Surrounded by the sounds of heavy breathing and sex, Clementine and I chase the inevitable high. She cries out as her body seizes atop mine, her legs trembling around me and her clit pulsing against mine. Her eyes flutter closed as her head falls back, and the undeniable euphoria on her beautiful face is my absolute undoing.

My own body arches off the bed as I shudder through my release, heat and exhilaration coursing through me. We ride out our orgasms, our bodies moving against one another, slow and languid, basking in the afterglow.

Reading my mind, Clem leans forward and captures my mouth with hers. There's less of the fire and frenzy, but the taste and feel of her are always so potent, so significant, so life changing.

She peers back at me, and I see the vulnerability in her eyes, the toll it takes on her to share her history, and the courage it takes to ask for what she truly wants. But it's nothing compared to the true smile that splits her face in two.

With a sated and relaxed sigh, she sags against me, my fingertips running up and down the length of her spine, enjoying the way her body rises and falls with mine. As the comfortable silence stretches between us, I find the courage to resurrect my question from earlier.

"Why is Arlo worried about you?"

I'm not surprised when she doesn't lift her gaze to meet mine, or that she doesn't answer instantly. Determined to show her that I'm patient, I continue to soothe her with my touch, waiting till she finds the words.

Eventually, she drags herself off of me and we're back to lying down on our sides and facing one another.

"Promise me something," she says, her tone serious. "Please don't get all weird when I tell you things about my past or my upbringing."

"Weird how?"

"I don't know." She shrugs. "Just don't pity me, okay?"

I feel my face fall at her request. "I would never pity you."

Needing to hold her, I hook my leg over her hip and throw my arm around her waist, bringing her impossibly close to me, my gut warning me whatever she says isn't going to be easy, but I want to be here for her.

For a moment she puts her palm to my cheek before

resting it on my waist, and for some reason it feels like she's comforting me instead of the other way around.

Her throat bobs, and I wait for whatever bomb she's about to drop.

"My birth mom was raped." I admire her eye contact as she tells me what has to be the most heartbreaking thing to ever come out of someone's daughter's mouth. "She was sleeping at a friend's house, and a friend of a friend was over and made his move."

She averts her gaze, and I realize she still hasn't delivered the final blow.

"It's how I was conceived." Her eyes fill with unshed tears as she tries to hide the emotions in her voice. "And because of that, I don't sleep away from home. Well, I haven't." She pauses, her gaze stuck on mine. "Until now."

My chest tightens for a plethora of reasons, namely because I couldn't imagine what it would be like to know those details about your conception. It can't be an easy thing to come to terms with, especially for a child.

I brush my knuckles along her cheek. "How old were you when you found that out?"

At this she closes her eyes, and my heart breaks for her. "I can't remember not knowing," she says, her voice just above a whisper. "It's the reason I was put in foster care. She couldn't—" Her voice cracks as she buries her face in my neck.

"Shhh, sweetheart." I try to soothe her, grazing my fingers up and down the knobs of her spine, my mind filling in the blanks, my heart absolutely shattered for the baby who paid for a mistake she never made. "It's okay, I've got you."

A muffled groan sounds throughout the room before she peers up to look at me, her watery green eyes doing nothing to hide her pain. "You really should've stuck to your no depressing talk rule."

I feel a sad smile tug at my lips as I run my thumbs under each of her eyes, wiping away the tears. "I'll listen to you talk about absolutely anything if it means I get to know more about you."

"Such a smooth talker," she teases, her soft smile turning serious all too quickly. "I'm sorry for crying. I haven't gotten that emotional about it in *years*."

"Hey." I hold her head in my hands, ensuring all her focus is on me. "I want to know everything about you. If that comes with tears more often than not, then so be it."

She mirrors my actions. "You know the same goes for you, right? If you ever want to talk about Lola, I'll always listen."

The mention of Lola feels like squeezing lemon juice into a paper cut, but unlike all the other times, where I hide behind a fake smile or lie my way through a conversation, I kiss Clementine, grateful that for once someone sees me. It's a strange and yet refreshing feeling to have someone know that sometimes everything isn't okay.

"Thank you," I say, feeling my eyes sting, grateful for this unexpected gift of a human who makes me want to open old wounds and ensure that this time they heal properly.

Her eyes narrow. "For what?"

I press my lips to hers. "For being you."

20
CLEM

I wake up as soon as the sun rises high enough to peek through the blinds. Working out with Arlo more often than not has ruined my ability to sleep in, even after the late night we had. I slowly climb out of the bed, careful not to wake up Zara. I head to her bathroom and quickly rummage through my duffel that I eventually brought in from Remy's car.

Finding my toothbrush, I quickly wash my face, brush my teeth, and tie my hair up on top of my head. I notice a robe hanging on the back of the bathroom door and reach for it, not wanting to wash the remnants of last night off any part of me just yet.

I wrap it tightly around me and am glad to see Zara still peacefully curled up around her pillow. Grabbing my cell, I walk back into the bathroom to grab my AirPods and then quietly make my way down to the kitchen.

Making myself at home, I start to look through the fridge, hoping to find something to put together for breakfast. The beauty of growing up and fending for myself is I can pretty much cook a meal out of nothing. But when I spot the full tray of eggs, a full bottle of milk, and a sealed package of bacon, I'm grateful I don't need to think too hard.

Slipping the AirPods into my ears, I press shuffle on one of my most recent indie rock playlists and let the music keep me company as I cook. I find pots and pans in a large drawer under the microwave, pull out the two I need, and set them up on the stove.

Finding a medium-sized silver mixing bowl, I do a quick sweep of the rest of the kitchen, piling up salt, pepper, bread, and a few utensils in my arms. Lining them all up on the counter, I start by cracking four eggs into the bowl. Then I add salt, pepper, and milk, and whisk it all together.

I turn on two burners and begin heating up the pans, filling one with bacon and the other with the eggs. When they're both hot enough, I scramble the eggs over the heat, and quickly switch off the burner as I search high and low for some lids to stop the eggs from going cold and the bacon from spitting at me.

"Found ya," I call out excitedly into the empty space, holding up the two lids in the air. When both pans are covered, I put bread in the toaster, but don't turn it on yet, and go back to the refrigerator to grab an avocado.

I'm bent over, reaching for the fruit, when gentle hands settle on my waist. I startle momentarily but am grateful for her perfect timing. Turning to face her, I pull one AirPod out of my ear and take in her barely-there sleep shorts and tank before holding the avocado up between us.

"Do you eat smashed avocado?"

Smiling, she nods before pulling me to her and pressing her mouth to mine. "Good morning."

Her lips are cool and she tastes like spearmint. "Morning."

"What are you doing?" she asks, glancing around the kitchen.

"Uh..." I follow her gaze. "Is it not obvious?"

She chuckles. "It is, but you didn't have to."

I roll my eyes playfully. "I know I don't have to. Maybe I just want to."

"And what if I wanted to make you breakfast?" she challenges.

"You're going to have to wake up a little earlier than me to make that happen."

"Why didn't you wake me up?" she says with a pout.

I smack her lightly on the shoulder with the back of my hand. "Don't give me that look. You looked so peaceful and I know how hard it is for you to sleep."

The fridge begins to beep. "Okay, so let's close this," I say, shuffling us out of the way.

Zara then tugs at the belt that's holding my robe together, pulling it until it hangs open, exposing my naked body. Her gaze glides over me like silk on my skin, and I fight the urge to ditch breakfast.

"You need to stop looking at me like that," I warn. "I made you breakfast."

Her tongue pokes out to lick her bottom lip. "I could eat two meals."

"Of that I'm sure," I say with a chuckle.

I wrap the robe around myself, tying it back up, and point to one of the kitchen stools. "Why don't you sit down and let me finish."

"Why don't *you* sit down and let *me* finish?" she counters.

"How does anyone ever manage to do something nice for you?" The question is rhetorical, and she has the decency to look sheepish, but the struggle to be still and let people wait on you resonates with me. "Do you want to plate it up?"

Relief is evident in her posture, and I hate that she feels a little put out when someone does something nice for her. She grabs us both plates and we stand at the stove as Zara dishes us up the eggs and bacon. I scoop out the avocado and smash it in a bowl, adding salt and pepper before finally toasting the bread and then sitting down to eat.

"Thank you," Zara says, kissing me on the cheek. "I don't remember the last time someone made me breakfast."

Despite knowing it's impossible, I still reply with, "I'll do it anytime you want me to."

She kisses me again, but this time it's interrupted by what sounds like the ringing of her cell coming from upstairs.

"Shit," she says, holding her egg-filled fork to her mouth. "That's probably Raine."

"Do you want me to run upstairs and get it for you?"

She shakes her head as she chews and swallows her food. "I'll call her back when I finish my breakfast. If she calls a second time within the first five minutes, that's usually when I stress and there's a problem. She's probably calling to see how my weekend with my mystery woman is going."

My body stills at her words, a cyclone of panic brewing in the pit of my stomach. "What did you tell her?"

Zara cautiously lowers her fork and pushes her plate away so she can move herself closer to me. She places a hand on either side of my legs, turning me on my seat so we're now face-to-face, my legs bracketed perfectly between hers.

"I didn't tell her anything incriminating," she reassures me. "I just don't like lying to her."

"I know that," I say a little too quickly, a little too defensively. "I don't want that either."

"I told her I was seeing someone," she says. "I told her I really liked this person and I want it to work out more than anything."

Her honesty silences me, because how am I meant to argue with a confession like that? I want all those things too. As I sit here in her kitchen, making breakfast for her after a night wrapped up in her body, I want *this* life more than anything.

"When you're ready, you tell her." She places her hands on either side of my face. "I won't rush you on that, but I at least want her to know just how important you are to me. I want to be able to say I'm going to see my girlfriend, and not have to lie about it."

I swallow at her confession, not at all disliking the word but disbelieving that a woman like her could truly want someone as inexperienced as me. "I'm your girlfriend?"

"Well?" She reaches for my hand, holding it between both of hers. "I don't want you to walk out of here on Monday morning thinking that you're anybody else's but mine."

"Zara," I breathe out, completely bowled over by her revelation.

"What?" I don't miss the hint of anxiety in her voice when she asks, "Do you not want that?"

I slide off my stool and stand between her legs, tipping her chin up so her eyes meet mine.

"I want it," I say, my voice earnest. "I want *you.* So

much. But I don't know what it's like to let myself want things."

The truth hurts to say out loud, that painful reminder that I have been unintentionally living a life based on everybody else's needs and Zara is the one single reason that I've started to question it.

Everything between us is new, but it's also very real. And the possibility of not having this woman in my life hurts just as acutely, if not more, as all the other things I've let myself walk away from, and yet I can't make all the pieces in my life fit together.

"I don't even know what I like." My hands flail wildly as I ramble. "What I dislike. I didn't even know I could be into women. I'm a hot mess."

"Hey." Her voice immediately soothes me as she curls her hand around the back of my neck, her thumb rubbing soft circles over my rapid pulse. "I don't care about how messy you are. I like you just the way you are."

"How?" I argue. "How, when you don't really know me? How, when *I* don't really know me."

I'm challenging her now, greedy for reassurance but asking for it in all the wrong ways.

"Do you know how many times one person can change in a lifetime?" she asks rhetorically. "Or how late in life some people discover and come to terms with their sexuality? I don't know where you got the idea that everyone but you is so put together, but we're not." Her voice loses its certainty. "I'm so far from put together, Clementine, but I want this with you all the same."

Her perception of herself is real-life proof that the person we see when we look in the mirror every day is almost never what everybody else sees. It should've been comforting that we're all walking around, struggling with imposter syndrome, and yet my insecurities do not give me the concession I know I deserve.

"I live in survival mode," I explain. "I always have. I do what I need to, to make sure my carefully constructed world stays the way I need it to."

"And how is that?" she asks, genuine curiosity in her eyes.

"I make sure everybody else is taken care of." I don't know why it leaves a bad taste in my mouth to say that out loud, but it's never felt like a burden till this very moment. "I make sure nothing can disrupt the peace, and if it does, I'm the only one who takes the hit."

"How is that fair?"

"It's not."

"So why do you do it?"

I shrug, feeling hopeless. "I'm just scared."

Her hold on me tightens. "Of what?"

So many things.

"I'm scared to be selfish," I say truthfully. "I'm scared to put myself first, to finally want things. For every one thing I could have, it's another thing I could lose."

I see the understanding settle on her features. The devastation of loss and just how irreparable life after it could be. I know she's lived it.

"We just take one day at a time," she says patiently. "That's all any of us can really do. That's all *we* can do."

Nodding, I know she isn't going to give me a chance to walk away from this, and despite all the reasons old habits and history told me to do so, I want to listen to her and I want so badly to stay.

Standing, she moves that little bit closer to me and

kisses one corner of my mouth. "What do you say?" And then the other. "Do this with me?"

I move my head, wanting her to kiss either side of my mouth again, before cradling her face, capturing her lips with mine and finally answering her question.

Yes. I say yes. I'll do this with you.

21

ZARA

"What are you doing?" Clementine's unused morning voice fills the room.

"Shh." I continue to bury my nose in her hair. "If we don't talk, then we're not truly awake, and if we're not truly awake, then we don't have to say goodbye."

It's the most ridiculous, childlike logic, but I'm here for it. Already curled around her, I tighten my arm draped across her waist and bring her back flush with my front. It's Monday morning; we both need to get to work, and Raine will be back in L.A. later this afternoon.

Of course I miss my daughter, but this bubble Clementine and I have created together has been everything I wanted it to be and then some. The only problem is that being with her, with no disruptions and complete access to her mind and her body, has solidified that I don't want to let this woman go.

Not for a minute.

Not for a day.

Not for a lifetime.

My feelings for her are big—*too* big, *too* soon—but I

can't seem to slow them down. And at this point in my life I don't think I even want to. I know Clementine thinks she's the inexperienced one out of the two of us, but just because I know my way around a woman's body doesn't mean I have any idea on what to do with a woman's heart.

Hers or mine.

"Maybe if we skip breakfast, we can stay here longer," Clementine suggests.

"But I was going to cook for you this morning."

It's a silly thing to fixate on, but I want to have my cake and eat it too. I want to pack our two days together with all the things we won't be able to do with one another while Raine is home. We're doing it all backward, not at all conventional, but nothing about my life has ever been conventional, so what's the point in starting now.

Turning, Clementine grabs my hand and guides it between us

"I think this"—she then mirrors the action on me, cupping my sex and making her intentions known— "might be a better use of our time."

The green in her eyes is alive and vibrant as I hold her gaze and slide my fingers through her folds, not even a little surprised to feel her arousal on my fingertips. She's insatiable, her confidence evolving every time we touch.

I lower my mouth to the crook of her neck, sucking on her skin as I tease and stroke her, my own body coming alive every time I touch hers. I hike my leg up and around her hip, opening myself wider to her as fingers slip inside me.

It never gets old, that full feeling, the deep sensation as she finds a steady rhythm, thrusting her fingers in and out of me. My mouth meets hers, teeth clashing and tongues feasting; a small spark morphing into an unmanageable flame in minutes. Desperation growing between us, our hands moving faster, the race against the clock heightening everything about this moment.

"Zara," she moans, her eyes boring into mine as my slick fingers continue to rub at her clit. "It's too much."

Even in the heat of the moment there is a vulnerability in both her expression and her words that steals my breath. She isn't just talking about her impending orgasm, she's talking about us.

Too soon, *too* big, *too* much.

My heart grows two sizes too big, my chest struggling to contain everything that is transpiring between us. I fuse my mouth to hers, using the only coherent form of communication I have available to me at this moment.

I want her to know I feel it too.

All of it.

The big and the small and everything in between.

Clementine cries against my lips, her orgasm taking us both by surprise. Her body shudders as she tightens around my fingers, her hard clit pulsating against my thumb.

Her fingers fumble as her body goes lax, and I replace her digits with my own, mixing her arousal with mine.

"Fuck, I'm sor—"

I kiss away her apology because I don't need it. It has no place here, because give and take comes in so many different ways and wants. This included.

Her mouth is hard against mine, unhinged almost, like even though she just came, she still somehow can't get enough.

My lips falter, a loud moan leaving my mouth when she unexpectedly slides her own finger against mine, pushing it inside me.

"Oh my God," I pant.

"I want to see you fuck yourself on our fingers." It's more demand and less request, and I'm happy to oblige. She looks down between us, and my gaze follows.

My hips rock as our fingers move, back and forth, in and out, wetness smeared all over them.

I've never felt so complete as incomprehensible words slip from between my lips. My body trembles as the orgasm rapidly courses through me, completely obliterating me. My legs automatically slam together, but Clementine stops me.

"I'm not done," she murmurs, eyes still fixated on my pussy. She slides her finger out and mine follow, but she's quick to bring both our hands up between us.

Neither of us miss the glisten that coats our fingers, and when Clementine puts all three digits in her mouth, a familiar heat stirs in my belly.

"I think I've created a monster," I whisper.

She smiles smugly around our fingers before slipping them out of her mouth. "But I'm *yours*, right?"

She is definitely mine, and everything we share in this bed is ours. My heart trips over itself hearing her acknowledge something she wasn't so sure of only a day ago.

"We have to get up now, don't we?" She sighs.

"I think we can at least squeeze in a shower together before we rush off and it feels like this weekend never happened."

She beams at me as I take her hand and drag us both out of bed. The shower is supposed to be quick, but we can't help ourselves from the wordless appreciation that takes place between us as we wash one another.

After rubbing shower gel over every inch of her body, I shampoo and condition her hair. It's the way she softens as someone takes the time to prioritize her that has me taking my time.

She rinses herself under the spray and my gaze follows her, entranced and enchanted. She runs her hands over her wet locks, pushing them out of her face, before walking me back until I'm one with the cool shower wall. Her hands are pressed against the tiles, one on each side of my head. "I want to take care of you the same as you take care of me."

"You want to wash my hair and body?"

She rolls her eyes and steps closer to me, one of her hands curling around the side of my neck. "Obviously, I can do that, but you know that's not just what I mean."

I don't know why the words and her intentions surprise me, but my chest aches in longing for mornings that start like this and days full of what she's offering. It's not that I need someone to take care of me, I've done well on my own, but her simple desire to *want* to do that for me, has warmth filling my chest.

"You think just because you say that you want me to be yours, it doesn't go both ways?"

I slide my hands around her waist, closing the space between us completely, our wet bodies flush against one another. "I'm yours, huh?"

"Absolutely." Her gaze darts to my lips and back to my face. "And if there's one thing I know how to do well, it's take care of what's mine, okay?"

"Okay," I say softly. "Take care of me, then."

She kisses me quickly before squeezing a generous amount of shower gel into her hands, rubbing them together to create some suds. She foregoes the loofah and explores every curve and dip of my body with her hands.

My eyes flutter close as I relax into her touch. She's gentle and reverent, like I'm precious to her in every way.

Tender hands wash my hair, and I feel myself become overwhelmed by unfamiliar emotions.

Clementine turns the water off and then drags a towel off the rack before wrapping it around me. She gives me a quick peck on the nose. "Do you think we still have time for you to cook me breakfast?"

22

CLEM

"That smile kind of looks weird on your face," Remy says as I make us breakfast.

I flip him off. "How about you feed yourself."

"It's too late now, you've already started."

I slide over his grilled cheese sandwich and glass of orange juice across the counter. "I won't be home till later tonight."

"Are you going out with Zara?"

I shake my head. "No, I'm just closing tonight."

It's been five agonizingly long days since the weekend Zara and I spent together. I underestimated how hard it would be to go back to my everyday routine knowing that a life like that, with her, was somewhat within my reach.

"Oh," he says, sounding a little confused. "I thought after spending the weekend with her, you would be with her all the time."

My chest pinches, knowing I am undoubtedly the only reason that she and I aren't seeing each other every other day. I told her I was scared, and I am. I'm scared to tell Raine and have to give Zara up completely.

The chances of it working out that way might be slim to none, but it's still too much of a risk for me to lose her now. Even this early in the relationship, I know it's something I won't be able to bear.

Not wanting to dive into the conversation with Remy, I offer a weak platitude of sorts, knowing he isn't one to pry any further. "We're both just busy."

Nodding, he picks up his sandwich and begins to eat. I do the same and let the silence stretch between us, my mind floating back to Zara. Even though I haven't physically laid eyes on her, the last five days have been full of late-night phone calls and all-day messages. There isn't a single passing second where we're not thinking about one another, and letting the other know. It's so new and different, and never in my wildest dreams did I think I would like the idea of "belonging" to someone, but I *love* the idea of belonging to Zara.

"You're all wearing that face," Remy says, interrupting my thoughts.

I take a sip of my juice before answering. "What face?"

"That love-sick face," he says. "First it was Frankie and Arlo with all the pining, then it was Lennox with Samuel and Rhys, and now you."

His observation has a laugh bubbling out of my mouth; he's kind of right. Two months ago it was Arlo, Lennox, Remy, and me living together, and now it's Arlo and Frankie rekindling their relationship, Lennox finding love after his hearing loss, and me trying to figure things out with Zara.

I playfully shove his shoulder. "Don't sit too close or you might be next."

"Yeah." He rises and walks around the kitchen to put our empty dishes in the dishwasher. "Hard pass on that one."

"Never say never," I tease. "Do you need anything from me before I head off to work?"

He shakes his head in the negative. "I'm good. I'm gonna jump in the shower, but I'll see you later."

We say our goodbyes and then I stop by my room to grab my bag and phone. I can't stop the smile that stretches across my face when I see Zara's name on the screen.

> Remember when you told Raine you were talking to me about your hair?

>> Yes?

I have no idea where this conversation is going.

> I have a cancelation in two weeks on a Wednesday, and I wanted to ask you if you wanted your hair done instead of me filling up the slot.

I mull it over; the idea of doing something different and fresh with my hair is very much appealing to this new version of myself, but the truth is, I can't afford to do it at a regular salon, let alone the upscale one Zara works at.

Another message comes through before I get the chance to answer.

> We wouldn't have to lie to Raine about seeing each other and this gives you enough time to check your schedule.

It sounds more enticing with every message she sends, but reality is a bitch, and if she wants to know every part of me, then this was included.

That sounds amazing, but I can't afford to get my hair done right now.

Three dots bounce on the bottom of my screen before disappearing and reappearing again. It happens another three times before my phone vibrates in my hand and Zara's name runs across the screen.

"Hello."

"Hey," she breathes out. "I tried to text but none of it was coming out right."

Not wanting to be late to work, I place the phone between my ear and shoulder, and lock up the house before heading to the nearby bus stop. "What's not coming out right?"

"I know this isn't going to sit right with you, and I'm not trying to overstep, but I don't charge my family when I do their hair," she says. When I don't answer, she adds, "That includes you. Nothing about that invite had anything to do with money. It didn't even cross my mind, I just wanted to do someth—"

"Zara," I interject. "Slow down."

There's no denying she and I are from different pay brackets, with very different life experiences, but there are ten years between us, and while it doesn't often pose a problem, I have to consider that there are going to be times when it's going to come up. Case in point.

And while I want to stand my ground and hold my own in every facet of my life, I don't want Zara to be tying herself up in knots in the process or miss the fact she included me in her family.

"Shit. I really fucked this up, didn't I?"

"No..." I pause, running my hand over my face. "This is part of it, right?"

I'm grateful she isn't pointing out the differences between us or offering to pay, because I'm protective over my independence, and I'm certain Zara knows that.

"If you're sure family doesn't pay, then I'll make sure I schedule myself off that day."

She exhales loudly into the phone, and I feel her relief as if it's my own.

"I'm sorry," she says again.

"I'm sure you can make it up to me," I tease, trying to lighten the mood.

"Do you have any ideas?"

"Actually," I drawl as an idea formulates in my mind. " I do. Are you free on Monday night?"

"I can and will be." There's no missing the priority she's placed on us, and my stomach fills with butterflies at her assurance. "I miss you."

"I miss you too," I echo before admitting, "Like really stupid amounts."

"I'm happy to know I'm not the only one."

"Talk to you tonight?" I ask.

"Always."

We hang up, and the smile that was on my face when I answered doubles in size. While the ache in my chest from missing her never dissipated, the happiness that fills me from being attracted to someone and exploring something so new and exciting with them fuels me.

My phone vibrates almost immediately, and I'm surprised to see Nina's name on the screen.

"Hello," I greet.

"Did the phone even ring?" Nina says as soon as she hears my voice.

"Sorry, it was in my hand and I just hung up with Zara."

"Oh." Her voice perks up. "And how is she? I wonder

what your ship name could be," she muses. "Zaratine? Or what about Clemra?

I groan. "Please stop. Both those sound like medication for STIs."

"I mean, you're not wrong," she says with a laugh. "But you need ship names."

"You could try using our actual names."

"Well, you're no fun. But either way, that's not why I called."

"Is everything okay?" The bus finally arrives at my stop, and I internally cringe at having to talk in front of the other passengers. "Are you okay?"

"Why do you do that?" she asks, her voice a little disappointed. "Do people only ever call you when something's wrong?"

I pinch the bridge of my nose. "Nina. Focus."

"Okay. Yes. Sorry." Her voice turns serious. "Are you able to house-sit at the beginning of next month and watch Dexter for the weekend?"

"Your dog?" I clarify.

"Well, yeah. How many other Dexters do you know?"

My shoulders sag in relief, proving Nina's theory about how I expect something to always be wrong, to be true.

"Just the weekend? And don't you normally just pay someone?"

"Dexter's getting old. He needs medication daily, and honestly, I don't trust leaving him with anyone but you," she explains. "And you'll have my car in case you need to get around. It can be like a mini vacation. And you could bring Zara."

This has my ears pricking up, because a few days with Zara at Nina's place is the equivalent of a holiday stay in a resort.

"I know how you get about fucking up your work schedule, so I wanted to give you some time."

I think back to Zara also checking in with me so I could work out whether or not I had to work. "Am I really that particular about work?"

"What? Where did that come from?"

"What you said just got me thinking."

"You're the manager. You have to fill the spots when people call out," she says. "It makes sense you don't want to make your life harder."

Her explanation actually makes me feel a million times better and less like some inflexible grump.

"So when do you need an answer by?"

"The weekend before is fine."

"Yeah, I can do that, but just text me the exact dates you want me there." I mentally note it down, knowing I'll put it in my calendar as soon as we get off the phone.

"You're the best," she says. "I'll text you now. Thank you."

Just like she said she would, Nina texts me the dates and I transfer it along to my calendar, realizing Zara never told me what time the hair appointment is.

> Hey, what time is that hair appointment?

2:30pm.

> Do you think you can get a few days to yourself at the beginning of next month?

> I got asked to dog sit for Nina, and her place is practically a resort. Thinking we could spend another weekend together.

A weekend with you? I'll make it happen.

My face stretches into another obnoxious smile. I like the idea of making plans with Zara. For once, I like thinking about the future, even more so a future with her in it. Not even caring how eager I sound, I send her another message.

I'm already counting down the days.

23
ZARA

Monday's are always slow, but counting down the hours till this evening almost killed me. It had been one week since I last saw Clementine and I've decided anything longer than this isn't an option.

I pull up to the curb as my GPS tells me I've arrived at my destination. Picking up my cell from the cup holder, I quickly send a text to Clementine.

> I'm here.

Her response is instant.

> I'll be out in a minute.

When Clementine asked me to pick her up from her house, part of me reveled at being allowed more insight into who she is and where she comes from. The house is a little older, the facade a little outdated, but it's neat and tidy, and I maybe googled the area to see if it's safe.

Thankfully it is.

When the front door opens I'm surprised to see three young men walk out, Clementine right behind them. Knowing enough to know that they're three out of her four siblings, I open my door and climb out of the car.

I'm a grown woman. I'm not going to sit here, like a girl in my teens, too embarrassed to step out of the car. Clementine is their sister, a woman we all respect, a woman I like a whole lot more than the weight that single word will ever hold.

I know how important these men are to her and I want them to know how important she is to me. Rolling my shoulders back, I make my way into their front yard and stand at the patio entrance.

Clementine pushes through her brothers. "I'm sorry about this," she says, completely unperturbed by my decision to get out of the car. "They aren't all usually home at the same time." She glances behind her. "Well, they're not all here; Lennox is with his boyfriends, but I'm sure it's only a matter of time."

Her snark has my mouth lifting in a smirk. I like this side of her. I'm certain this is the version of her that holds her ground against her brothers, the version of her that says "I love you, but I will not take your shit."

"Arlo." Clementine points at the biggest of the three, with his muscled body and long brown hair. She then points to the man who's holding Arlo's hand, who's the same height but not the same build. His body is slender and more swimmer-like. "This is Frankie," she explains. "And this is Remy." Remy is very obviously the youngest, and from the way Clementine nudges him, I can tell they're close. Eventually, she drags her gaze away from her brother and turns to meet mine. Pools of green soften as she says, "This is my girlfriend, Zara."

Pride bursts inside my chest. Having her say it out loud to the people she loves the most, gives me hope we're moving a step in the right direction, that we're on the same page, and this is most definitely going somewhere.

"Hey," I say as I hold my hand out to greet each of them individually. "It's nice to meet you all. Clementine's told me so much about you."

"Who is Clementine?" Arlo asks, a smug smile painting his lips.

She flips him off and then steps toward me, sliding her hand into mine before rising to her toes and kissing me on the lips.

"Hey," she murmurs against my mouth. "We're going to be late."

I glance back at her brothers, and the three of them are staring at Clementine like she's grown two heads, but none of them are bold enough to say anything to her, and I like that. She tugs on my hand, and I dutifully follow her back to my car.

Before she climbs in, she calls out to them. "Bye. I'll see you all in the morning."

"Safe to say meeting the girlfriend was a success," I joke.

She smiles. "They were so insistent on meeting you when they saw your car pull up, but when I agreed, they seemed to have swallowed their tongues."

"I think it went well," I add.

"I enjoyed shocking them." She then leans over the center console and kisses me. "Hi again."

I smile against her mouth. "Do you think your brothers are the type to be peeking through the windows?"

She laughs and pulls away, situating herself back in the

passenger seat. "I don't think so, but we should get going anyway. I don't want to be late."

"Where am I taking us?" I bring up the GPS on my screen. "I don't know where I'm going half the time, but I'm happy to drive."

"I'm sorry, I should've asked to borrow Remy's car." She types in the address and On The Horizon comes up as the destination.

The only reason we would be going there again is if it's Clementine's turn to volunteer. "Are you sure?" I ask, almost feeling guilty to be invading something that is so important and personal to her.

"Yes," she assures me. "I asked if I could bring someone with me, and they're always excited to have an extra set of hands."

An unexpected onslaught of emotions lodges itself in my throat. This woman is so unsure and uncertain of whether or not she has anything to offer, and yet here she is opening up her very private life to me, including me, allowing me the privilege to see every single side of her.

"Thank you," I manage to say. "I know how much this means to you, and I know how close you keep this to your chest."

She offers me a soft, wistful smile as her eyes fill with unshed tears. "I want you to know me."

Unsaid feelings and declarations fill the air around us as we make the rest of the drive. Hands clasped together as we both no doubt get lost in our own thoughts about life and maybe, just maybe, love.

There's a small little parking area behind the house that can't be seen from the street, and Clementine instructs me on where to park my car. My heart beats rapidly as we walk up to a back entrance that is secured with a gate that you need a code to access.

"Do they have a lot of people visiting here that shouldn't be?" I ask, feeling every bit of my privileged life and the hint of shame that comes with it.

"It happens," she says nonchalantly as she punches in the numbers on the keypad. "Parents fighting over custody, parents with protective orders against them. You also need to make sure that everybody who comes in has been verified with some kind of background check and has been approved to work with children."

This has my steps faltering. "I don't have one of those."

"I know," she says, sliding her hand in mine and leading me inside. "I spoke to Rochelle, and you're just going to be observing. And you need to be with either her or me the whole time, but if you want to come back, I can help you get one."

"Only if you want me to come back," I say, still cautious of invading her space.

"Of course." The words leave her mouth without a second thought, no hesitation or issue with having me around.

Clementine rings the doorbell. "Just don't decide till the night's over, because it might not be everything you think it is."

I stare at her as she waits for the door to open. "I'm certain it's everything I think it is."

The door swings open and I reluctantly drag my eyes away from Clementine, trying to push away the urge I have to throw myself at her and tell her how amazing she is.

"Clem." A woman at least ten to fifteen years older than me greets her with excitement. "It's so good to see you."

Clementine blushes. "It's only been a month." The

women hug each other before Clem brings me to her side. "Rochelle, this is—"

"Oh you must be Zara," she finishes. "Clem mentioned she was bringing someone with her tonight."

"Clemmmm!" The high pitched squeal gets closer as a girl no older than five, with dark brown curls, runs into Clem's legs and hugs her tightly. "You made it."

Clementine crouches so she and the little girl are eye to eye. She bops her nose. "And how's my favorite five-year-old?" Clementine asks, confirming her age.

The little girl bounces on the balls of her feet. "I'm not five anymore, Clem. I'm not five. I turned six." She holds up six fingers. "Rochelle said you were going to make me a birthday cake."

"Well, you know the rules. We have to cross a few things off our list before we make dessert."

"I did my homework," she exclaims. "And I just finished my dinner."

Clementine stands and extends her arm out to the little girl, who comfortably places her hand in Clem's. She leads her farther into the house while Rochelle stays back with me, both of us following a few steps behind.

"She's a wonder with these kids," Rochelle praises. "Even when it isn't her month, she makes sure to never miss an opportunity to make any of them a birthday cake."

Images of a little blond-haired girl growing up in this place with nobody making her birthday cakes breaks my heart. It's obvious her intention now is to make sure these kids know they were wanted, that someone is celebrating their existence.

I marvel at her empathy and her selflessness. I marvel at this woman who does so much for so many people without any true realization of the lives she's changing because *she* exists.

"Have you known Clementine for a long time?" I ask as Rochelle takes me on a tour of the group home.

"I started here the year Clem began volunteering," she explains. "I think it's been five years now."

"Wow," I breathe out. "Do a lot of kids come and go in that amount of time?"

We walk into the kitchen area, and it's bigger than one that's traditionally seen in a standard sized house, with its bare counter space, double sized stove and oven, and huge kitchen sink.

There's a large adjoining area with a few teenagers sitting around doing what looks to be homework.

A few other children are cleaning up after dinner, each of them clearly having a task they need to complete. From the outside it looks like a well-oiled machine, something I'm not too naive to know isn't always the case.

Rochelle lowers her voice, bringing her mouth closer to my ear. "For most kids it's in and out. But there are kids who truly have no one and spend a big part of their childhood in places like this."

Just as Rochelle's words land painfully in my chest, Clementine walks in from another entrance, this time four other residents following her, each one a different age.

They join the teenagers around the table, and Clementine glances up, smiling widely when she notices me. She whispers into the little blond girl's ear, and the girl leaves her and walks straight to Rochelle and me.

She puts her hands on her hips. "Clem said that everyone has to help make my cake and that includes you two."

"Well, someone has to watch the rest of the house," Rochelle says. "But you can take Miss Zara."

I hold my hand out to the little girl. "I'm Zara. What's your name?"

"I'm Madison." She places her hand in mine, then drags me to the table toward Clementine, clearly not wanting to waste cake time with talking. "Clem, I brought Miss Zara. Does this mean we have everything we need? Can we start baking now?"

Clementine's eyes twinkle as she taps two fingers to her lips in concentration. "Well, if Miss Zara's here, we definitely have everything we need."

24
CLEM

Zara and I climb back in the car, with two slices of cake wrapped up on my lap, a gift from Madison. Zara surprises me when she turns in her seat instead of starting the car.

"Thank you so much for bringing me tonight," she says. "I really can't explain how grateful I am, and just how great those kids are."

Zara doesn't say it with any disbelief, but I know from experience just how misunderstood children of the system truly are, and all it takes is to make the time to spend with them to know they're all products of their circumstances. But children are like many things in life; if you nurture them positively, they can and will flourish.

"I'm glad you had a good time. I think Madison traded me for you by the end of it."

"She's so cute," Zara coos. "She's the youngest in the home, right?"

"The age ranges are usually eight to twenty-one, but you will rarely find anybody who turns eighteen and chooses to stay unless it's a court order," I explain. "And sometimes, like in Madison's case, they have to make exceptions because there's nowhere else for her to go."

It isn't my place to delve into or discuss anyone's history. I listen when Rochelle tells me the things I need to know and I help where I can. In Madison's case, it's hard being so young and not truly understanding the details of your own life, so if I have an opportunity to make her smile, I take it.

Zara nervously runs her fingers across her lips. "What was it like when you grew up there?"

I could tell from her expression that the question has sat on the edge of her tongue for a while, and she's just been waiting for the right time to ask. I mirror her pose and rest my back on the car door. Talking about my upbringing isn't as painful as people would think; it's more just a sequence of events that led to a sequence of revelations that led me here—and sometimes thinking about that makes me sad.

"It was fine," I say truthfully. "I moved around a bit before I got here, but when I found out I was staying, Frankie and Arlo took me under their wing, and eventually Remy came along and then Lennox. And we found our family in each other."

"I can see how much they love you," she says. "The way they came out of the house when I picked you up was typical big brother behavior."

I huff out a laugh. "Sometimes adulthood is harder. We've all been through a lot together. Arlo's recovery, Frankie moving to Seattle, and Lennox's hearing loss."

"He lost his hearing?" Her brows knit together. "The brother I didn't meet, right?"

Lennox's hearing loss has been a journey, one that's paralleled with me finding out who Zara was. Unintentionally, she's been the perfect distraction, and I've found myself giving Lennox the space he needs—more space than I would if Zara weren't in the picture.

It's a little bit selfish, but it turns out, no matter how hard you want to be there for the ones you love, you're not always the only one they need.

"Yes," I reply. "He lost it after a football accident where he hit his head."

Her hands fly over her mouth. "Oh my goodness, that's so horrible."

"I was so upset about it," I continue. "And that's why Raine invited me over to your place that night. I find that I tend to overreact just a little when unexpected things happen."

"I mean, is there such a thing as overreacting in those circumstances?" she challenges.

"Remember what I told you about my mom?"

She nods. "Of course."

A humorless laugh slips out of my mouth, wondering if Zara is truly prepared to hear how deep my neurosis runs. "I kind of developed this obsession with trying to control everything, because if I could plan our days, and keep us safe and in line, there was less of a chance of something from the outside ruining it all.

"I have had years to think about my mother's choice to give me up. I have gone through the seven stages of grief over the life I could've had." I keep my voice steady as I continue. "Some days I feel gross and unwanted and unworthy, but other days, *most of the days*," I emphasize, "I have come to realize for some of us the world is a cruel and cold place.

"I can't begrudge a woman for not wanting to relive the single worst experience of her life every time she held her daughter." A tear drops on my cheek, and I know now that the words have left my mouth, all my emotions will follow. "I can be sad as a daughter without a mother, but as a woman who lives in a man's world, this is just par for the course, right? A woman paying for a man's mistake."

I hiccup as a sob escapes me when I notice the tears that are now streaming down her face. "She's stripped of her safety and of her experiences as a first time mother, and I'm left as an orphan. And I couldn't even tell you if they caught that man and if he even went to jail."

"Clementine," she breathes out.

"So," I say as I wipe the tears off my face. "Long story short, when things happen that are out of my control, I panic and overreact, because my mind takes me straight to the worst case scenario."

"And that's why you live in survival mode," she says. "And that's why you do what you have to, to make sure your carefully constructed world stays the way you need it to."

Zara repeats the exact words I said a week ago, and all the puzzle pieces finally come together for her. Her eyes stay locked on mine, her stare soft, chocolate brown eyes filled with empathy, understanding and something I dare not name.

Leaning forward, she wraps her hand around the nape of my neck. "Come here."

She captures my mouth in a searing kiss, and I taste the salt of her tears.

"You're so amazing," she says against my lips. "And I know we shouldn't be kissing here, but there is no way I could keep myself away from you for a second longer."

I reach for the side of her face. "I think one more kiss won't hurt anyone."

I press my lips to hers, my chest feeling so light, the usual dark cloud that sits over me, lifting, as if sharing the ugliest parts of me with her has made me feel just that little bit more beautiful.

"In case nobody has ever told you," Zara says, "you are the very best kind of person there is. You've grown into a loving, giving, and selfless human being."

Our next kiss is slow and languid. "You did that," she reminds me. "When people praise you, and they will, for the person you are—remind yourself that you. Did. That."

"You better get us out of here," I murmur against her lips. "Because if you keep sweet-talking me, I will not be responsible for the things I do to you."

She reluctantly pulls her mouth away from mine.

"You're right," she says. "We need to go, because I can't afford to get into trouble when I plan to come back here."

"You do?" I ask, finding it even harder now to keep my hands off her.

"Once my background check comes through, and if you're okay with it," she says. "I'll do a different evening so it doesn't encroach on your time with them."

I appreciate her offer, but it's completely unnecessary. "No," I say firmly. "I want you with me."

Her smile is filled with endless amounts of gratitude, and my heart stutters at just how breathtaking she is when she looks at me like that.

I hold my hand out to her and she places hers in mine. "Let's get out of here, huh?"

As we hit the highway, her phone rings and Raine's name shows up on the car screen. Zara squeezes my hand reassuringly as she presses a button on her steering wheel and answers the call.

"Hey, babe."

"Hey," she greets. "I'm sorry for calling, I know you're—"

Zara cuts her off. "You know there's nothing for you to apologize for. Are you okay?"

"Are you going to be late?" Raine asks. "Because I burned my dinner and I was hoping you could pick me up some food on the way."

Zara glances at me, rich brown eyes filled with remorse and indecision, so I bring the top of her hand to my mouth and kiss it comfortingly.

There is no need for her to feel guilty, it has no place here, because there's no choice between Raine and me. I would proudly put myself second, because there is nothing that is more honest and attractive to me than Zara putting Raine first.

It doesn't matter how much or how little Raine needs her; I want her to know she could and would be there for her, and I will support that every step of the way.

Understanding settles on her features as she finally opens her mouth to respond. "I'll be home soon," she tells her. "Text me what you want and I'll pick it up on my way."

"Yes," Raine cheers. "You're a lifesaver, Mom. Thank you, and tell Aubrey I'm sorry for calling."

This has me bristling.

"Aubrey?" I silently mouth.

"I'm not with Aubrey tonight," Zara corrects.

"Oh, that's right, you're with your mystery woman," Raine teases, not even the slightest bit put out by her mother's dating life. "What did you say her name was?"

"You're funny," Zara deadpans. "You know very well I didn't give you a name."

This has Raine chuckling. "Fine. Fine. Fine. Well, tell her I'm sorry, and I'll see you when you get home."

"Don't forget to text me," she reminds her. "I'll see you soon. Love you."

"Love you, Mom."

When the call ends, I can't help the words that rush out of my mouth. "Do you still see Aubrey? She's the woman who was at your house that day, right?"

"I haven't seen her lately," Zara says, and I don't know why I hate that answer more. "And yeah, that's her."

Jealousy churns in my stomach, unwanted and unfounded, and yet it's there all the same.

"Clementine, she's just a friend," Zara says, attempting to placate me.

"But you could've been more, right? If it weren't for me?"

Zara shakes her head. "Actually, no. I put her in the friend zone right after our first date, and that was before you showed up at my place."

"But why? She's perfect for you, and you wouldn't have to lie—"

Zara loosens her hand from mine and rushes to put it over my mouth, silencing me.

"You better stop that, right now," she warns. "If I wanted Aubrey, I would be with Aubrey." She gives me a meaningful look. "There is no such thing as somebody else being perfect for me." She drops her hand. "It's only you."

"Fine," I say on a pout. "But it probably would be easier."

"Maybe," Zara concedes. "But it still wouldn't be you."

25
ZARA

"Your two thirty is here," Georgie, the junior stylist, says as I finish blowing out my client's hair.

I glance up at the large clock on the wall, noticing Clementine is fifteen minutes early. Thankfully, my day has stayed on schedule enough that she won't be waiting too long.

"Do you want me to bring her in?" Georgie asks.

Shaking my head, I switch off the hair dryer and place it on my cart. I run my hands through the ends of my client's hair and bring the strands over her shoulder, making sure her new cut is even.

Grabbing my handheld mirror, I hold it behind her head so she can see the back of her hair through the reflection. "What do you think?"

She angles her head to the left and then to the right, the smile on her face enough to make me feel confident that I managed to get her hair to look exactly the way she wanted. Even after more than a decade, I will almost always tie myself in unnecessary knots over the end result.

It doesn't matter how long I've been doing it, hair is

such a personal preference, with such a public audience, there is no room to get it wrong. Especially in the day and age of social media, because if you're not careful, someone is blasting you on the internet somewhere, ruining your reputation.

It's been a while since someone has left my chair unhappy, though, and as my gaze quickly scans the salon for Clementine, I hope it stays that way.

Georgie takes my current client to the front of the salon to finalize their payment, and instead of waiting for Georgie to bring the woman I've been wanting to see all day through to my chair, like she usually does, I follow her to the waiting area, surprising Clementine.

She rises to her feet, smile restrained. "Hey."

From the look on her face, I'm not surprised when she places a hand on my chest when I lean in to kiss her. "Everything okay?"

"I think everyone is staring at us," she whispers.

"Is that a problem?" I ask, my own lips now starting to curve.

"I don't know, is it?"

"No." I laugh. "Unless you don't want to kiss me?"

"I didn't know if you had rules or something like that at work."

Besides Raine seeing Clementine's hair and her knowing that I did it, there's a chance Raine could come in and someone would joke with her about her mother's new girlfriend. But the specifics and connection between the two would be lost on everyone here. And, quite frankly, I'm only a few conversations short from telling Raine myself that I'm in a committed relationship, because as far as I'm concerned, that's where my head and heart are right now. Committed to Clementine.

My hands find her waist and bring her to me, less than an inch of space between us. "Stop worrying and kiss me."

It's too quick and makes me miss her in my arms almost instantly. We've been doing our best to see each other whenever we can, but we've only managed the night at On The Horizon and today, both still not enough for me, and I don't know if it ever would be.

I want the stability and routine of knowing when and where we would see one another. I want that small hole in my chest to close up entirely, instead of gradually getting bigger the more serious things become.

Hand in hand, I walk her through the salon, and just like she said, everyone is glancing our way. Ignoring them, I gesture for her to take a seat at my station. Georgie is quick to follow, draping a cape over her and asking what she would like to drink.

Clementine's cheeks fill with that familiar shade of pink, and I know she's a little bit uncomfortable with all the attention being on her. When Georgie walks away, I catch her gaze in the mirror and run my fingers through her hair. "Is there anything specific you have in mind that you want to do?"

She shrugs. "This really just started out as an excuse for me to talk to you without Raine being suspicious, remember?"

"Okay, so maybe a cut? Or a color?" I probe.

"You decide," she says with confidence. "I trust you."

"Are you sure?" I smile. "The last time someone gave me full control, I shaved all their hair off."

"You did what?" she gasps. "I hope they liked the end result."

"Well, Leo, Raine's papa, didn't care," I tell her. "But

since we did it to piss Jesse off because he loves Leo's hair, someone didn't like the end result."

"Do you cut all their hair?" she asks.

Georgie returns before I get a chance to answer, placing Clementine's iced mocha in front of her. "Is there anything I can get you?" she asks me.

"Can you bring over a color chart, please?"

When Georgie is out of earshot, I answer Clementine's question. "Jesse calls it an initiation," I explain. "But I just do the hair of the people who matter to me the most, and I take it personally when they let someone else cut or style it."

She smirks. "But what happens while you live here and Jesse and Leo live in Seattle?"

I think back to the first time Leo needed a haircut after I'd left, and he said *"I'll fly to you if I have to, but please don't be upset with me."*

"They can get it cut by someone else, but every time we see one another, they have to need a haircut so I can do it."

Her eyes are filled with adoration as she digests my words. "So as long as you cut their hair when you see them, it doesn't bother you if they have to go somewhere else in between?"

"Oh, no, it one hundred percent bothers me," I confirm. "But it's the best compromise we could come up with."

"So, what you're saying is, you doing my hair is a big deal?"

Our gazes stay fixed on one another through the reflection as I read in between the lines of her question.

"I'm saying that if you need to know how important you are to me, or how I feel about you, then this is a dead giveaway."

———

"Okay, are you ready?" I ask Clementine, holding the black towel on top of her head, the moment of truth about to take place in seconds.

She puts her hand over mine, stopping me from removing the towel. "I just want to say, I know it's going to look amazing, because *you* did it, and that's really the only thing about this that matters."

"Are you trying to make sure my feelings don't get hurt if it turns out you don't like it?"

"Maybe," she deadpans before both of us crack up laughing.

"First off, I'm not too concerned," I tell her, because I'm not, and I know after washing her hair that it turned out perfect. We chose a nice, deep red that was easy to switch to from her natural blond. But whether she likes it or not is really where my worry sinks in. "But if you hate it and don't tell me, I can't fix it."

"Surely, you know me well enough by now to know there's no way I'm telling you if I hate it."

I do know that, and that's why I'm sending prayers out to the universe that she falls in love with it.

I rid her head of the towel and start sectioning her hair so I can blow it out. It's harder to talk with the sound of the hair dryer between us, so I'm motivated to be done quickly and hopefully have a few moments alone with her before my next client.

Clementine's fingers are strategically flying over her cracked screen before she looks up at me, a little flustered. I switch off the hair dryer. "Is something wrong?"

She shakes her head. "I asked Lennox to meet me here, is that okay?"

Eager to meet her remaining brother, I nod. "Of course it is."

Not too long after, I finish the blowout, and show off every angle of her hair through the handheld mirror. I'm entranced by the way her features shift as she takes herself in, green eyes filled with nothing but wonder, almost like she can't really believe what she's looking at.

Her gaze catches mine through the reflection, and I don't miss the slight change in her posture or the way she holds her head a little higher.

She has always been beautiful to me, my attention absolutely consumed by her since that very first night, but now she's coming into her own, finding herself, emanating confidence that makes my attraction to her run beyond skin deep.

"You look stunning."

I don't miss the subtle lick of her lips, the rise and fall of her chest, or the flush that creeps up her neck at my words. She's speechless, but her body is telling me everything I need to know.

It's extremely unprofessional, especially in a place as upscale as this one, but I figure I'll worry about it later. I dart a glance around the place, and while I know my colleagues will notice my disappearance, I make sure I'm not leaving any clients unattended or waiting.

Holding out my hand to her, I tug her to her feet and walk her to the back of the salon, away from prying eyes. We have an aesthetician who works here a few days a week and thankfully she isn't here today and her room is empty.

Closing the door, I press Clementine up against it. Her hands find my face and she slams her lips to mine.

"How did you know?" she murmurs.

"That your new hair made you horny?"

"That word is so weird." She kisses me again. Hard. "But yes, that."

I smile against her lips as my hands cup her ass and she wraps her legs around my waist. "You feel sexy, baby. Own it."

The kiss deepens and Clementine rolls her hips against me just as someone knocks on the door. She stiffens in my arms when Georgie's voice comes through from the other side of the door.

"Zara," she says. "Your four thirty is here."

Clementine slaps a hand over her mouth, her eyes sparkling with mischief.

"I'll be out in a second," I tell her.

Clementine drops her head to my shoulder. "This is so embarrassing."

"Look at me." She raises her eyes to meet mine. "Own it, remember?"

With Clementine's hand in mine, I open the door, and Georgie's eyes are incredulous, her smile wide. "Um..." She reaches over and flattens the top of Clementine's hair before looking at me. "Maybe quickly go over the back."

Clementine anxiously follows the motion with her hands, and I drag them off her head. "Sit back down and I'll fix it."

She turns and mouths, *"Oh my God."*

And I just tap her ass and wink.

Sitting down, she grabs her phone while I make it look a little less like sex hair at the back. In the mirror, I catch her smiling at the screen before glancing around. There's a young man waiting at the front, and next to him is a young girl who could only be Raine's age or a little bit older.

"That's Lennox," she informs me as she waves at the young man.

As I finish up, I lead her to him, just in time to hear him say, "I never imagined you as a redhead, but now I can't see you as anything else."

I watch their interaction curiously as she responds to him proudly, shaking her head from side to side and then splaying her right hand against her chest before pulling it away and making her middle finger and thumb come together.

I know she's learning how to sign, but I still have no idea which is what, and it almost feels like I'm intruding.

"I love it," he says before his gaze almost knowingly darts to mine. Whether his brothers told him who I am, or he could just tell by the constant stars in my eyes I have for Clementine, he's onto us.

When Clementine looks back at me, I tuck some of her hair behind her ear before kissing her on the cheek. It'll have to do, even if I wish we could wind back the clock to ten minutes earlier.

Lennox and his friend laugh, catching our attention, and Clementine signs again, rubbing a fist over her chest.

Lennox shakes his head. "We aren't in a rush."

He guides his friend to the front door, leaving Clem and I to say our goodbyes.

"Sorry I didn't introduce you two properly," she says. "I sometimes forget about his accident, and my mind scrambles at the last minute to make it easier for him."

"It's fine," I assure her, leaning forward and kissing her on the cheek. "I'm pretty sure he caught me staring at you like you hung the moon, and figured it out anyway."

"I hang the moon, do I?" she teases, a smirk on her lips.

"I don't know about anyone else's, but you definitely hang mine."

26

CLEM

My phone vibrates against my mattress, and I don't need to check the screen to know it's Zara. We're very much in a predictable routine of calling each other before bed and Zara hanging up every time I fall asleep mid-conversation.

"Hey," I answer.

"Hey, sweetheart." Despite the endearment, Zara's voice is uncharacteristically flat. "How are you?"

"Fine," I answer cautiously. "How are you?"

"I'm okay," she says a little too quickly. "How was your day?"

When I don't answer, the silence shifts, now awkward and uncomfortable. I know I can fill the quiet, but I don't do well with miscommunication, and I don't enjoy that her decision to not share things with me makes me feel like I've done something wrong, even though I *know* I haven't.

Eventually, she lets out a long exhale. "I'm sorry. I've just got a lot on my mind."

The tension in my shoulders eases only slightly at her words. "Anything I can do to help?" I ask.

"No." She sighs. "But I can't do that weekend with you at Nina's place."

"Oh." Disappointment settles in my chest, but I quickly cover it up, my voice a little too high pitched now. "That's okay, things come up."

Instinct tells me she wouldn't bail on me unless it's something important, and more specifically something to do with Raine, and if that's the case, I'm willing to let it go. I'm not in competition with Raine, and until I find my big girl panties and tell her about my relationship with Zara, this will be how the cookie crumbles for the foreseeable future.

"I have to go to Seattle with Raine," she states. "I got my dates confused and thought it would be the weekend after."

She sounds so defeated, I can't be sure if she's upset about missing out on a weekend with me or about going to Seattle. She doesn't talk much about Lola, but I know she came here, to L.A., for a fresh start after what happened, and my intuition tells me she isn't too pleased to be going back. The only problem is, I don't know why. She keeps her cards close to her chest, and I respect that, but I also want to know everything about her and be there for her if I can. I guess I just can't do that if she doesn't want me to.

"I wish you were going with me." As if she could hear my doubts, her revelation has them all disappearing. It wasn't an invitation, because we both know I've already agreed to help Nina out, and Raine still doesn't know about us, but it's enough to make me feel wanted and needed by her.

And I *want* to be wanted and needed by her.

"Maybe it's time we talk to Raine," I suggest. "That way, next time, maybe I can go with you."

"I think we should wait," Zara says, completely blind-siding me.

"What?" I practically spit out. This whole conversation is giving me whiplash. "Am I missing something here?"

"Fuck," she breathes out. "No, it's nothing like that. She's just going through a lot right now, and I think we should wait."

It wasn't truly awkward having Raine as a friend and dating her mother until this very moment, because I know things about Raine, and I know things about Zara, but they both know one another better than I would ever know either of them.

It makes sense.

It's normal.

And yet, I feel like I'm on the outskirts of it all, and I don't like that feeling at all.

"I guess I can wait," I eventually manage to say. "Maybe you can tell me when you think it'll be a good time."

"Of course it'll be good to tell her," she agrees. "Just not yet."

Zara is undoubtedly distracted from the conversation, and the unease I felt when I first heard her voice returns tenfold.

"Are you sure you're okay? Is Raine okay?" I ask again, my mind toggling between concern and annoyance. "You know you can tell me whatever it is that's bothering you."

"I know."

When she doesn't follow up with anything, I decide to call it a night, because I really have no idea what I'm doing here. If she were one of my brothers, I would just flat out ask, and yet here, with Zara, I don't even know what I'm asking.

She told me she couldn't spend the weekend with me,

and that she was annoyed about it. Though it doesn't exactly feel like the truth, I know I have to swallow it like it is.

"I'm going to go," I announce.

"Yeah," she agrees. "I can feel a headache coming on. I think I need to try and get some sleep."

We say goodbye, the words exchanged in a monotonous daze, and a sadness unlike anything I've ever felt before washes over me.

I don't like the unknown. I don't like uncertainty.

Just as my eyes feel heavy enough to close, my phone vibrates with an incoming message.

I'm sorry I wasn't good company tonight.

I stare at the lit-up screen, but the urge to respond to her doesn't come. Instead, I reach for her necklace off my nightstand and stare at the heart and lock pendants that hang from the chain. There is a little inscription on the two teeth of the key. One is an R and the other is an L.

Raine and Lola.

By the time I realized just how important this necklace meant to her, too much time had passed to give it back. But here it is, my one connection to her, and what is clearly her connection to them.

It feels significant.

It feels like an answer to a question that hasn't been asked yet.

It feels like an answer to a question *I* haven't asked yet.

Another message comes through.

Goodnight, sweetheart.

Choosing to leave her second text unanswered as well, I place the phone and the necklace back on my nightstand, then bury my head under my pillow and try to ease my anxiety. I don't like feeling this way, especially because I can't pinpoint why.

For now, I need to sleep and hope that tomorrow is a better day. For both of us.

———

"Cle—"

"What?" I snap. My colleague Priscilla's face falls, and guilt immediately washes over me. "I'm sorry," I say. "You didn't deserve that." I put my half-eaten muffin down. "Is everything okay?"

She cautiously steps farther into the break room. "There's a lady here looking for you."

There is only one lady who ever visits me here at work, and I'm not really sure if I want to see her. I slept like shit last night, and my chest aches in confusion, and I have no idea what to say to her or how to get us back to where we were before the phone call.

Part of me wonders if it was all in my head, but the fact that she's here validates my feelings, even if just a little.

"Do you think you could bring her back here for me, please?"

If Priscilla is confused she doesn't bother voicing it, instead hurrying out of the room and returning only a few seconds later with an apologetic looking Zara, whose eyes are tired and sad. And I realize very quickly, despite feeling the exact same way, I don't like seeing her like this.

Priscilla closes the door behind her when she leaves, and Zara takes the few steps to close the gap between us.

She crouches down before me, placing her hands on my knees, looking up at me, brown eyes full of contrition.

"Hey," she says softly.

Because I can't help myself, I place my hand over hers. "Hey."

"You look tired," she muses. "Like you might've had a shit sleep because someone upset you before bed."

Something similar to a chuckle and a huff leaves my mouth. "Something like that."

"I'm so sorry." She shakes her head as she searches for her next words. "I had a lot on my mind, and I kind of just shut down."

I squeeze her hand. "If something is wrong or bothering you, you could just tell me, you know."

"I know that," she confirms. "I was really looking forward to that weekend with you, and I don't really want to go to Seattle."

"I wish I could go with you," I say honestly, hating that my need to be a good friend is intruding on my ability to be a good girlfriend. "You know that, right? If I could, I would."

She nods. "I do. And knowing that is enough."

Leaning forward, I cup her cheek and press my mouth to hers. "I hated the way we said goodbye."

"I'm sorry," she whispers against my lips.

With my hand still on her face, I use my free one to guide her up and onto my lap. Straddling me, she wraps her arms around my neck and deepens the kiss, repeating her apology over and over again. With every swipe of her tongue, it feels like there is a seismic shift between us, like the bump in the road only highlighted just how deep into this we both are.

"Let me make it up to you," she says in between kisses.

Pulling back, I raise a brow. "In here?"

Zara rolls her eyes. "Not like that. Well, like that, but not here."

"I'm not following," I say, thoroughly confused.

"A weekend away," she clarifies. "Before I go to Seattle."

"And Raine?" I question.

"I could get us a hotel room," she suggests.

I shake my head, but she puts her index finger against my mouth, silencing me. "I'm apologizing, am I not?"

"But do you have to spend copious amounts of money to do so?" I half heartedly argue.

"I don't, but until we tell Raine, this is how it's got to be if we want to spend more than a few fleeting hours together," she explains. "And I feel like accepting the apology is the only way you'll let me pay for it."

"You have a point." I kiss her again. "So we're still on the same page about telling her? You'll tell me when it's the right time?"

"I will," she promises.

"Is she okay?"

"She will be." Zara brushes her fingers along my cheek. "And I'm sure she'll let you know if she's not."

"In that case, I don't think I can do a whole weekend," I say. "But I could finish early on a Saturday night and start late on Sunday."

"That works for me." She kisses my nose. "Now, how much longer do you have left of your lunch break?"

"I don't know." I press a finger to my chin thoughtfully. "I think I might need a few more of those apology kisses."

27
ZARA

"Wake up, sleepy head." Clementine's voice is a soft whisper against my skin as she slips under the covers and curls her body around mine. I'm in nothing but my underwear and a t-shirt, not wanting to sleep in my jeans and bra.

"You're here," I say groggily.

"I am." She kisses my neck. "Sorry I'm later than I said I'd be."

"It's okay. Work is work. What time is it?"

"Eight."

Slowly, I open my eyes, noticing that the sun has set and the only light in the room is from the two lamps that sit on either side of the bed.

"Are you hungry?" I turn in her arms, now facing her. "Do you want to go and get something to eat?"

She shakes her head. "I'm too tired to move." Her stomach rumbles loudly.

"Room service, then?"

Laughing, she leans forward and kisses me. "That sounds perfect."

"I think the menu thing is on your side," I tell her.

Clementine nuzzles her face in my neck. "Just let me stay here for a bit."

Hiking my leg over her waist and an arm around her, I close the gap between us, basking in the silence and the ability to just lie here and hold one another without having the rest of the world rushing in. The weeks have been passing by so quickly, and the trip to Seattle is getting closer, both of those things making me uneasy. I just want to be in this moment with Clementine, where I don't have to think about anything else but her.

"Are you okay?" I ask her.

"Better than okay," she says while pressing open-mouthed kisses up my neck. "Right now everything is absolutely perfect."

Clementine rolls me onto my back and strips off her jeans before she straddles my waist. She peers down at me, the low light of the lamps casting the perfect glow across her face, her red hair now accentuating the green of her eyes.

She grips the edge of her t-shirt and drags it up her body, my eyes eating up her exposed skin. I hook a finger in the front of her bralette and drag her down to me, until her mouth fuses with mine. I slide my hand underneath the material and press my palm against her heart, loving its steady rhythm. We kiss, slow and languid, like we have all the time in the world. We kiss as if it's a slow climb to the top before we both fall.

Because that's what we're doing. We're falling. I can feel it in her touch and her kiss. I can feel it in the air, wrapping around us, keeping us in this bubble that was only made for us. And I want to let myself fall. Fall into her, into this moment, into this life I've only ever dreamed of. This life I now only ever dream of with *her*.

Clementine loosens her lips from mine, our faces only a breath apart, her hair falling around us like a curtain, hiding us from the rest of the world.

"I've been waiting for this all day," she whispers

"Waiting for what?"

"You." Even in the dimly lit room, I recognize the look in her eyes, and my heart beats wildly inside my rib cage at the sight of it. "Just you."

She presses her lips ever so softly to mine and we both sit here.

Still.

Breathing one another in.

Even with very few words, I know what she means, because it feels like I've been waiting too. But not just today, or even the last two and a half months. It's like I've been waiting since that very first night—waiting to be this version of myself that only exists in the now, with her and because of her.

Clementine's mouth moves against mine, firmer now, her tongue slipping between my lips, hungry. I match her stroke for stroke, tasting and teasing as the temperature between us rises. My hands travel down her body, cupping her ass. I rock her back and forth against me, heightening the friction between us, loving how she feels on top of me.

Her lips trail down my neck as her hands push up my shirt. She sucks on the skin above my collarbone, and my breath hitches when she lowers her mouth to my breasts, teasing and licking my nipples. There's something about the way she greedily sucks that has me certain I could come from her tongue and mouth alone.

She's like an eager student, and I'd be lying if I said I don't get off on being the one to teach her. She moves her way back up my body and to my lips, need and arousal coursing through me. "I want to see you touch yourself." My words come out shakier than I expect them to. "I want to watch you."

She sits up and her hooded green eyes lock on mine. Heat travels up her neck, settling on her cheeks as she dutifully follows my orders and slides her hands beneath her underwear. Wanting more, I hook my finger over the waistband of her panties and pull the material down, stretching it, giving myself the perfect view of her pussy.

Her fingertips slide up and down her wet center, and when my gaze darts back to hers, she's looking at me expectantly, and I love it.

"Show me," I breathe out. "Show me how you make yourself come."

She uses one hand to spread herself wide, and the other to play with her clit. She rubs and rolls the sensitive bundle of nerves, slow and fast, occasionally sliding two fingers inside herself and slipping them back out, wet and coated with her arousal.

She gasps when I replace her fingers with mine, pushing them in and out as she continues with the steady rhythm on her clit.

"Have you ever played with any toys?" I ask her, my eyes flicking between the inward and outward slide of my fingers and her face.

She shakes her head, her expression demure, the complete opposite to the desperate way she's rubbing at her clit.

"In my mind I'm using a vibrator on you, watching you fuck yourself on it, the way you're fucking yourself on my fingers right now." I watch her as our hands move in tandem, and the imagery of my words has her chasing her release. "I would have you laid out before me, teasing and taunting you till you're begging me to stop."

My hand stills and she cries out my name.

"Just like that."

"Zara, please," she begs.

I drag my fingers out of her and slip them into my mouth.

"I need more of this," I say, smacking her thigh. "Climb up here."

Clementine leans forward, placing her palm against the wall and maneuvers herself above me, just right. One of my favorite things about her is the trust she has in me during sex; she never second guesses and she never feels too shy. She allows herself to feel all the things she's supposed to feel, relishing in her newfound sexuality, and it only makes me want her more.

The view of her above me is mouthwatering, her pussy wet and glistening, and her beautiful face in the background, looking down at me, eyes burning with desire. I keep my eyes on hers as I swipe my tongue over her clit.

She's so keyed up, her thighs shudder around me, and I know it won't take long for me to have her coming on my face. I go back and forth, up and down her opening, before going deeper, tasting more of her, memorizing the way she feels on my tongue.

I alternate between gently biting and sucking her clit, loving the way her gasps and moans echo around the room. Finding her stride, Clementine rocks her cunt up and down my face, her arousal coating my mouth and chin.

Her thighs begin to tremble around me and her clit pulses on my tongue. Grabbing her hips, I hold her in place as the orgasm sweeps through her, leaving her sensitive and breathless and chanting my name. My tongue lazily laps at her, unhurriedly indulging in the sweet taste of her cum.

"Oh my God," she cries out. "I think I'm going to fall on you."

I can't help but smile against her, but I squeeze her hips, letting her know I've got her. She slowly angles her leg over me and then collapses onto the mattress, her chest rising and falling rapidly.

"Fuck," she breathes out. "I don't know how, but the orgasms just keep getting better and better with you."

My face splits into a huge smile. "It's a good thing you don't plan on getting them from anyone else," I tease.

Turning on her side, Clementine props her head up with her hand. As if she just noticed her arousal on my lips, she traces the shape of them with her finger. "It's a good thing you don't plan on getting them from anyone else either."

With only a hint of a smirk, her voice doesn't hold the same humor as mine; it was more of a statement that bordered on a question, like she needs reassurance. And that bothers me.

"Hey." I mirror her pose and lean in to kiss her. "Not only don't I plan on getting them from anyone, I don't want them from anyone else either. It's just you, Clementine. I thought you knew that."

Her gaze darts from my eyes to my mouth before it's her turn to press her lips to mine. "I like tasting myself on you," she murmurs.

"Are you distracting me?" I say, kissing her back.

"Trying and clearly failing."

"Clementine," I say firmly. "You know it's just you, right?"

Her tongue peeks out, wetting her bottom lip. "I do."

When the silence feels a little too long, I push. "But..."

"Some days it just all feels so surreal." She gestures between us. "Being disgustingly happy is kind of new for me."

I understand that more than she knows. A year ago, the only thing I was certain of was being Raine's mother—it felt like there was nothing else more to me and there never would be.

I didn't know who I was without her. Every emotion and life experience was tied up with her, and by extension Jesse and Leo. There wasn't a single thing that was just mine, except for Clementine.

Her smile.

Her laugh.

Her body.

Her heart.

I hope.

It's all mine.

28

CLEM

Wearing plush white robes, Zara sits up against the headboard of the bed while I have my head resting in her lap. The hotel television is on, the volume low, playing some movie in the background that neither one of us are paying attention to. We'd had sex, we'd showered and eaten, and now my eyes are threatening to close as she gently runs her fingers through my hair.

I'm so relaxed and content, it's like I'm floating on air. The comfort I feel at being in Zara's presence is so foreign but addictive.

Life always feels like a rat race, but in this moment, and every one I spend with Zara, the world goes still. Everything is silent, and the only thing that matters is the two of us.

I don't know if it's because we're so meticulous when planning our time together, that we've become protective over it, or if it's because my priorities have been shifting since the moment I met her.

There is no longer an extreme focus on everyone else's life; the good and the bad. Because of Zara, I can see how we're all outgrowing our codependency, learning to live for ourselves instead of one another.

I suppose Frankie did it first, but I mistook his choice to leave as selfishness, when in actuality, he did the best thing he could for both himself and Arlo, and it took hindsight to see that.

Now I'm watching Lennox do the same thing as he navigates both his new disability and his new relationship, but I'm understanding it in real time.

Life is complicated and complex, and every part of it has a learning curve. You can plan and prepare all you want, but if life has other plans, you have to get on board or get left behind.

And I don't want to get left behind.

I don't want to be the one to turn my back on something good just because it's different. It's a sobering thought to realize the life you wanted was so mediocre to the life you could have.

And that's what life before Zara truly was. Mediocre. It was existing versus living. It was a muted, dull version of happiness that was just enough to keep me going.

"I think I want to get a new job," I blurt out, plucking out one single line of thought from the mixed bag that is currently my mind. "Something less monotonous."

Zara continues to thread her fingers through my hair. "Do you have anything specific in mind?"

I glance up at her. "Rochelle offered me a part-time job at the group home."

"Oh my God." Zara's eyes widen in excitement. "When? What did you say?"

"She called me on my way here," I explain. "Said there was a spot opening up and that my volunteer history was enough experience to be eligible."

"I've seen you with those kids," she says proudly. "You're more than eligible."

My stomach flutters in excitement at the thought of something new and different and challenging. "You make me feel like I can do anything," I say, surprising myself. But it's the truth. Making the choice to pursue this relationship with her makes me feel like I can have anything I want.

"That's because you *can* do anything."

Her eyes are full of emotions as she looks down at me; some I recognize, some I don't, but all of them are just for me.

Both my heart and pulse thud with want as we stare at each other. The air shifting, the tension thickening. It's close to midnight, and I'm exhausted, yet I need to be close to her.

Wordlessly, I sit up, letting the robe slip off my shoulders and pool around my waist. I reach for Zara, pushing the heavy material off her body till we're both topless.

Switching off the lamp beside me, I climb in between the sheets, and Zara follows. Naked, I wrap her body around mine, my back pressed to her front, and guide her hand in between my legs. It's a dull ache, a gentle throb, and it's one I don't want to dissipate.

I want to fall asleep with her knowing just how much I need her.

"Hold me," I whisper into the dark.

Without question or judgment, Zara cups my sex and kisses the back of my neck. "Goodnight, sweetheart."

———

"Morning," Zara says softly. The smell of fresh pastries has me lifting my head up from underneath my pillow. "I bought you some breakfast."

I turn my head to find her already dressed, sitting cross-legged on her side of the bed, sipping an iced mocha. In front of her is a large white paper bag, filled with what I assume is baked goods, and a drink for me.

"How come I didn't feel you leave the bed?" I ask groggily.

"I made an effort to be super stealthy, but also, you were too tired to notice," she explains. "The snoring kind of gave you away."

I gasp, mortified. "I do not snore."

Zara chuckles. "Well, not all the time, since I don't remember you snoring at my place or when you fall asleep on the phone."

Playfully, I attempt to throw a nearby pillow in her direction, purposefully missing her and the drinks. "I don't know what you're talking about."

"It's kind of cute," she remarks. "But it also makes me worry you're not sleeping enough."

My heart never fails to trip over itself whenever she voices her concern, because it's so rare that anybody reminds me to stop and take care of myself.

"I probably just sleep better next to you," I say truthfully.

Everything feels better with her, and the last twenty-four hours only solidified that. I want more of it. I want what Arlo has with Frankie and what Lennox has with Samuel and Rhys. I finally understand what it's like to want something for myself, and I'm determined to keep her.

"When we get back from Seattle, I think it'll be a good time to tell Raine." Her voice perks up. "And then maybe we could have more sleepovers. Tell her you need it to sleep better."

I smile at all the possibilities. I'm giddy over telling Raine, a far contrast from the anxiety I felt early on. I know it will be a hiccup, no matter what, and Raine will be entitled to all her feelings, but it won't be the end of us that I predicted. Of that I'm sure.

"What's the time?" I ask

Zara casually grabs my phone off her nightstand and hands it to me. It takes a few moments for my sleepy eyes to register what I'm looking at, but when I notice, I whip my head up. "Did you fix my screen? How did you even...? Where did you go?"

A smirk tugs at her lips. "When your alarm went off this morning and it took me forty whole seconds to turn it off without slicing my fingers, I decided it was time. I searched the area online and found something nearby."

"Zara." I sit up, covering my naked body with the sheets, warmth filling my chest at the gesture. "You didn't have to do that. I was going to—"

"I know," she interjects. "And this isn't about me doing it because I thought you couldn't. Nothing I do for you is because I think you can't do it for yourself. It's because I *can* do nice things for you." She carefully transfers the food and drink to the bedside table and then scoots herself closer to me, resting a hand on my cheek. "Because I want to, Clementine. Can't I be the person who gets to do nice things for you? And watch your face light up with surprise, knowing I'm the one who put that look there?"

"You are that person." I put a hand over hers, so grateful that she can read me like an open book, knowing how to ease all my insecurities at just the right time. "You're so much more than just that person."

"Good." She kisses me on the nose. "Now, enjoy your phone screen and your cut-free fingers and let's eat what I bought from this bakery I found."

She hands me my iced mocha before tearing open the bag to reveal two of everything. There are sweet pastries and savory pastries, and far too much for just the two of us.

"Is anybody else joining us this morning, because there's no way this is all for us," I say before taking a sip of the cool liquid.

"My stomach couldn't make its mind up."

I reach for a chocolate cinnamon roll and groan at the first bite. "These are so good."

My eyes dart to Zara, who's just staring at me.

"What?" I ask

"I just wasn't prepared for you to have an orgasm over baked goods."

I laugh and then point to her empty hands. "If you eat one, we could orgasm together."

She raises a brow at me. "If I eat *something*, we could most definitely orgasm together."

"I don't know." I shrug playfully. "These are really doing it for me."

Zara shakes her head. "You're going to regret that when you're at home with only a sugar high to keep you company."

She's absolutely right, but two can play this game. "I don't know," I say in between bites. "I ordered a few toys the other day that I think could—"

Zara interrupts me, grabbing the half-eaten pastry and my drink out of my hands and then arranging everything off the bed. "I'm sorry, I thought I just heard you say you ordered some toys."

"I did," I answer nonchalantly.

"What toys?"

There are no toys, but curiosity had found this cat a few nights ago, and I'd gone down a rabbit hole I definitely want to revisit after the vivid image she so eloquently described of me with a vibrator.

"I don't know." I hike up a shoulder. "Which ones can you imagine me with?"

Heat dances in her irises. "That's a very, very loaded question."

"Lucky I didn't actually buy myself any, then," I confess. "But, coincidentally, I did go on a deep dive the other night and made a mental comparison table. You mentioning a vibrator last night definitely sealed the deal."

Zara inhales deeply. "I'm not going to lie, it's so fucking sexy hearing about you making a comparison table for sex toys."

I laugh, my chest feeling so unbelievably light, loving the way we volley back and forth about anything with such ease. "I want to be sure they're good for both of us."

"Oh, you don't need to worry, sweetheart, anything that's good for you, is absolutely going to be good for me." She situates herself on her haunches and then leans forward till I fall back on the bed and she's hovering over me. "Now, tell me more about this comparison table."

29
CLEM

"Are you ready for your weekend in Seattle?" I ask Raine.

The lunchtime rush is finished and Raine and I finally have a moment to ourselves. It's been a while since we've hung out properly, but I know college is kicking her ass, and I spend every free moment I have either helping Arlo and Frankie move into their new place or sneaking around with Zara.

It won't be Raine's first trip back there this year, but knowing her mother is going with her this time, selfishly has me a little bit more interested.

Raine shrugs, the usual bounce in her step very obviously missing. "I wish I didn't have to go," she admits, and this surprises me.

"Why not?" I ask. "I thought you love visiting your dads."

Instead of answering me, she sighs before giving me her back, and my concern for her escalates immediately. "What's wrong? Are you okay?"

She continues to ignore me.

"Raine," I say more firmly, and she eventually turns around, unshed tears filling her eyes.

Glancing around, I'm grateful the café is quiet. I grab her by the wrist and drag her to the nearest booth, leaving Mel, one of the other workers, behind the counter on their own. We slide along the leather benches and her gaze finally finds mine.

"Talk," I say. "Now."

Raine's eyes dart down to her hands as she picks at her cuticles. "I had a sister."

Her words are only a little bit louder than a whisper, but they hit my heart hard. A loss like theirs is insurmountable and it doesn't matter who I heard it from or how many times it was said, I feel their grief each and every time.

"Two years ago," she informs me. "Her name was Lola, and it was a stillbirth."

Extending my arm across the table, I cover her hands with mine, comforting her. I hate already knowing this information about Raine, but I also know because of my relationship with Zara, it would be inevitable. I just didn't realize how unprepared I would be when it happened.

"We're going to Seattle for her birthday." She shakes her head in confusion. "Or is it a memorial service?"

My hand tightens around Raine's for reasons that have nothing and everything to do with her unexpected confession. I can feel my heart shatter into a million different pieces at the realization that Zara never told me why she's going. That Zara *chose* to withhold that very important piece of the puzzle.

She knew I wasn't going to question her when she said she had to be there for Raine. I took the explanation at face value, because truthfully, why wouldn't she tell me?

More importantly, why *couldn't* she tell me?

"So, you're both going to Seattle to celebrate Lola's life?" I ask, trying to make it all make sense in my head.

She nods. "My papa, he didn't really..." She pauses, her tears falling this time. "My papa didn't really deal with her death well, and my dad kind of put all of his energy into saving their marriage," she explains as she wipes her eyes. "My dads are in a much better place this year, and I know it'll be good for all of us to be there together. I just hate seeing them so upset like that. Remembering how close they were to getting a divorce."

"And what about you?" I ask, slipping into friend mode. "What's it like for you?"

"I love the times my family is together, but I'm always going to hate the circumstances." I watch as her chin quivers. "I remember being so excited about being a big sister. Being at home with Mom, counting down the days, lying down with her as Lola spent the night kicking."

My own eyes sting at the idea of Zara pregnant. What it must be like to hold everyone's joy in your body, only for it to be taken away.

Raine gets lost in her own thoughts and I get lost in mine, because I hear the worry for her fathers and I hear her own grief, and I'm here right now for her, but who is there for Zara? Who was there then and who's going to be there now?

"Raine," I say, the seriousness in my voice surprising us both. Her brows furrow together as I finish my thought. "I need to tell you something."

Raine straightens her spine, perplexed by my tone. "What is it?"

"I know this is really shit timing, but..." I blow out a breath and rip the Band-Aid off. "I'm dating your mom."

Awkward laughter bubbles out of her throat as she pulls her hand away from mine. "What?"

"I'm dating your mom," I say again.

Her expression turns pensive as she keeps her gaze on mine. "*You're* the mystery woman?"

I swallow down my nerves and nod. "Yeah, I'm her."

"But how?" She scratches at her temple. "She said she met her... you before?"

"We did," I confirm. "Meet before. I met her before I met you. I was out for my birthday and she was out with friends from work and—"

"I'm sorry, are you saying you had sex with my *mother*?" she shrieks.

My head swivels around the café in mortification. "Raine," I plead. "Please keep your voice down."

"You had sex with my mom," she whisper-shouts, this time the words more of a statement and less of a question.

"Okay, so, I had sex with your mom," I whisper-shout back. "But can we maybe circle back to that, because I need to meet you both in Seattle, and you can't tell her I'm coming."

This has Raine's whole expression turning serious. "I'm not following."

"I need to be with your mom this weekend," I explain. "But I'm not sure she wants me there. And I'm telling you about us so you're not shocked when I show up."

"Oh, wait, are you telling me this is serious." Her eyes widen. "This is *serious*. Like, you and her?"

"Yes," I answer honestly, thinking of how these last few months have unfolded, from our first night together, to the night we just had in the hotel. It's beyond serious. I'm pretty certain that woman is my forever. "I'll answer any question you want, but I can't not be there for her this weekend."

I can tell she doesn't understand my urgency, because she doesn't understand the depth of her mother's grief, or just how little Zara has allowed herself to show that grief, especially in front of her family. But I hope she can at least see how much I care for Zara, and that if anything, that alone will be enough.

"Okay," she concedes. "I'll give you our flight details, my dads' address, and whatever else you need."

My body sags in relief. "Thank you. So much."

Raine continues to stare at me in silence, and I can see her trying to wrap her brain around the enormity and disbelief of the bomb I've just dropped.

"I don't know if this makes a difference to you, but it was my choice to keep it a secret," I reveal. "Your mom wanted to tell you from the get go. So if you're mad at anyone, be mad at me."

I appreciate that she doesn't rush to absolve me of any guilt or try to calm the situation. She has every right to know all the facts before she settles on a way to feel about Zara and me dating.

Raine leans forward, forearms resting on the table. "Why do you want to come to Seattle so badly?"

"She's there for all of you," I tell her. "And I just want to be there for her."

In order for Raine to understand, it's really that simple. She doesn't need to know all the unexplainable details of why Zara didn't tell me in the first place or how that makes me feel, because I don't even know them, and the intricacies of our relationship aren't her business.

The bell on the café door interrupts us and the possibility of our conversation going any further.

"If you need to go home and pack," I say as I stand up, "I can cover you here."

"Are you sure?" she asks, stepping out of the booth. "Because I kind of need to work out how to face my mom without telling her I know."

Guilt courses through me. "I'm sorr—"

Raine raises a hand to stop me. "I feel like there's going to be a lot of apologizing over the next few days, so let's save it for now."

I put my own hands up in surrender. "That's fair."

Making my way behind the counter, I plaster a fake smile on my face and help Mel with service, trying not to fixate on the last half an hour or the upcoming weekend. I have so many things to worry about, including how the fuck I'm going to afford to fly to Seattle and back on a last-minute flight.

When Raine leaves the café, I quickly duck out to the back and drag my cell out of my back pocket, sending Nina a text.

> Hey. I'm so sorry, but I can't dogsit this weekend.

What? Why? Are you okay?

> I'm fine. Something came up with Zara, and I need to go to Seattle and see her.

She's in Seattle?

> I'll explain later.

> I'm so sorry.

It's fine. We'll catch up when we're both back.

Just before I put my cell back, a text from Raine comes through with all the details I need for the weekend. I forward the text to Remy, knowing he'll help me without asking questions I don't have all the answers for, and then send a follow-up message.

> Can you please book me flights to Seattle that sync up with these times?

> Remy: Do you need accommodations?

I have no expectations for this weekend. Despite my feelings being hurt, it isn't the time to make it about me; I just want to be there for her, and that includes sleeping wherever she is.

> No.

> Okay, I'll have it all sent to your email.

> I'll pay you back.

I press send on that last message and feel physically ill at not having some extra savings I can dip into when I need it.

> There's no rush.

Needing a moment, I find a nearby seat and fall into it, just breathing.

Inhale. Exhale. Inhale. Exhale.

I rub a hand over my chest, trying to rid myself of the ache and heaviness resting there. I'm hurting for Zara, hurting for me, hurting for us. It feels like a chasm has formed between us overnight. One day our whole lives lined up, and the next everything was off center.

Another text comes through as I sit there, only it isn't from Remy, Raine, or Nina.

> Zara: I miss you.

It's bittersweet to read and bittersweet to respond, but I know I will anyway, because I do miss her. Somedays it feels like I miss her endlessly. I missed her before I knew why she was going to Seattle, and I miss her even more now that I do.

With a heavy heart, my fingers move back and forth, type and delete, settling on the only thing that rings true.

> I miss you too.

30
ZARA

"Mom, are you okay?"

It was the seventh time Raine asked me, and at this point I'm not sure what answer she wanted me to give her. I'm not okay. Not even close. And every time she asks, I crumble that little bit more inside.

"Yeah, babe, I'm fine." I quickly run my hands through my hair, attempting to style it. "More importantly, how are you?"

"I'm good," she says, and I can hear the truth of her answer in the tone of her voice.

She's my inspiration. Her impressive ability to coexist with her grief and to incorporate Lola into her everyday life without it hurting too much never ceases to amaze me. It could be her age but is probably because she's more like Jesse that way, and in this instance I'm glad.

A phone beeps and annoyance trickles through me when I notice it isn't mine. I've texted Clementine a few times since arriving and have received no response. And even though she doesn't owe me one, it's so unlike her, it puts me on edge.

Raine's fingers fly across her screen, and it takes everything in me not to ask who it is. She's been on it all morning, and my mind has gone through a million different scenarios, every one worse than the one before. It's irrational and completely over the top, but being here is a lot more stress inducing than I'd prepared myself for.

If I let myself think about it, I could admit that I should've asked Clementine to come.

We're staying at Jesse and Leo's place this weekend. Me in the guest room and Raine in her childhood bedroom. I'd wanted to book a night in a hotel, to give myself a place to decompress, away from prying eyes, but secrets in this family are too hard to hide, and my absence would be suspicious.

"How much longer do we have till we leave?" I ask Raine, grabbing my toiletries bag.

"Dad said we have to be at the cemetery by eleven and then we have a lunch reservation when we're done," she answers.

Nodding, I head to the main bathroom to finish off my hair and makeup. My eyes are tired and flat, both things I haven't seen in my reflection since moving to L.A. I hate how uncomfortable I feel in my own home, because that's what this place is. With Raine and Jesse and Leo, my home is wherever they are. And I should be at my happiest with them.

And yet, it has never been more obvious how incomplete my home is, now that I'm here without Clementine.

There's a knock on the bathroom door, and I put the last coat of waterproof mascara on my eyelashes before opening up.

Jesse stands on the other side. "Hey."

"Hey," I answer wearily. "Everything okay?"

"Yeah, I'm just checking on you."

First Raine and now him—I feel like I'm missing something. "Is everyone okay?" I huff. "Because between you and Raine, the questions feel more like an inquisition."

"We can't be worried about you?"

"Why are you worried about *me*?" I ask defensively. "It's a tough time for all of you, but I'm fine."

I know Jesse can read me like a book, but he also knows never to call me out, especially when it comes to Lola. It's still always too awkward, because I don't allow myself to grieve in front of any of them. Instead, when Jesse, Leo and Raine figured out a way to commemorate Lola's memory, I asked them not to include me. I said I wasn't her mother the way that I was Raine's, and they were not responsible for me and my feelings.

I was nothing more than a surrogate and I was here for *them*.

It's the biggest lie I'd ever told, but I'm determined to take it to the grave.

"Leo and I are going to leave now," he says. "We have to stop by the florist first. I'm going to leave you his car, and you can drive there with Raine."

My lungs deflate in relief for the little bit of reprieve this would allow me. "That sounds good. Thank you."

He leans forward and kisses me on the forehead. "I love you, you know that."

My eyes threaten to fill with tears and I quickly close them, hoping to evade the onslaught of emotions. "Love you too," I manage to croak out. "Now go so you're not late."

After he leaves, I give myself a once-over and head back to my room to return my toiletries bag, and find Raine lying down on the bed with her eyes closed. Climbing up on the mattress, I lie beside her.

"What are we doing?" I ask her.

"Talking to Lola," she answers casually.

My chest tightens. "Can I ask what you talk to her about?"

"Normally, yes. But this time it's just some sister stuff," she says. "A girl's got to have secrets, you know?"

My shoulders shake, laughing. "You better not be keeping any secrets from me."

Her cell alerts her to another message, and I sit up and glance at her over my shoulder. "Mother's intuition is telling me something is up."

Her expression never falters as she reads and responds to whoever texted. "Mother's intuition would be correct."

I jokingly smack her thigh, thoroughly enjoying the lighthearted distraction between us at this particular point of time. "Raine."

Sitting up, she smirks before throwing her legs off the side of the bed. "We better get going."

Following her, I lock up Jesse's house and then throw her the keys. "Want to drive?"

She catches them, and together, we climb into Leo's car. L.A. traffic is so bad, there was no point in investing in a second car there, but here she could put that license to good use and drive her mother around for a change.

We arrive at the cemetery just in time to see Leo and Jesse make their way to Lola. They have balloons and flowers, and Leo is holding a cute little plush horse under his arm that I know he'll take back home and add to her collection.

The last time I was here with Jesse and Leo, they couldn't even look at each other or hold one another, their grief insurmountable. I had put all my energy into making sure Raine was okay and hiding just how much they were suffering from her, whenever I could.

But this time almost feels like the first time for me, because I have nothing else to focus on but myself. Raine is older, wiser, and her fathers are in the right headspace to be able to be the ones to support her this time around, and I... I'm just me.

We gather around the headstone and my breath shudders at the sight of it. The grass around it is beautifully manicured, and the pristine marble shines under the midday sun.

It reads:

Lola Ricci-Hunt
Beloved daughter and sister.
Here for a moment, loved for all of eternity.

Raine sits down in front of her sister, and Jesse and Leo crouch down on either side of her. My heart aches and mourns for what they lost, and it simultaneously beats with pride for how much they have overcome.

But as usual, I'm on the outskirts—by choice and by default—and I can't stop the tears from falling down my face if I tried. Selfishly thinking I'm nowhere and nothing. I don't exist in their circle, and Lola isn't a daughter or a sister to me.

I cover my mouth to hide the sob that threatens to slip from between my lips as an avalanche of shame and heartache washes over me. Not wanting to interrupt their moment, I take a few steps back and unexpectedly collide with somebody. I'm about to open my mouth, when familiar arms wrap around me, stopping me.

"I'm so sorry I'm late."

Clementine's voice in my ear obliterates any control I

thought I had on my emotions, and I completely fall apart. It isn't silent or stealthy or even a little bit subtle. I turn in her welcoming arms and let her hold me and shield me from the rest of the world.

I'd been holding it all in for too long, and now she's here, and I can let it all out. I'm not alone. Not anymore.

"What are you doing here?" I ask through sobs.

I notice she glances behind me, and for the first time ever, I don't care who witnesses my breakdown. I'm knee deep in my own grief and there's no turning back. I notice Clementine doesn't answer my question, just runs her hand up and down my back, soothing me instead.

My cries quiet and the fog eventually clears, awareness prickling my skin. The one thing I didn't want to do, I've done.

I made it about me.

I glance up and meet Clementine's eyes. They're full of sadness and pain and hurt; a hurt that I can see isn't *for* me but *because* of me. Nervously, I turn and find Jesse, Leo, and Raine staring at me.

Shit. Raine.

"Raine," I start, but Clementine's hand on the small of my back stops me.

"I told her," she says quietly. "I wouldn't spring this on her like that. I wouldn't do that to you."

I don't know if she's having a dig at me, but I feel guilty either way. My eyes take in the three sets staring back at me, all soft and full of empathy, the judgment and resentment I expected at ruining Lola's day nowhere to be found.

With my index fingers, I wipe at the excess tears underneath my eyes and straighten my stance. "I'm so sor—"

Leo raises his hand and steps forward. "No, *we're* sorry."

Jesse places his hand on Leo's shoulder, as if to show his

solidarity. "He's right," he echoes. "We didn't know you were still struggling."

Surprising me, Clementine steps forward. "Is it okay if Zara and I hang back here and meet you at the restaurant in a bit?"

"How about the three of us go and pick up some food so we can eat at home instead?" Leo suggests. "That way you can come back home whenever you're ready."

Struggling to find my voice, I let Clementine make the decisions for us. I watch as she and Raine have a quiet exchange, before Raine picks up a bag I'm assuming is Clementine's, and plants a kiss on my cheek. "I love you, Mom."

The air turns cold as they leave, Clementine and I, shoulder to shoulder, both staring at Lola's headstone.

It's her voice that breaks the silence first. "Why didn't you tell me why you were coming to Seattle?"

Grateful we're not looking at one another, I give her the answer I gave myself. "You had already committed to—"

"Try again," she interjects. "Why didn't you tell me why you were coming to Seattle?"

31
CLEM

The anger brewing in my veins surprises me, and I try to rein it in, because despite how hurt I am, I also hate how broken Zara looks right now. We're standing side by side but the distance between us feels endless, like we're no longer the same couple we'd been only forty-eight hours before.

The silence stretches and my mind goes haywire trying to find ways and things to say to fill it.

"Zara." My voice is full of defeat as I move to stand in front of her, waiting for her gaze to meet mine. "Please just tell me."

Pained brown eyes stare back at me.

"Tell me what I missed," I practically beg. "Tell me why you thought you needed to come and do this alone."

Zara shakes her head as unshed tears fill her eyes. "You didn't miss *anything*," she whispers. "It was just too late. By the time I realized I wasn't okay, it was too late." She reaches for my hands and intertwines my fingers with hers. "You've spent your whole life worrying about everyone else, and I wanted to be the one thing you didn't have to worry about," she explains. "The one person who takes care of you instead of needing to be taken care of."

I let out a soft, humorless laugh as I squeeze her hands. "Do you know how unrealistic that is? To think that there will never come a time when you need me or that I wouldn't drop *everything* to be what you need?"

"I didn't want it to be this," she admits, and I see the shame that's etching itself into her features. "I didn't want it to be this, and I didn't want it to be today."

She sounds almost frustrated with herself, as if there is ever the perfect time to not be okay. As if it doesn't make sense to feel the most vulnerable and broken on the day that reminds her of the biggest tragedy in her life.

"If not today, then when?" I challenge. "Because you never speak about it. You never speak about her. You never speak about how sad you are or how you moved states because you couldn't handle the reminder. You can talk about how hard it was for Raine, how hard it was for Jesse and Leo, and I love how much you worry about them, and I have no doubt they hurt too, but what about you, Zara?" I tug her to me, dropping her hands and gripping her face. Her chin quivers as tears run freely down her cheeks. "What. About. You?"

My question seems to be her undoing as she buries her head in my chest and cries. Big, painful sobs rack her body, and I hold her through every single one. I hold her as she cries for the woman she was, what she lost, and who she is now. I hold her as she cries for her family's loss and their future. I hold her as she remembers the baby she carried for nine months; the baby she loved and lost.

My hands roam up and down her back as the shaking of her body against mine subsides. The sobs turn to little hiccups, and eventually, she leans back to look at me, her eyes swollen, her nose red, her mouth wet from her tears.

Using the edge of my sleeve, I wipe under her eyes, under her nose, and dry her cheeks. She is beautiful. Even sad and broken, she is still so beautiful. And she's mine. With every fiber of my being, I know this woman is mine, and I would go to hell and back to keep her.

"I love you." The three words roll off my tongue with such ease, I say them again, convinced it was a fleeting thought and she didn't actually hear me.

"I love you," I repeat, this time taking in the way her eyes widen ever so slightly, and the way the light and life slowly returns them. "I love you, Zara. And not just on the good days. Or the days where you make me feel like I somehow deserve this beautiful life with you.

"Life is hard and complicated, but if you'll let me, they're the days I know I'll love you the most."

Closing the distance between us, I lower my mouth to hers, tasting nothing but her heartache. "I love you the most today."

"Clementine," she breathes against my lips, and I put a finger between us, silencing her.

"I need you to know how I feel way more than I need to hear you say it back."

I kiss her. Gently.

"You have changed my life."

I kiss her. Tenderly.

"I found myself because of you."

I kiss her. Softly.

"My life is infinitely better with you in it."

I kiss her again, but this time I let my mouth fill in the blanks to all the words I can't say and all of the many unsaid reasons I do love her. I use the kiss as a reminder of all the little moments we've shared over the last few months; how we started, how we changed, and what we are now.

Zara's hands reach up to cup my cheeks, deepening the kiss. Her mouth moves against mine, and it's my turn to listen to her unspoken words, to her unspoken feelings. To feel her gratitude and her love. Because it's there... It's been there for a while now, blossoming, filling in the empty space between us.

"Tell me about Lola," I say softly.

I wait, patiently, and when she sits down in front of the beautiful headstone, I have my answer. Lowering myself to the ground, I sit behind her, situating her between my legs. Flowers and balloons surround the headstone, and Zara keeps her hands busy arranging and rearranging them all in a beautiful display. Eventually, she leans back into me and I wrap my arms around her neck and rest my chin on her shoulder.

She slides her fingers through mine as she starts talking. "I didn't think twice about being a surrogate for Leo and Jesse," she says. "There was not a single doubt in my mind that it was a perfect plan. A foolproof plan.

"I welcomed the IVF procedures, the morning sickness, the swollen feet, even the weight gain." My brain conjures up images of Zara at every stage. "There were tough parts, but the excitement of it all outweighed everything.

"And I loved being pregnant that time around," she says. And even though I can't see her, I can hear the smile in her voice. "As an adult who didn't have the same worries a sixteen-year-old girl had, I truly loved it."

"And you weren't worried about giving her up?" I ask.

"But I wasn't giving her up," she says matter-of-factly. "Not in the traditional sense. Because I would be there, loving her and watching her grow, the same way Leo loves Raine. The three of us were built for this type of life."

Even from the very limited interaction I've had with Jesse and Leo, I could see what she meant about being built for this life. Raine was proof of just how well it could work.

"And then I woke up one morning and everything felt off." Her body sinks against mine, and her grip on my fingers tightens as her mind takes her back. "She wasn't moving. I called the hospital and they told me to load up on sugar, certain it would get her moving. A few hours later, still nothing. I felt nauseous from the food or from the dread, it didn't really matter. My intuition screamed at me to get to the hospital, so that's what I did.

"Jesse, Leo, and I sat in a hospital room as they told us there was no rhyme or no reason. It was like she went to sleep and never woke up." I expect her to take a moment to pause, but I realize she's too deep into the story now, and she was ripping the Band-Aid all the way off. "I remember feeling like someone had sliced my chest open with the news, but it was nothing compared to having to give birth to her."

My own eyes start to sting. I wasn't a mother and I'd never carried a baby, but I know enough about how hard it was for my own mother to give birth to a baby she didn't want, and I could only imagine how much worse it was when it was a baby you did.

"I tried to detach myself from it all instantly. Mentally telling myself everybody else's pain was worse, and there is a very real part of me that believes that." I feel a tear drip onto the top of my hand, and I hold her tighter. "I just didn't realize how much that same sentiment was eating me up inside.

"She grew in me," she whispers. "I have marks on my

body that are hers and hers alone, and I don't know how to let any of that go."

"But why should you? Who told you to let those things go?"

"Because I'm not her mother," she counters.

"I call bullshit," I say, feeling myself getting heated. "You're *a* mother, you're a parent, you're an amazing human being, with a heart two sizes too big, and I have no doubt you would've loved her with every inch of it. It was never going to be out of sight, out of mind. You gave birth to her sister, your best friends are her fathers; no matter what, you would've been somebody to that little girl."

I try to taper down my emotions, old and new ones rising up to the surface.

"Take it from me, a child who didn't have it. You can never have too much love, Zara. You can have little or none, but there is no such thing as too much." I let out a shaky breath before pressing a kiss to the side of her neck. "You deserved to let yourself mourn her the same way you would've loved her. With everything you have."

32
ZARA

The drive back home to Jesse and Leo's house is quiet, but I sit with a sense of peace I did not expect to possess on a day like today. Clementine was right, and my choice to be the martyr and sacrifice myself for everyone else was the wrong one.

Hindsight is a bitch like that.

There is no propriety on grief. We're not all carbon copies of one another, and there is no hard and fast rule about who can and cannot grieve or how much is too much or not enough.

I glance over at Clementine, who is comfortably driving Leo's car back.

"Just turn right over here," I instruct. "It's the third house on the left."

I point to their driveway, and she parks with ease beside Jesse's car. We climb out and Clementine waits for me to lead the way at the bottom of their porch steps.

"I'm going to need to talk to Raine *and* Jesse and Leo," I tell her

"Of course." She tucks some of my hair behind my ear. "I'm here for you, in whatever way you need."

My hands reach for her waist. "You're amazing, you know that?"

"I think you may have mentioned it a time or two," she says, a soft smile teasing her lips. "Are you ready to go in?"

"Not even a little," I say honestly. "Before we go in, can you tell me what happened with Raine?"

"She was upset at work, and I remembered you said it wasn't a good time for her, so naturally, I asked what was wrong," she explains. "She told me, and as soon as the words left her mouth, I knew I was following you here."

My heart beats fiercely for this woman, for her kindness and her friendship with my daughter and for all her thoughtfulness, especially when I was so thoughtless.

"I'm sorry," I say, closing the distance between us. "For not telling you. It was never my intention to keep it from you like some sort of secret."

"It's okay. I get it."

She places a hand on the side of my face, and I cover it with my own. "I didn't want you to worry about me. I didn't want to be one more person you have to take care of."

She brushes her thumb across my cheekbone. "Remember when you said sometimes you want to do nice things for me because you can?"

Reluctantly, I nod, knowing exactly where her line of thinking is taking us.

"Well, it goes both ways, Zara. You are not one more person I have to take care of. You are the *one* person I *want* to take care of. Knowing you would be here alone?" She shakes her head, as if the thought itself is too much to bear. "I was mad and hurt and so fucking worried."

"I'm sorry," I repeat. "I'm sorry for making you feel that way. I'm sorry for forcing your hand with Raine."

She presses a finger to my lips, silencing me. "I don't need your apologies. I just need you to be okay."

I'm not, not right now. But with her here, I know I will be, and that makes me feel lighter than I have in two years.

"And Raine," she adds. "I planned to tell her anyway."

"How did she take it?"

Her shoulder rises and falls. "She was shocked, but there kind of wasn't any time to process. I told her that I'm the one who wanted to keep it a secret and to not blame you for that, and that if she helped me get here on time, she can ask us anything."

"Did she help you?" I ask, knowing my daughter well enough to already know the answer.

"She did. She even thanked me for being here for you before she left the cemetery." Clementine's expression turns empathetic. "I'd say right now she's more worried about you than she is about us."

Isn't that the truth.

The fact that I had attempted to shield my grief from Raine, Jesse, and Leo, only to have this very public breakdown, has a sliver of shame trying to settle heavy on my chest, almost like a little voice telling me I failed. Instead of listening, I focus on Clementine and do my best to push it all away, knowing there's no sustainability in the way I was trying to handle Lola's death.

"Are you ready to meet my family?" I ask, distracting myself from my thoughts and easing her to the front door.

"I was up until now," she jokes.

"They'll love you." Her expression softens, and I let those three words sit between us. Three words I've wanted to say for weeks, and now they don't seem even close to being enough.

"Thank you for being here." I press my mouth to hers and whisper against her lips, "Thank you. Thank you. Thank you."

The kiss is quick but comforting, for the both of us. With her hand in mine, I open the front door and let myself in. It takes all of five seconds for three sets of eyes to find us, and the look of concern on each one of their faces makes me feel even more guilty than I already do.

The three of them are seated around the square dining table, Leo and Jesse on one side, Raine on the other, and two plate settings are set up for Clementine and me opposite the two men.

Jesse's the first one to break the silence, rising up off his seat and gesturing for us to sit down. "Come," he says. "Food always makes everything better."

When we reach the table, he holds his hand out to Clementine. "I'm Jesse," he says, introducing himself. "And this is my husband, Leo."

Clementine shakes his hand and then takes Leo's, who is now standing beside him. "I'm Clem. Zara's girlfriend."

She said the word with such pride, I can't help the smile that spreads across my face, remembering just how hard I had to convince her to give us an actual go. Now I'm certain she would wear a sticker on her forehead if I asked her to.

As we take our seats, I can't help but glance at Raine. "Is this okay?"

I know there's no rush to get all the hard conversations out of the way, but my brain just wouldn't let sleeping dogs lie, even for a little bit. There's a huge elephant sitting in the room with us, and I can't sit here and eat with everyone if I don't at the very least address some of it.

Looking at me pensively, Raine ignores my question and asks her own. "Are you okay?"

I imagine what she's asking to be the one thing everybody at the table wants an answer to, and for the sake of ridding my daughter of the concerned expression on her face, I nod.

"Things just caught up to me," I say truthfully. "I thought I had dealt with Lola's death, but in reality, I neglected myself while worrying about everyone else."

"Zara." Hearing Leo say my name across the dining table has more tears filling my eyes. I know how much guilt he holds for the way he dealt with his daughter's death, and I don't need him to feel guilty about this too.

"Raine," I say gently. "Will you excuse your dads and me for a little bit? I need to talk to them in private."

Her eyes dance between the three of us as she nods. "I guess I can hang out with my mom's girlfriend."

An unexpected laugh slips out of my mouth, appreciating her levity more than she'll ever know.

"I think you'll get along just fine," I tease.

When my eyes land on Jesse and Leo and I tilt my head to their back door, they both stand to follow me. Before I get up, Clementine's hand squeezes my thigh as she leans in, lowering her mouth to my ear. "I love you."

She kisses my temple, and I breathe in the strength her words give me.

Just as we're about to step outside, their doorbell rings, and Jesse's expression turns sympathetic. "Fuck. I'm sorry," he says. "We invited Julian and Deacon to come here after lunch."

His voice trails off and I fill in the blanks.

"But I had a major breakdown," I blurt out, only half joking.

"Well, I wasn't going to put it so bluntly," he murmurs. "Do you want me to tell them to leave?"

I wave him off. "Absolutely not. They're your friends, and I know how supportive they were to you both after Lola died."

Deacon is Jesse's boss, and Julian is his husband. They played a pivotal role in helping Leo and Jesse move forward last year, so it isn't surprising that they were invited to spend time commemorating Lola today.

Leo grabs my hand and looks up at Jesse. "Take your time settling them in, we'll be in Lola's room."

My whole body stiffens. I've never been in Lola's room, and he knows it.

"Leo," I breathe out, his name filled with both reluctance and a warning. "I don't know if I can."

"Of course you can," he coaxes. "It's time."

Leading me down the hallway, he squeezes my hand reassuringly before he opens the bedroom door and guides me in. The room is custard yellow and there are pictures and writing all over the walls.

"What's all this?" I ask, completely unprepared for the sight in front of me.

"This was Raine's idea," he explains. "She spends hours in here when she's home, writing on all the walls, talking to her sister. She's only recently started to include pictures."

My feet lead me farther into the room, until my fingertips are running across the wall, tracing all the words Raine has written.

"You know," he says, "Raine is something else. That daughter of yours—"

"Ours," I snap, glancing over my shoulder, correcting him. "She's *ours*."

And just like that, it all makes sense. The key fits perfectly into the lock, the missing puzzle piece is found.

"She's ours," he repeats, and I know we're no longer talking about Raine. "She was *always* ours."

Leo closes the distance between us. "How many times did you tell me Raine was mine? That blood and circumstances didn't matter, that she was unequivocally mine?"

I had said those things to him. I had repeated them over and over when insecurity plagued him, reminding him that he was part of our misfit family and nothing would ever change that.

"So why is it different for you?" he challenges. "Why is Raine mine and Lola not yours?"

Tears fall down Leo's cheeks as Jesse's strong arms wrap around me. He kisses the top of my head as my sobs fill the room.

"I'm so sorry I missed this," he says.

I shake my head, trying to talk through the tears. "It wasn't your job to notice."

"Yes it was," he argues. "My gut told me something was off every time I asked you if you were okay, but I just couldn't connect all the dots."

"He's right," Leo says. "We should've picked up on it sooner."

"Everybody was struggling." I wipe my eyes. "And I chose to hide the truth from you. I did that with purpose, and that blame lies with me."

"No more," Jesse says with finality. "No more hiding the hard stuff, thinking we're doing one another favors, because we're not. We're suffering in silence, and I don't want to do that anymore."

He's right, it was crippling and suffocating, and we're suffering. But one look around this room is proof that we had it all wrong. Because it isn't just about the loss, it's about the love, and Lola is loved.

We may have buried her two years ago, but she is very much alive and well.

In every thought.

In every breath.

In every sunrise and sunset.

"Can I have a pen?" I ask.

"Of course." I watch as Leo strides over to a chest of drawers that sits along the back wall of the room. He opens the top drawer and pulls out a handful of pens.

"Raine insists we have a variety of colors," he explains.

I pick out a green Sharpie and find a spot to call my own.

I miss you.

33
ZARA

The three of us walk out of Lola's room and into the living area, where Deacon and Julian are staring at Clementine with smiles on their faces as she cradles a baby, no bigger than four months old, wrapped in a light-green baby blanket, and Raine excitedly stands beside her.

Jesse had told me Deacon and Julian finally welcomed their baby girl into the world, but it didn't even occur to me that I would be seeing them this weekend.

"I'm just going to make room in the refrigerator since we're clearly not eating any time soon," Jesse says.

"Shit, Jess." I grab his forearm. "I'm sorry."

"Please." He waves me off. "I would rather all of us be here and smiling exactly like this. The food isn't going anywhere."

My eyes return to Clementine as she stares down at the newborn, her eyes full of wonder. And when her gaze finds mine, she smiles. Big.

Big enough that my heart stutters over itself as I bear witness to a version of her I didn't even think to consider.

"I've never held a baby," she whispers.

Striding toward her, I stand on the opposite side of Raine and take in the baby's sleeping form.

I glance up to look at Julian and Deacon. "What's her name?"

"Reese," Deacon answers, his voice so full of love and adoration. "Reese Sutton."

My eyes sting with tears, emotion thick in my throat. But for the first time today, they're not tears of sadness. Because it's so hard to look at men like Julian and Deacon, who are two of the most honest and loving men to ever walk this earth, and see them so enamored by their brand new daughter and feel anything but genuine happiness.

"She's beautiful," Clementine says.

I press a kiss to her cheek and notice Raine watching me.

"Want to take a walk?" I ask her.

She nods. "Let me just grab a sweater. I'm getting too used to the Californian sun."

When she's out of earshot, Clementine turns her head to face me. "Everything good?"

"Better than good." With every mention of Lola today, I'm knocking down fortified walls I've spent two years building, and I know my conversation with Raine will allow for the final piece to fall.

"Ready," Raine calls.

"I won't be long."

"I told you," she says softly. "I'm here for you."

I kiss her again and then take one more look at the sleeping baby.

"I'm going to need to hold her when I get back," I say to Deacon.

He gives me a two fingered salute as I follow Raine out the front door.

"Maybe I should've gotten a sweater," I muse. The air is cooler now with the midday sun hiding behind the clouds.

"Do you want me to run back in?" Raine asks.

"No." I loop my arm with hers. "I think I'll be fine once we start walking."

A comfortable silence settles upon us as we start the walk down the driveway and onto the street. I don't know which conversation I want to have with her first, so I nudge her shoulder and try for a joke instead.

"So, what do you think of Clem?"

She turns to look at me, her eyes incredulous, her smile smug. "You mean, what do I think of *my friend* Clem?"

"The one and the same."

"I mean, you already told me you were really into somebody, and she told me it was her decision not to tell me straight away."

"How do you feel about that?" I ask. "Her not wanting to tell you straight away?"

She shrugs. "Honestly, I have more feelings about her knowing how upset you would be today before I did."

Her words are like a swift kick to the stomach, and I deserve them. We aren't ones for secrets, but sometimes the lines between us blurred, and she mistook my desperation for protecting her as me keeping secrets.

"Raine." I halt my steps, in turn stopping her too. She turns around so we're now facing each other on the sidewalk. "You lost your sister."

"I know that," she snaps back.

"Do you?" I close the distance between us and grab her face in my hands. "Sometimes I think I raised you too perfectly and too selflessly, because you losing your sister and your grief surrounding that are the only things that matter." Her eyes fill with unshed tears as I continue. "My sadness and heartache should never be your responsibility. That's not how this mother daughter thing works."

She wraps her hands around my wrists. "Sometimes I think I'm not sad enough."

"What?"

"Papa couldn't get out of bed for months, and the way you cried today was even worse than when I used to catch you crying after you came home from the hospital." The words rush out of her in a hurried breath. "And I don't feel like that. Am I supposed to feel like that?"

"Hey," I say calmly. "Take a deep breath."

I inhale loudly and she exhales, we do this a few more times as I hold her still. "We are all different people." She works her throat over and averts her eyes. "Look at your dad. You and he are very similar. Do you think he's not sad enough?"

"No," she answers quickly. "I don't think that about him at all."

"Then why would you think that about yourself?" When she doesn't answer, I choose to drop my hands from her face and resume our walk.

"You know what I learned today?"

"What?"

"I learned that there is no right way or wrong way to grieve," I say. "We need to let ourselves feel the sadness when it comes, and we need to celebrate the life of our loved ones when the sadness goes. Sometimes the sad days will turn into weeks or even months, and other times, you'll be able to lie down on a bed, close your eyes, and talk to your sister as if she's sitting right next to you, without even thinking twice. They're both right, Raine."

"I just want you to be okay," she says, this time looping her arm into mine. "That's the only thing I care about right now."

I rest my head against her shoulder. "I promise. I'm going to be fine."

———

Raine and I step back inside the house, and I'm surprised to see Clementine lying on the couch, eyes closed and baby Reese sleeping along her chest. Julian is sitting on the floor right beside them.

"Umm, what's going on?"

Julian glances up at me, smiling. "I think they're attached to one another, and I wanted to make sure I caught Reese if Clementine happened to roll over or let go of her."

"I told you neither of those things were going to happen," she says, her eyes still closed.

"Are you planning on sharing?" Raine asks. "Because I'd like to be in the running for the title of 'favorite person other than my parents.'"

"You'll come back here and see her all the time," Clementine whines. "Stop being so selfish."

"Stop being so dramatic," Raine says. "You're dating my mom, you'll be back."

I've never seen this side of them, the way they interact, the comfort and banter, almost like they're sisters. It makes me giddy for the way each of our relationships would evolve from here on out.

When Clementine finally opens her eyes, she finds me almost immediately. "Hi," she says softly.

"Hi."

Raine makes a gagging noise. "Okay, we're going to need some ground rules if you two are going to stare at one another like that all the time."

"Stare at each other, how?" I ask.

Hands land on my shoulders and I turn to see Jesse behind me. "I'm so glad she was young when I started dating Leo. The worst thing she did was convince him to always bring gifts for her when he came over."

"Oh, I remember that," he says with a laugh. "I fell for it every time."

Leo and Jesse go back and forth, and I drown them out as I watch Clementine slowly maneuver Reese into a football hold before handing her back to Julian. She's so tender and gentle, and I fall in love with her all over again. As soon as her hands are free, she strides toward me, all the love she has for me blatantly written on her face.

Her hands grip my waist, pulling me close to her. "I don't know if I can kiss you or not, but I would really like to do that," she says loud enough for Raine to hear. "And soon."

"And that's my cue," Raine announces. "I'm going to meet up with Jamie. Julian, can I take Reese since my mother stole my friend?"

"I think she's a little too young for parties," he answers without missing a beat. "But maybe next time."

I bite the inside of my cheek to stop myself from laughing. "Is this going to be a thing between you and her?"

"Can't you tell it's going to be so much fun?"

"Okay, I think we're going to head off too," Deacon says.

"And Jesse and I have to go pick something up from the store."

Everyone is giving us some space, and if I wasn't so desperate to be alone with her, I probably would be a little embarrassed. But the last few hours have been a lot, and after all the talking and crying, I just want to bury my head in her neck and let her hold me till I fall asleep.

"Are they doing what I think they're doing?" she whispers.

I nod. "I don't know if it's weirder to stand here and wait for them to leave or just hide out in the guest room now."

"Just go now," Raine interrupts. "I'm leaving now anyway."

"You can't just eavesdrop on our conversations," I reprimand. "You'll end up hearing something you don't want to."

"It's fine, it's fine." She surprises us by giving us each a kiss on the cheek. "I love you," she says, her eyes darting between us. "Both of you. Now I've gotten that off my chest, I'll see you all later."

We watch as she waves goodbye to Julian and Deacon and then kisses her dads goodbye. When Jesse gives me a knowing look, I drag Clementine into the guest room and breathe a sigh of relief when I can finally close the door behind me.

"Wow," I breathe out as I walk farther into the room. "Today was a big fucking day."

Clementine wordlessly guides me to the edge of the bed before stripping me of all my clothes. She drags my pants down my legs and then slowly undoes the buttons of my silk shirt. She pushes the material off my shoulders and lets it fall to the floor.

"What are you doing?" I manage to ask.

Instead of answering, she drops to her knees, and every nerve ending in my body hums. She pushes me to sit on the edge of the bed before spreading my legs wide and raising her lust-filled eyes to meet mine.

My stomach coils in anticipation as she presses her lips to the inside of my thigh. I watch with bated breath as she kisses up my leg, slow and full of reverence. When she reaches my hip, she bypasses my sex, and my breath hitches in disappointment.

"Clementine," I breathe out.

Her mouth moves to my other knee, pressing the same open-mouthed kisses up my thigh, mirroring her previous movements. She brushes her lips over my covered pussy, and it takes everything in me not to beg for more.

Fingertips skate across my stomach, dancing along the bittersweet lines that are etched into my body. Her lips follow, a brand new tapestry, the shape of her love, now sewn into my skin as she kisses.

Adores.

Worships.

My eyes sting, my chest tightens, and my breath shudders. "What are you doing?"

"I told you," she says. "I'm here just for you."

34
CLEM

It's dark out, and despite the initial plan of the day to be visiting the cemetery and going to lunch, Zara and I eat an early dinner with Jesse and Leo before I watch her give them both hair cuts. Knowing they keep their hair long so Zara can cut it whenever they see one another makes a warm feeling spread through my chest.

It's one thing to know the woman you love is also important to other people, but it's another thing to see just how much. After spending time with them, the three of them enjoying one another's presence on such a bitter-sweet day feels like a privilege to witness. And now we're both fresh out of a shower and climbing back into bed.

It feels both scandalous and liberating to be having sex in Leo and Jesse's house, because A: it's nice not to be hiding, but B: they undoubtedly know what we're doing behind closed doors.

The only reason I'm less in my own head about it is because Raine hasn't come home yet.

Zara and I are sitting in our favorite positions, her back

against the headboard and my head in her lap. "How cute was Reese?" she asks.

Smiling just thinking about the little girl, I tilt my head back to look at her. "I am amazed how small a baby is, and she's already four months old," I exclaim. "I kind of felt a little bit sheltered that I'd never seen a baby that size up close and personal before."

"They're so cute and tiny," she agrees. "And you were so good with her."

"I'm surprised Julian even let me hold her."

"Do you want kids?" Zara blurts out, and for a second I almost think I misheard her.

"Did you just ask if I want kids?"

"Yeah."

Not wanting to have the conversation while her face is upside down, I sit myself up on my haunches and turn to look at her. "Is there a right or wrong answer here?"

"Oh my God, no." She leans forward and collects my hands in hers. "I just saw you holding Reese today and my mind kind of ran off on this wild tangent, and I..."

Zara lets out a shaky breath, and I'm surprised to see a wave of nervousness wash over her.

"What is it?"

Moving closer, she shifts herself till her legs are underneath her, and holds our hands in the air between us.

"I love you." She delivers those three words on a relieved exhale, like it's been painful for her to have to keep them in this long. "And I want forever with you."

"Forever," I echo.

"Yes." She nods with certainty. "Forever. But when I saw you with Reese, I panicked for the first time, thinking our visions of forever could look very different."

"What does your forever look like?"

With her heart in her eyes, she brings my hands up to her mouth and kisses them.

"It looks like a beautiful, selfless woman with a bleeding heart. It looks like nights wrapped up in your body and days filled with the sound of your laughter. It looks like fighting with your best friend and making up with your lover. It looks like firsts and lasts and everything in between."

A single tear slides down my face, and Zara's thumb is quick to catch it.

"It looks like you, Clementine," she says. "Today and tomorrow and the day after, my forever is all you."

I rub a hand over my heart, the amount of love almost too big to hold, too much to feel.

"And this forever... Is it with or without kids?" I ask.

We both know this isn't an easy topic for either of us. We're two women tethered to birth experiences for very different reasons. There's trauma and history, and so much of it we don't want repeated.

"I don't think I can carry another baby," she confesses. "And I don't even know if I could manage my own anxiety if you carried the baby."

She's being raw and honest, and her feelings are completely understandable.

"Come here." I tug us both back down so we're lying on the bed, curling myself around her.

Her heart beats rapidly underneath my palm, and my own heart cracks that even the mere mention of either of us being pregnant brought on this reaction.

"It's okay," I say reassuringly. "I don't want to get pregnant."

This has her turning around to look at me. "You don't?"

I shake my head. "I don't want biological children. Do you know how many unwanted and unloved children there are in the United States alone? Children like me?

"We both know blood doesn't make you a family, and I don't need blood to make my family. I know it's a lot to ask, but if you do want kids, I want to foster. And if you don't want that, there are hundreds of ways I can help those kids without bringing them home."

"What was it that I said?" She kisses me on either cheek. "A beautiful, selfless, bleeding heart. I love you, Clementine."

"I love you too."

"I want forever with you," she repeats. "I want *that* forever with you."

I want it too. I want more, and I want it with her.

She leans in to kiss me, but I hold a hand between us, stopping her. "Wait, there's something I have to tell you."

"Okay," she responds tentatively, her fingers skating across her lips, like she already misses me. "Is something wrong?"

"Maybe?"

"Clementine," she says apprehensively, clearly confused by the sudden change in my direction.

I quickly kiss her cheek. "I love you."

Hating myself for not doing this sooner, I rush off the bed and walk toward the overnight bag I brought with me, and pull out the velvet pouch I always keep with me. Climbing back up onto the mattress, I cross my legs and return to sitting opposite her. Her brows are drawn together in confusion, and I know there's absolutely no way I can erase that expression without explaining myself. And soon.

"Here," I say, handing her the pouch. "Open it."

She wastes no time, sticking her hand inside the velvet bag and then pulling out her necklace. Her eyes stay trained on the piece of jewelry, and when she finally recognizes it for what it is, her eyes dart back to mine, widening in disbelief.

"I've been looking for this for months," she says, raising it in the air so the overhead light catches on the small diamonds that rest in the pendants. "How do you have it?"

"It must've fallen off you that first night at the hotel," I explain. "You'd already left, and my first instinct was to keep it and find a way to return it, but then I told myself that would be too awkward, and before I knew it, I was just wearing it.

"It reminded me of you and that night," I confess. "Sometimes I don't know if you realize just how out of character that whole thing was for me, and yet, in hindsight, I don't think I've ever felt more myself than I did with you.

"So I kept it, because I wanted to be closer to you, or closer to that version of me." I shake my head. "I'm not too sure."

Reaching for it, I take it out of her hand and turn the key around to show off the engraved letters. "I know it means a lot to you, and when I realized these letters were for Raine and Lola, it made it harder to give back. And in the end I kind of thought..."

My voice trails off as I try to find better words to get my point across.

"You kind of thought what?" she prompts.

Shame courses through me, but I have the decency to keep my gaze locked on hers as I explain.

"I kind of thought if we didn't work out, at least I would still have something to remember you by."

Zara takes it back out of my hand and puts it around her neck, her fingers playing with the lock and key. "I bought this for myself the first Mother's Day after Lola died." She raises the heart pendant. "This is supposed to be my heart. And this"—she raises the key—"is Raine and Lola. Because they're the only ones who would ever have my whole heart," she explains. "The only ones who would ever have every part of me."

She lets out a huff. "Tell me you didn't think, for even a second, that you having my necklace meant any of what I just said to you would change. Or change how I feel."

I shrug, years of insecurities and always expecting the worst rushing to the surface. I want this life that I had no idea existed or could ever be within my reach, and that meant every moment I was scared that something could take it away.

"I want you to know something," she says. "When I say forever, I mean it. The good times and the bad, Clementine. I will not walk away from you, even if you begged me to."

An unexplainable amount of relief settles in my chest. Loving Zara means realizing everything before her was like living with your eyes closed, and I don't want to go back to life before her.

"I love you."

Our mouths fuse together, heated and passionate. The kiss is filled with clarity and confirmation, an ode to finding your person and being completely different yet very much the same. As certain as the sun and the moon, I know we will show up for one another every day.

When it's easy and when it's hard.

When she's happy and I'm sad.

When tears stream down her face and my smile is too big to bear.

We will break. We will heal. We will love.

The kiss is as fierce as a promise and as soft as a prayer, with every swipe of her tongue against mine, her kiss tells me. This. Is. Forever

I love you hard. I love you soft. I love you always.

EPILOGUE
CLEM

"Oh my God," I squeal. "How much longer are you going to be?"

"You know better than to rush me," she scolds. "I'm shaving your legs, and cutting you isn't an option."

I roll my eyes. "You know I can do them myself, right?"

She drags her eyes away from my legs and meets my gaze. "And where's the fun in that?"

"Everybody is coming over in an hour," I remind her. "You said it would be a quick bath."

"Sweetheart, when have we ever been naked and anything be quick?"

I smack the water with the back of my hand, splashing her. "Are you saying I should've known better?"

"Absolutely," she quips. "Now, stay still."

We sit opposite one another, my leg propped up on the lip of the bath as Zara runs the razor over my soapy skin. She does this often, finds a million and one ways to show me how much she loves me, how much she cares for me... how much she wants to take care of me.

"I love you." I smile at her. "But maybe you shouldn't have invited everyone over," I say a little more seriously. "It doesn't have to be this big deal."

She shifts her gaze to mine again. "But it does, because it is."

"It's just community college," I argue.

"Firstly, it's getting accepted to community college *and* your birthday." She maneuvers my leg back into the water, places the razor on the niche beside us, and slides closer to me, wrapping her arms and legs around my body, her perfect breasts pressing against mine. "Secondly, and most importantly, do you think the children's lives you're going to change give a fuck about whether you went to community college versus a big university?"

"Okay," I scoff. "Changing lives is a bit presumptuous," I state. "And also, it's so sexy when you say the word 'fuck.'"

She bites her bottom lip. "Sexy enough for you to let me *fuck* you before everyone gets here?"

"How much time do you think we have?" I ask rhetorically.

She buries her head in my neck, nipping at my collarbone. "There's always time for you."

My body coils at the seduction in her words, the need between us almost never abating. It's been a whole year since that first night together, and every day I wonder if a lifetime will ever be enough.

I lean in to kiss her. "I'll make you a deal. You let me finish shaving my legs so we can get dressed and not be naked when Jesse, Leo, and Raine come back home."

She laughs. Loudly. "Do you even know how deals work? You didn't say what I get if I let you shave your own legs."

"Oh." I gesture to my naked body. "You get me. But at a later time."

She rolls her eyes dramatically but pushes herself up to her feet anyway.

"Thank you," I drawl as I grab the razor and continue on with the job she started.

Stepping out of the bath, she quickly runs the shower to rinse off any excess soap, then steps out and dries herself. My hands move quickly and then it's my turn to jump in the shower and do the same.

Within fifteen minutes we're both dressed and down-stairs, and Zara's got five bowls of chips and five different dips set up across the kitchen counter.

She does this stuff on autopilot, like she's the perfect hostess and never flinches at having too many guests; it's a world and then some away from the life I knew. And yet everything we do together feels so natural and normal. When I moved in two months ago, she insisted that my brothers feel welcome enough to visit me, and now, at least one of them, if not all of them, are over having dinner here once a week.

It's surreal in the best kind of way.

Standing in the middle of the kitchen, I run my clammy hands up and down my denim-covered thighs.

"Everyone comes over all the time," I state. "So, can you tell me why I'm nervous?"

"Sweetheart." She stops fidgeting with the food and reaches for my hand, tugging me to her. "Why aren't you proud of yourself?"

"I am," I say half-heartedly.

"Try again," she coaxes.

"I am," I answer more confidently. "But I'm not the first

or last person to go to college, and I'm not the first or last person to have a birthday."

"It's not about being the first or last," she argues. "It's about doing the things you want to do. Living the life you want to live. And birthdays are for celebrating."

The doorbell rings, interrupting us, and Zara quickly kisses my forehead. "And sometimes when you're as loved as you are, people want to be around you no matter what."

I think it's that part that has me so overwhelmed; the wholesome family unit we've all turned into, surprises me at every turn. When Zara reaches the door, I expect to see my brothers, but Raine is standing in the doorway flanked by Leo and Jesse.

"Why are you ringing the doorbell?" Zara asks Raine as the three of them file in. "You have house keys. You live here."

"I left them at the rental by accident," Raine explains.

Jesse and Leo often come to visit. And when they do, Raine always spends the week with them wherever they're staying, catching up. Just yesterday we picked them up from the airport for their current week-long stay in L.A.

It's a nice reprieve. More for her than us, because ever since I agreed to move in with her and Zara, I'm extremely mindful of not overstaying my welcome. There's a difference between moving in as the best friend and moving in as the mother's girlfriend, but lucky for me, their easygoing relationship with one another makes it all even easier for me.

"Happy Birthday," Leo says as he kisses me on the cheek. Jesse greets me next and then it's Raine's turn.

"Happy Birthday." She hip checks me as we both lean on the kitchen counter while Jesse and Leo talk to Zara. "How was your night in the house without me?"

"Could barely sleep," I deadpan. "Tossed and turned all night."

"Exactly what I love to hear."

I chuckle and then nudge her back. "How was the rental?"

"Dad and Papa are always great," she says. "But I'm starting to feel perpetually single because of my own parents."

I chuckle. "I thought the goal was to finish college, then date?"

"It's still the goal," she says. The silence stretches and she adds, "But you ever wake up one day and realize, *shit, I think I want to have sex with my friend*?"

I shake my head. "Literally, never. Your mom, on the other hand..."

Raine shoves her hand in my face. "Stop talking, immediately."

I'm about to ask her who this "friend" is, when I hear Zara greet Remy and then follow up with the rest of my brothers.

She rises up on the tips of her toes to kiss Arlo on the cheek. "Thank you for picking this up for me."

"Not a problem." He hands her a white box that she quickly rushes into the kitchen and then he beelines for me. "Happy Birthday, Clementine."

Ever since hearing Zara call me Clementine, my brothers have turned it into a running joke, that only they think is funny.

The rest of them all pile in after him; Frankie, Lennox, Samuel, Rhys, and Remy each carrying pizza boxes.

"Um." I thoughtfully place a finger on my lips before brushing it down over my open palm and then using my left hand to sign the letter Y and press it to my right hand. "What's this?"

My signing has improved immensely, and it helps that Zara and Raine also started learning, making it easier for the three of us to practice on nights we're all at home.

Lennox is almost exclusively signing now, using his voice less and less. He puts two open hands in front of his chest and moves them in a circular motion before pointing his middle finger to his chin and then his chest.

Happy Birthday.

I ensure my hand is open and flat, bringing my fingertips to my chin, then moving them away to say thank you just as Remy begins to open all the pizza boxes along the counter.

"Um, why is there a missing bite from a slice of every pizza?" Raine asks.

I cover my mouth with my hands in shock. "Oh my God, you didn't."

"What?" Zara says conspiratorially. "I asked your brothers if they knew a way to celebrate your birthday and you getting accepted into college to complete your social work degree."

"Oh my God," Raine squeals. "You got in?"

She's the first one to throw her arms around me and then Arlo, Frankie, Lennox, and Remy are all up in my space, kissing and hugging me.

My eyes start to sting, the amount of love and emotion in the room overwhelming me. My gaze searches for Zara, and when it lands on her, she's already looking at me with this soft smile on her lips and an endless amount of love in her eyes. Like she's known all along that this life was mine for the taking. That I could have hopes and dreams, and happiness, and that she's been showing me how I can have them all with her.

I raise my hand, close it in a fist, and then release my thumb, forefinger, and pinky all at the same time.

I love you.

She signs it back, and we just stare at one another as I hear Remy explain to Raine why every pizza box is sans one bite of pizza.

"So whoever brings the pizza home is responsible for eating one bite from a slice out of every box?" she confirms.

He nods as she opens each box to check that they've, in fact, fulfilled the tradition.

"Huh," she muses. "That's both absolutely ridiculous and kind of cool."

"Right?" he agrees with a chuckle. "We kinda can't not do it now."

My gaze follows Zara as she makes her way over to me.

"Happy Birthday, sweetheart," she says when she reaches me, wrapping her arms around my neck. "How's twenty-five feel?"

"It's already the best year yet." My eyes quickly scan the room, taking in all the people I love the most under one roof. "Thank you for insisting I have everyone over to celebrate."

"I will never walk away from an opportunity to show you just how loved you are. And you are so very loved, Clementine." It's her turn to quickly look around the room. "I will always love you the most, though."

This makes me smile. "You will?"

She presses her lips to mine.

"The most." Kiss. "The hardest." Kiss. "The longest."

"Can I steal you away for a second?" she asks me.

"You don't need to ask for permission."

She intertwines her fingers with mine and weaves us in and out of everyone standing in the kitchen until we're making our way back upstairs.

"Seems a bit risky to come back up here while everyone is downstairs," I tease.

She chuckles as she leads me to the chest of drawers that sits against one of our bedroom walls. Opening the top drawer, she pulls out a familiar velvet pouch.

"What's this?" I ask.

She places it in my hand. "Have a look."

Carefully, I tilt the pouch until the familiar piece of jewelry lands in my hand. "I've been meaning to ask you why I haven't seen you wear it in a while," I muse.

"This isn't my necklace."

I bring it up in front of my face, letting it hang before me. "What do you—"

And that's when I see it, the little Z engraved on the key.

"Zara," I breathe out, lowering my hand so my eyes meet hers. "It's beautiful."

"It is," she says, her gaze on me and not the necklace. "It matches mine."

My brows furrow in confusion as she reaches into the drawer, this time pulling out her own necklace and handing it to me.

I place it over her head and let my fingers linger as they move down to the key. My breath hitches as I turn it around, feeling both expectant and surprised at the sight of the letter C on the stem.

"Because you have all of me," she says softly. "The whole pieces and the broken bits. The things I love about myself and the things I don't."

I reach for my pendant, my fingers tracing the simple Z,

over and over again, as the sight of the three letters resting on her chest make it all feel permanent. Everlasting.

We're all there, the most important people in her life: Raine, Lola, and *me*.

———

Did you enjoy Unlikley?

If you want to see more of Clem and Zara go to my website to read a bonus epilogue.

https://www.marleyvbooks.com/bonus-epilogues

———

Want to know more about Arlo and Frankie?
Find out what happens in Unwanted, the first book in
The Unlucky Ones Series: A second chance, gay romance

———

Want to know more about Lennox, Rhys and Samuel
Find out what happens in Unloved, the second book in
The Unlucky Ones Series: A polyamourus romance

———

Want to know more about Jesse and Leo. Find out what
happens in <u>What We Broke</u>, A Marriage in Crisis
romance

———

Want to know more about Deacon and Julian in Without You. Find out how they got together before they found their Happy Ever After.

———

Want more LGBTQIA+ Romance from Marley Valentine?

<u>Devilry: A Teacher/Student Romance</u>
<u>Unforgettable (Vino & Veritas)</u>
<u>Want You Still</u>

Tragedy brought us together, but something stronger made me want to stay.

Julian was the boy next door. My brother's best friend, he fit with my family in ways I never could. While he and Rhett went on to play house, I left the only life I knew, desperate for a fresh start.

Until everything changed.

Heartache came along, and the aftermath of my brother's death was here to stay. I was now face to face with Julian more than I ever wanted to be.

Being around him brought up all my insecurities, forced me to deal with hard truths, and conjured up feelings I had no business entertaining. He wasn't the man I thought I knew. He was complex and layered, and inherently beautiful in all the ways I'd never noticed.

Not on another person.

Not on another man.

Not until him.

PURCHASE WITHOUT YOU: A BROTHER'S BEST FRIEND ROMANCE

From USA Today Bestselling Author, Marley Valentine comes a brand new, marriage in crisis, hurt/comfort, standalone, gay romance.

If someone asked me to describe our love story, I would only need to use two words.

Before and After.

When I met Leonardo Ricci, he was determined I would only be a fling, while I was certain he was my forever.

Seven years later, we're the perfect couple. Happy, married, and in love–in sickness and health, till death do us part.
At least until the unthinkable happens.

Now we can't look at each other. We don't sleep in the same bed. We can't even be in the same room. The loss is too great and the pain runs too deep.

But this man is the love of my life. I convinced him once, and I would be damned if I couldn't do it again. I would be damned if I couldn't fix what we broke.

PURCHASE WHAT WE BROKE: A MARRIAGE-IN-CRISIS ROMANCE

I couldn't tell you when I fell in love with Gael Herrera, but I wish I knew how to make it stop.

Falling in love with a straight man is a rookie mistake. But falling in love with my soon-to-be-married-to-a-woman best friend is nothing but heartache.

Through all the years, and all the men I've fooled around with, he's always been at the back of my mind. An unrequited crush I wish I could shake. A dream that was never going to come true.

When I whisk him off to a surprise bachelor party weekend in Vegas, I surrender to the idea that this is an opportunity for me to finally let go of my feelings for him and say goodbye.

But after a heated exchange and an even hotter kiss, everything I thought I knew about our friendship changed.

Maybe I had it wrong. Maybe, after all this time, we were more than best friends. Maybe, just maybe, he felt it too.

PURCHASE ACHE: A FRIENDS TO LOVERS ROMANCE

Two halves of a whole, Arlo Bishop and I were both
unwanted kids brought together by the foster system.
Dealing with the aftermath of neglect and abandonment,
we grew up side by side and found solace in one another.

We wanted.

We needed.

We loved.

Desperately.

But somewhere along the way, Arlo wanted and needed
and loved drugs more. So, I did the only thing I could and
broke my own heart to save his.

Now, four years later, I'm back in L.A. and face-to-face with
my past. Not only does the pain and hurt of our mistakes
linger between us, but so do our feelings.

I didn't plan on a second chance, fear of history repeating
itself making it hard to forgive and even harder to forget.

But with only one touch, one kiss, I was taken back to
where it all started.

Two halves of a whole, Arlo Bishop and I were made for for
each other. But we were no longer the unwanted foster
kids.

We were grown men.

And I wanted nothing more than him.

<u>PURCHASE UNWANTED: A SECOND CHANCE ROMANCE</u>

We longed. We lost. We loved. *Desperately*.

I thought I had my life all figured out. But after a college football accident leaves me deaf, I was learning how to live all over again.

I expected the anger, the frustration, and the struggle to readjust, but what I didn't expect to happen amongst the chaos, was to fall in love.

Especially not with two men.

Rough-edged puzzle pieces, Rhys, Samuel, and I were nothing but aching memories, painful realities, and hidden scars.

We were products of our pasts, abandoned and unloved, messy and complicated. Individually we had baggage; together we had mountains to climb.

But when the three of us were tangled up in one another, spilling secrets in the dark, hearts beating in sync, nothing else mattered but them.

We needed to break the cycle, because they deserved love... And who knows, maybe I finally did too.

<u>PURCHASE UNLOVED: A MMM ROMANCE</u>

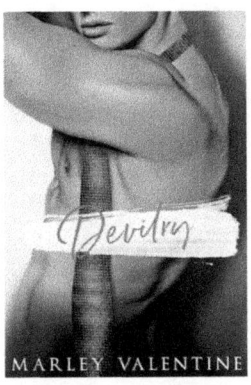

Attending King University was at the top of my bucket list. Falling in love with my professor wasn't.

Earning a full scholarship to King University was my hard earned ticket out of hell. I'm happy to be away from the small town I grew up in and all the equally small minded people who live there.

King was going to be my safe haven. A place where I could leave the old me behind and finally grow into the young man my family had desperately tried to hide away.

Diving head first into new experiences, new friends, and parties, I didn't expect to run straight into the one thing I wasn't ready for.

His arms are welcoming, his body is addictive and his lips are heaven. Cole Huxley is everything I could fall in love with, except for one problem... I never wanted to fall for my professor.

PURCHASE DEVILRY: A TEACHER/STUDENT ROMANCE

One night with Reeve Hale wasn't enough. I knew it when I kissed him, I knew it when I slept with him, and I was certain of it when I walked out of his motel room the very next day.

So when the shy, gorgeous man is introduced as our newest employee at Vino and Veritas, I can't help but conjure up all the ridiculous ways to convince him to repeat that unforgettable night. Like asking him to be my fake boyfriend at my sister's upcoming wedding.
Only, I didn't expect him to say yes.

Playing pretend shouldn't feel this real. Especially when Reeve is planning on leaving Vermont after the summer.

We agreed to one night. We negotiated a fake relationship. But I'm the one who broke our terms. I wasn't supposed to fall in love and he was never supposed to be so unforgettable.

PURCHASE UNFORGETTABLE: A WORK PLACE/ FAKE RELATIONSHIP ROMANCE

ACKNOWLEDGMENTS

If you made it here, you made it to the end of the book and I hope you truly enjoyed it.

I am so grateful Zara and Clem let me write their beautiful story and I hope you all enjoyed my foray into sapphic romance—I know I did.
If you love it, thank you. If you don't then hey, I have a few other books you can choose from.

Firstly I want to thank everyone who is always in my corner. You make the impossible days a little less so and I don't think you know how much that means to me.

Kacey, Laura, Jodi, Elizabeth and Tanya so much for sticking through me on this one. There were truly times where I wanted to throw in the towel and you all carried me over the finish line when I couldn't do it myself.

Shauna, thank you as usual for being so accomodating, so encouraging and the greatest at your job. I am indebted to you.

The Author Agency, thank you so much for all you do on release days.

My mum and my sister, you can retire for the year lol. No

more books scheduled. Thank you so much and no words will ever be enough to say thank you for helping me make my dreams come true.

To Andrew and my boys: I love you. x

Until next time. Much Peace and Love.And that's it from me.
Until next time.
Much Peace and Love.

ABOUT THE AUTHOR

Marley Valentine

Living in Sydney, Australia with her family, Marley Valentine is a USA Today bestselling author and a former social worker who uses her past experiences to write real life, emotional and heartfelt contemporary romance.

She enjoys mixing it up with all types of romance pairings, incorporating all forms of life, lust and love as her characters embark on their journey to their happily ever after.

When she's not busy writing her own stories, she spends most of her time immersed in the words of her favourite authors.

Marley enjoys interacting with her readers so please feel free to reach out to her via Facebook, Instagram, email and/or subscribe to her newsletter.

Other Books by Marley Valentine

Reclaim | Revive | Rectify

MM Romance Books

Devilry | Without You | Ache|Unforgettable | What We Broke | Want You Still

The Unlucky Ones
Unwanted | Unloved | Unlikely

Find Marley

Facebook | Facebook Reader Group | Amazon Author Page | Goodreads Author Page | Twitter | Instagram | Website | BookBub | Newsletter